'A rollercoaster of intrigue ... d
suspense and, er, saunas. H ...

'If you are familiar with A ...
humour then you will acc ... nd
its way into the most ord ...
out' European Literature Network

'An intense and darkly funny murder mystery novel. I devoured it
in one sitting and particularly enjoyed the contrast of the drama
with the descriptions of the story's setting ... in rural Finland'
TripFiction

'Weaving domestic life with a murder mystery is done rather well
in *The Burning Stones*, with added dark humour'
Bookmarks and Stages

'I love how Antti Tuomainen takes such an unassuming, and
widely popular, Finnish pastime and uses it as a method of murder
– a particularly gruesome one' Jen Med's Book Reviews

'Antti Tuomainen has taken the concept of the whodunnit and
stood it on its ear with his signature brand of quirkiness'
Loopy Kaz

'Nobody else could use the off-the-wall scenarios, comedy and
crime, and still make it engaging and utterly page-turning'
Books 'n' Banter

'Creepy and tense in places, a little comical in others, full of
interesting, eccentric characters' Simply Suze Reviews

'Original, hilarious, tense and addictive ... totally brilliant'
Emma's Biblio Treasures

'Antti Tuomainen's writing is top notch, as always'
Cal Turner Reviews

'Nordic noir the Antti Tuomainen way is an absolute joy'
Brown Flopsy

'Razor-sharp characterisation, vivid sense of place and a plot which
effortlessly switches between droll humour and a compulsive race
against time ... Tuomainen at his warm and witty best'
Hair Past a Freckle

'I'd happily live in the worlds Tuomainen creates' Café Thinking

'Full of dark humour, intrigue and insightful commentary'
A Little Book Problem

'A beautifully written and engaging murder mystery' Fully Booked

PRAISE FOR ANTTI TUOMAINEN

WINNER of the Petrona Award for Best Scandinavian Crime
Novel of the Year

SHORTLISTED for the CrimeFest Last Laugh Award

SHORTLISTED for the CWA International Dagger

SUNDAY TIMES THRILLER OF THE YEAR

'The funniest writer in Europe' *The Times*

'A refreshing change from the decidedly gloomier crime fiction for
which Scandinavia is known' *Publishers Weekly*

'Right up there with the best' *Times Literary Supplement*

PRAISE FOR *THE BURNING STONES*

'Suspense is uppermost in this adroit mix of psychological thriller, whodunnit and middle-aged rom-com' *Sunday Times* Book of the Month

'Finnish author Tuomainen has a talent for creating offbeat characters ... [a] tense, pacy novel, laced with the author's trademark laconic humour' *Guardian* Book of the Month

'It may seem hard to find good comic crime-writers, but clearly we haven't been looking in Finland ... simultaneously thrilling and evocative of the mundanity of life, and also very funny indeed' *Telegraph*

'Hilarious, beautifully penned and startlingly inventive. No other writer can come up with more ways to kill you in a sauna, and *The Burning Stones* cements Tuomainen's position as the king of the humorous crime caper' Abir Mukherjee

'Showcases Antti's trademark deadpan humour and crime plots focused on intriguingly quirky individuals. An utter delight' Vaseem Khan

'Laconic, thrilling and warmly human – hugely enjoyable' Christopher Brookmyre

'Antti turns the heat up with this wryly comic thriller. You'll sweat along with the characters!' Douglas Skelton

'Just what you want from Antti Tuomainen, the brilliant moulding of apparent mundanity into a which-way-now thrill ride, with humour drier than a desert snake's belly' Ian Moore

'You don't expect to laugh when you're reading about terrible crimes, but that's what you'll do when you pick up one of Tuomainen's decidedly quirky thrillers' *New York Times*

'Deftly plotted, poignant and perceptive in its wry reflections on mortality, and very funny' *Irish Times*

'Fresh and witty' Chris Ewan

'A thrilling and hilarious read' Liz Nugent

'A wonderful writer, whose characters, plots and atmosphere are masterfully drawn' Yrsa Sigurðardóttir

'Charming, funny and clever' *Literary Review*

'A delight from start to finish' *Big Issue*

'Original and brilliant storytelling' Helen FitzGerald

'Tuomainen is unique in the Scandi-crime genre, infusing his crime narratives with the darkest humour … [his] often hilarious, chaotic narrative never vitiates the novel's nicely tuned tension' *Financial Times*

'Tuomainen continues to carve out his own niche in the chilly tundra of northern Europe' *Daily Express*

'Quirky crime capers don't come more left-field than the Rabbit Factor trilogy … extremely funny, with a wicked line in social satire' *Daily Mail*

'*The Beaver Theory* is a fun and clever thriller in which a hero finds the right balance in all pursuits' Foreword Reviews

The Burning Stones

ABOUT THE AUTHOR

Finnish Antti Tuomainen was an award-winning copywriter when he made his literary debut in 2007 as a suspense author. In 2011, Tuomainen's third novel, *The Healer*, was awarded the Clue Award for Best Finnish Crime Novel and was shortlisted for the Glass Key Award. In 2013, the Finnish press crowned Tuomainen the 'King of Helsinki Noir' when *Dark as My Heart* was published. With a piercing and evocative style, Tuomainen was one of the first to challenge the Scandinavian crime-genre formula, and his poignant, dark and hilarious *The Man Who Died* became an international bestseller, shortlisting for the Petrona and Last Laugh Awards. *Palm Beach, Finland* (2018) was an immense success, with *The Times* calling Tuomainen 'the funniest writer in Europe', and *Little Siberia* (2019) was shortlisted for the Capital Crime/Amazon Publishing Readers Awards, the Last Laugh Award and the CWA International Dagger, won the Petrona Award for Best Scandinavian Crime Novel and will be coming to Netflix in 2025.

The Rabbit Factor, the first book in a trilogy that includes *The Moose Paradox* and *The Beaver Theory*, is now in production for TV with Amazon Studios, starring Steve Carell. *The Moose Paradox* was a Literary Review and *Guardian* Book of the Year and shortlisted for CrimeFest's Last Laugh Award.

Follow Antti on X/Twitter @antti_tuomainen, or on Facebook: facebook.com/AnttiTuomainen.

ABOUT THE TRANSLATOR

David Hackston is a British translator of Finnish and Swedish literature and drama. Notable recent publications include Kati Hiekkapelto's Anna Fekete series (published by Orenda Books), Katja Kettu's *The Midwife*, Pajtim Statovci's *My Cat Yugoslavia* and its follow-up, *Crossing*, and Maria Peura's *At the Edge of Light*. He has also translated Antti Tuomainen's *The Mine*, *The Man Who Died*, *Palm Beach, Finland*, *Little Siberia*, and *The Rabbit Factor* trilogy for Orenda Books. In 2007 he was awarded the Finnish State Prize for Translation. David is also a professional countertenor and a founding member of the English Vocal Consort of Helsinki. Follow David on X/Twitter @Countertenorist.

The Burning Stones

ANTTI TUOMAINEN

Translated from the Finnish by David Hackston

ORENDA
BOOKS

Orenda Books
16 Carson Road
West Dulwich
London SE21 8HU
www.orendabooks.co.uk

First published in the United Kingdom by Orenda Books, 2024
This B-format paperback edition published 2025
Originally published in Finland as *Palavat kivet* by Otava, 2023
Copyright © Antti Tuomainen, 2023
English language translation copyright © David Hackston, 2024

A catalogue record for this book is available from the British Library.

Hardback ISBN 978-1-916788-32-9
B-Format Paperback 978-1-916788-43-5
eISBN 978-1-916788-33-6

Orenda Books is grateful for the financial support of FILI, who provided a
translation grant for this project.

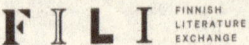

Typeset in Garamond by typesetter.org.uk
Printed and bound by Clays Ltd, Elcograf S.p.A

For sales and distribution, please contact *info@orendabooks.co.uk*

For Anu

'Tis a dim and dusky evening,
and sauna chimneys billow.

—Kaarlo Sarkia

PROLOGUE

Aaaaahhhhhh.

The steam spread over his skin like a hot, damp blanket and flowed evenly and satisfyingly slowly across his whole body, first his back and flanks, of course, which made his ears tingle, then gently squeezing his calves. Ilmo Räty concluded, once again, that having a sauna by yourself certainly had its benefits. It allowed you to concentrate, to throw as much or as little water on the stones as you wanted, to sit on the bench for as long and for as many times as you liked, and simply to enjoy the sacred, holistic experience that was ... the sauna.

And that's exactly what he had been doing for over an hour. He had just returned from a short dip in the lake to cool off – his third that evening. The lake was still and pleasantly warm, and the flicker of the fire chamber lit up the sauna like a lantern. He had added a few more logs, just enough to keep the temperature at a steady 80°C.

The shorter, darkening August evenings were made for bathing in the sauna, for bathing was exactly what this was, in every sense. In the old days, before running water, the sauna was considered a bathhouse – an almost holy place where families would come together and spend time washing themselves.

Right now, however, his thoughts were racing, galloping far beyond the confines of the sauna, which was, perhaps, understandable. He was about to be appointed CEO of the company. He had to admit, even he had been a little taken aback by the announcement.

That spring hadn't exactly been the finest period of his life.

His wife, Saija, had left him after he'd had a foolish dalliance at a skiing resort. The affair with a skiing instructor considerably his junior had ended with him learning to ski and the skiing instructor learning that after a hard day's skiing a man in late middle age doesn't have the energy for both dancing *and* romance. Not for more than a week, at any rate. To cap it all off, his adult children weren't speaking to him because they had heard from their mother that he had sent the skiing instructor (who was their age) a series of high-resolution photographs of his penis. They baulked at his explanation about the fateful combination of drink and impotence drugs taken at the wrong time – it was a whim, a moment of madness – and now they considered him just a dirty old man. All this meant that he'd had difficulty concentrating, difficulty sleeping, difficulties in general. But despite this – he was the chosen successor, and soon...

Why was his bottom suddenly tingling and tightening?

The steam couldn't get underneath him; and when he had sat down, the wood had been damp. Now it felt as though the bench had been replaced by a stove, and he was sitting on the red-hot stones, as though the stones themselves were on fire. He had to stand up...

The pain was the same as if something had exploded within his skull, as though every nerve ending had shattered into a thousand separate parts. He couldn't stand up, he was unable. It wasn't possible. He was ... stuck to the bench. How could this have happened?

And what was that noise coming from the changing room? He recognised the sound. Someone was taking logs out of the box then slamming the lid shut. The door into the sauna opened, and in walked...

The intruder, who was wearing a tight-fitting black outfit, complete with balaclava, turned directly towards the stove, opened the hatch and began piling fresh logs into the fire chamber.

Ilmo Räty asked what this was all about and again tried to stand up. Still to no avail. His buttocks and the back of his thighs were glued tight, perhaps even melted into the wooden bench. He thought – in fact, he was sure – that his superglued backside and the intruder putting more logs into the stove must somehow be linked. The intruder closed the stove's hatch with a clank, slipped out of the sauna and pressed the door firmly shut.

Ilmo Räty started to shout. First in an enquiring tone, then more stridently.

The logs in the fire chamber got to work. The temperature began to rise – and rise. The stove rumbled like a forest in a storm.

The intruder returned, added more logs, then left again.

Ilmo Räty had been in the sauna-stove business for almost ten years. He bathed several times a week. He knew a great deal about the effects of the sauna, both mental and physiological. He knew saunas were a clean and safe space – so much so, women used to give birth in them. But right now, that knowledge did little to calm him down; quite the opposite. He knew what lay ahead. And that's why he had to make at least some effort to resist.

The next time the figure in black stepped inside (by now, all Ilmo could see was a blur), he hurled the water ladle towards the door, managing to strike the intruder right in the forehead. But this did not stop the intruder, who once again filled the fire chamber with logs and left. But not immediately, not before wagging a reproachful forefinger at him.

That gesture! He knew it from somewhere.

He was certain of it. One last time, he tried to focus his gaze, but it was impossible. Then he remembered.

That finger!

Now he knew who the intruder was, who had adhered his backside to the bench, and who had wagged a finger at him.

At times he was unconscious, at times awake. The latter began to feel the stranger of the two. He thought to himself that somewhere there must surely be someone else who had sent penis pictures to his skiing instructor, then taken a 150-degree sauna and survived, but the idea began to feel increasingly improbable.

He wasn't sure whether he was imagining it or whether the sauna door did open, and the figure dressed in black did stand in the doorway one last time. Then the door closed. And it was closed regardless of whether he had imagined it being opened or not.

Ilmo Räty thought of the intruder again.

The thought surprised him.

Because now he knew why this had happened, why he was enjoying his sauna for the last time.

Why the temperature was continuing to rise.

In this sauna and in many other saunas too.

1

I steered the car into the lay-by and stepped out.

It was a warm morning, August still in full bloom. There were only a few scattered strips of cloud in the sky, gentle white brush-strokes far away along the horizon; another sweltering day to add to the week and a half of sweltering days that had just passed. I had driven a hundred kilometres, and there were about another three until I arrived at my destination. I was well ahead of time, and there was a good reason why.

Sixty-four hand-crafted wood-burning sauna stoves. It was a lot. Perhaps not in the grand scheme of things, perhaps not for factories that churn out mass-produced stoves, but for us, and for me, this order was a big one; it could even be make-or-break. Above all, it felt like a reward, because I'd been laying the groundwork for this deal since early spring.

I took a deep breath. The forest still smelt of summer, of blossoms, greenery and life.

I had plenty of experience of situations just like this one, and I don't think I'd misread the signals; I was certain that today we would finally seal the deal and place that order.

I was fifty-three years old, and I'd been selling handmade sauna stoves for twenty years. I'd met this potential customer several times, and as far as I could tell we understood each other's needs. I was intimately acquainted with every stage of the manufacturing and retail process, right from the original stove design to the bliss of bathing in the steam, from the initial brochures to closing the deal. Sometimes it felt as though I understood stoves better than anything else in my life.

I'd sold more stoves than anyone else in the history of Steam Devil, with the exception of the company's founder, Erkki 'The Stove King' Ruusula. I'd been able to match any and all offers made by our competitors – on both price and quality – and had gained people's trust one week, one phone call, one email at a time. And when, two weeks ago, I'd made another short phone call and asked if I could come and visit the site again, I was welcomed in the warmest of terms.

I watched a group of birds fly from one dark-green edge of the forest to the other. They crossed the marshlands quickly and effortlessly; they didn't have to worry about getting themselves stuck in the boggy ground. It didn't seem like a bad way of approaching my own situation.

I filled my lungs with the forest's fragrance one last time and felt better than I had done in a long while.

I returned to the car and started driving.

〰

'Anni Korpinen, the master saleswoman, in the flesh,' said the man as soon as we were within speaking distance. His name was Lauri Kahavuori. He was the founder and owner of Kaha Cabins Ltd, a semi-detached chalet conglomerate – as he called his medium-sized business. I was about to respond to his greeting when he continued: 'Quite the situation you've got going on.'

Of course, I knew what he was referring to, and his curiosity was understandable, but the utterance still took me by surprise. As did his expression, his body language. They had somehow changed since our last meeting a week and a half ago. Of course, a lot had happened at Puhtijärvi since then.

'It was a terrible shock,' I admitted, candidly, and I was reminded that one and a half weeks after Ilmo Räty's tragic death

I still had no more information on the matter than what the staff at Steam Devil had heard the day after the fire: a lakeside sauna had burned down, the fire brigade had discovered Ilmo inside, and the police had reason to believe that the fire had been started deliberately.

'The police are looking into it,' I said eventually. 'And, naturally, we're helping in any way we can.'

I hoped the subject was now dealt with and that we could move on. All the speculation and rumination on the matter had begun to feel voyeuristic, and as the days passed, it felt futile too.

'Quite,' said Kahavuori. 'I'm helping too.' His eyes seemed to sharpen.

I didn't understand what he meant. 'So...' I began, waited a moment, then continued. 'Obviously, I'm here to get things moving with those stoves and—'

'Of course,' he nodded. 'Always a good idea to get things moving.'

Kahavuori turned, the car-park gravel crunching beneath his shoes. We climbed up a small hill and passed a row of incomplete semi-detached chalets. The whole hillside was dotted with them. Thirty-two semi-detached chalets in total, each unit to be fitted with its very own sauna. And that meant sixty-four stoves.

Kahavuori came to a stop about halfway along the cluster of chalets, where a stretch of the terrain had been levelled flat.

'The sun is shining,' he said. 'These things almost build themselves, you know. Everything's going great.'

'I'm glad to hear it. So, we have—'

'And yet,' he said, and raised his hand, moving it in a horizontal line from left to right, from right to left, as though trying to sculpt the air in front of him. 'There are shadows, over there, over there, over there.'

Throughout the spring and summer months, Kahavuori had

turned out to be a tough negotiator. But I could never have imagined there would come a time when I genuinely had no idea what we were talking about.

'Of course, it's none of my business,' he added, 'but I have a few thoughts on the matter.'

'Thank you,' I said, still unsure what he was referring to. 'That's good to know.'

I remained silent for a moment, then decided to give it another shot. 'In our last counteroffer, we agreed that—'

'Seeing as we're talking about stoves, what say we talk in the sauna?'

This obviously wasn't an invitation to bathe with him. He meant the sauna facilities of the unfinished semi-detached chalet next to us.

The chalet was still nothing but a skeleton. The floors were nothing but bare, unsmoothed concrete. Our footsteps scuffed through the dim interior. I followed Kahavuori across the living room, into the utility room then through the changing room into the sauna. And with that, the glare of the summer's day was gone. Inside, the sauna was almost dark, and the sounds of construction work, which only a moment earlier had surrounded us, were now muffled echoes. Naturally, this sauna was only a sauna on paper; the wood panelling was missing, as was the stove, not to mention the benches. But nonetheless, here we were in the sauna, just the two of us, far away from the world outside.

'Jeffrey Dahmer,' Kahavuori almost whispered. 'Ted Bundy.'

'Excuse me?'

'I mean, for instance,' he said, and his voice was different now, coarser, closer to me. 'Someone who seems just like anybody else, roaming about the village of Puhtijärvi. Of course, those are extreme examples. Our guy wouldn't have to dismember his victims, keep their body parts in the fridge and turn them into dinner, or help the lonely by day only to turn into a bloodthirsty killer by night.'

Kahavuori's expression was expectant, and I couldn't see any other option but to answer him.

'No,' I said. 'I suppose not.'

'But the principle is the same,' he continued in that gravelly voice, 'because we know how many of them start by lighting fires. It's not so much the exception as the rule. And we know how many of them were the guy next door that everybody liked. Then afterwards everybody says, oh I'd never have thought Ed or Dennis or Asko from down the road could do a thing like that. What if this is, you know, a serial killer who's just getting started on his … series? I mean, it's always a possibility. That's all I'm trying to say.'

It was clear that Kahavuori's thoughts were focussed on something other than the sauna stoves. There was an intensity in his angular features, something I'd never seen before. His sharp nose looked more like a tool than part of a human face.

'It could be me,' he said quietly.

We looked each other in the eyes. He had turned his whole body to face me and was standing very close. There were several walls between us and the late-summer's day outside. I could hear neither Kahavuori's breath nor my own. I didn't think it particularly likely that he was about to kill me and then eat me, though I did worry that we were straying dangerously far from the topic of the stoves. But I didn't know what else I could do but engage with the discussion he had started, and moreover, do so on the wavelength he had chosen.

'Anything is possible,' I said eventually, in the gravelliest voice I could muster.

Kahavuori's expression brightened. 'That's what I mean,' he said. 'It could be somebody you know. I watch a lot of true crime, and I look into old cases. I'm really inside the discourse.'

'Is that so?'

Kahavuori nodded. 'As an escape from all this,' he said, waving his hand, and immediately sounding a little less enthusiastic. 'The building trade can be heavy stuff.'

Now he looked stressed, even a little troubled.

'So, to bring us back to these stoves,' he said and pointed to the small space in the corner where the stove belonged. 'You know I want a genuine Steam Devil stove, right there. The product is second to none, as they say, and the offer was very well put together – I would expect nothing less from you and the company. But ... we're a family business – we sell our houses to families – and the cornerstone of our brand is reliability and a certain ... decency. So, if, under the present circumstances, we install a Steam Devil, and then a nice, happy, sauna-loving family arrives here on holiday and sits down on that bench right there...' Kahavuori indicated the empty space on the wall where the benches would eventually be situated '... and they throw some water on the stones and see the company insignia on the side of the stove,' he continued, and I was sure I even heard a sigh, 'then they might start wondering which of them is going to be brutally murdered first. If nothing else, it'd be a vibe-killer. And that wouldn't be the kind of happy family moment that we're known for, that I want people to know us for. The attraction of Kaha Cabins lies in their harmony and security – not serial-killer stoves.'

I looked at him. He seemed genuine in what he said. A feeling began to rise within me, and I quickly realised it was panic – or maybe simply horror. But it wasn't horror at the idea of murder or dismemberment – real or imagined – it was at the possibility that I saw forming before me. I had to get this conversation back on track.

'I'm sure there are no serial killers roaming the streets of Puhtijärvi,' I said calmly, though I could hardly believe such a thing needed to be said. 'And I don't believe that our stoves will in any way—'

'I'm afraid I can't commit to the purchase right now,' Kahavuori interrupted. 'Not before we've got to the bottom of the matter.'

Now I knew precisely what he was getting at.

Something enormous descended onto my shoulders, a great burden, and at the same time the ground disappeared from under my feet. I caught my breath, trying to do so as imperceptibly as possible. I could smell the building materials – the wood, the paint, the coatings. I was certain that, outwardly, I looked the same as when I'd arrived – calm and confident – and I reminded myself that twenty-two years' experience of selling sauna stoves and fifty-three years of life experience were distinctly good things. Say what you like about middle age; at least it gives you the chance to slow down.

I looked again at Kahavuori, and I knew with the fullness and certainty of all that experience that he wasn't going to change his mind.

I said I was sorry and that I was very sad to hear that. I told him I would get back to the matter of the stoves as soon as the other, more unfortunate, matter had been cleared up, which would be very soon indeed, and that we could then continue from where we had left off. Kahavuori nodded; he genuinely seemed to agree. I glanced at my watch, thanked him for the meeting and said that I had to get going.

Kahavuori seemed to perk up. 'I have a couple of alternative theories...'

We exited the chalet, walked back down the hill to my Volvo, and Kahavuori talked. He certainly did have theories, most of them even further removed from Puhtijärvi than the afore-mentioned American cannibals.

The day was getting sultrier by the minute. I could only see a single sliver of cloud in the sky. It occurred to me that only a short while ago I'd felt the power and vitality of the day inside me. Now it just felt hot, the air almost glued to my skin.

We arrived at the car park. I got into my car and started the engine. I reversed, turned, then slowly pulled up next to Kahavuori. I rolled down the window to remind him that I would get back to him very soon, but he got there first. His sharp nose seemed to jut right out of his face and felt as though it was poking its way into the car.

'You know,' he said, 'saunas can be fatal.'

2

I was clenching the steering wheel. Tight.

I only realised it when I reached a long, straight section of road. I loosened my grip a little and adjusted my position in the seat, but now it felt like something was tightening its grip on *me*. And it couldn't all be because, instead of signing on the dotted line, my client had volunteered his help in hunting down notorious cannibals. A delay to the deal would be a huge headache, though, and if it were cancelled altogether, it would be a catastrophe, like a bucket of cold water thrown over an already dangerously cooling stove.

No, this sense that some greater force was clenching me in its grip was the result of an even greater uncertainty, one that had far-reaching implications.

It had all started at the end of January, when Erkki 'The Stove King' Ruusula, founder and main shareholder of the sauna-stove factory, informed us of his intention to step down from his position as CEO and reduce his stake in the business considerably. On the surface, this decision wasn't exactly unexpected. Erkki was seventy-five years old, the sauna-stove business no longer seemed as close to his heart as it once was, and he had become a little distant and even inconsistent in his decision-making. He'd told us that ever since becoming a widower, he'd felt very lonely in his vast lakeside villa, that he needed a little more sunshine, while in the same breath mentioning the terraced house he owned on the Costa del Sol and all the wonders that awaited him there: fresh figs in the bowl on the balcony table, the Andalucian vigour of the local

masseuse – a firm tenderness, he called it – and flamenco. Some
of these things I'd heard from him directly, others I'd picked
up elsewhere. All in all, it was in many ways perfectly understandable that he was keen to pass on responsibility for the
company to someone else.

Erkki's children didn't seem particularly interested in hand-
crafted sauna stoves, though, except when it came to their
annual dividends, so he had plumped for another solution. He
had announced a competition would be held to select his
successor from the ranks of the company, and a few months
later the winner was named as Ilmo Räty. Who, a few weeks
later, ended up dead.

And now, nobody appeared to know what was going to
happen next.

Not that the future of Steam Devil had been clear while Ilmo
Räty was alive, either. For a long while, Ilmo had said that as
long as you agree on a price, everything else should be up for
renegotiation – even the company's independence and its
geographical location. Like our five other employees, I too had
been in the race to succeed Erkki, and I had completely
disagreed with Ilmo. I still did.

For me, in order for Steam Devil to survive, it had to remain
independent, and it had to remain in Puhtijärvi. On more than
one occasion, I'd pointed out that I had been in the sauna-stove
business long enough to know what would happen if we were
to sell off parts of our company and end up being absorbed into
a larger concern. The big stoves always swallow up the smaller
ones, like wood for their fire chambers; then they puff them up
into the sky, producing very little heat in the process.
Relocating would do the same: Steam Devil would lose first its
steam, and eventually all the devils who worked for it.

The idea plagued me now too, as I sped between the walls

of dark-green forest slightly in excess of the speed limit, all the while trying to resist the temptation to drive even faster. The risk of colliding with an elk, which the road signs warned me about, was very real.

I knew that I thought about Steam Devil – and stoves in general – far too much. And while I was a middle-aged woman in the prime of her life and not a hand-crafted premium stove, I did seem to be taking the matter very personally, as though every stove was a small part of me, and if something threatened them, it threatened me too.

Not only that: the way I thought of Puhtijärvi seemed to have changed recently. I still enjoyed the small, peaceful village with all its bays and coves, the village where I'd spent my whole life. I truly believed that this was where I belonged. But I'd felt more conflicted about it in recent weeks than I had for a long time. For thirty years, to be precise. For some curious reason, Puhtijärvi now felt the same as it had back then, all those years ago – small and claustrophobic, and placing restrictions on my movements.

Everything suddenly felt more alive to me than it had in years, but I couldn't say why, nor why my mind was constantly and repeatedly pulling up flickering, fleeting memories of that autumn evening thirty years back.

Each image like a flash in a dark theatre.

The nocturnal lake.

The rocking boat.

The bloodied lure.

My trembling hands.

The flashes were followed by a familiar heaviness, familiar shadows – of things I'd learnt to live with but that seemed more and more reluctant to stay where I had thrust them.

Perhaps this was why Kahavuori's refusal to sign on the dotted line had felt so bad.

I knew what it felt like when the sky came crashing down on your shoulders. And I was afraid it might happen again. I was afraid that everything would collapse, and I instinctively thought that cancelling the deal would set off a chain reaction that would lead directly to that collapse. I felt as though something frightening was on its way, something that had been biding its time beneath the surface, something that would change everything.

The phone rang, and I flinched back to reality. When I saw the caller's name, I was perplexed. I flicked the button on the steering wheel, and Erkki Ruusula's voice filled the car.

'How did you get on with Kahavuori?' he asked.

I paused for a moment.

'In what sense?' I asked, playing for time, because I had no idea how he'd found out about my meeting. I'd certainly not told him.

'Is he going to order our stoves?' Erkki asked. 'For his cottage conglomerate?'

'I'm working on it,' I said.

'What's the hold-up?'

American psychos. I decided not to try and explain this to Erkki. It would only lead to an even less productive conversation than the one we were having right now.

'Just some minor details about the stoves,' I said. 'I'll go back again early next week.'

Erkki was silent for a moment.

'Do you want me to come with you?' he asked.

I was unable to answer. Erkki hadn't suggested anything like this for years. I had always worked pretty independently, to put it mildly. For Erkki, results were all that mattered. Which might in fact have been the reason for his surprise suggestion. We both knew I'd fallen short of my usual sales targets this year.

But what he was suggesting was not a solution to the matter. It was the polar opposite.

'Kahavuori and I have established a strong line of communication,' I said, and this was certainly true. 'But if the situation changes or I need some help, I'll let you know right away.'

Again, Erkki was silent. The grey road and the blue sky stretched out in front of me.

'I'm only too happy to help,' he said. 'And you'll remember, I have all kinds of experience when it comes to selling stoves.'

'Thank you,' I said, then waited a second, two... 'Yes, I remember. You managed to sell stoves to Oman.'

I admit, this last bit was flattery: a reference to Erkki's own favourite anecdote about how he sold a turbo-stove to people living on the edge of a desert, a place where the temperature in an outdoor sauna would have been 60°C even without a stove. But I had to avoid, at all costs, a situation in which Erkki decided that a joint sales mission was the solution to our problems. I hoped that flattering him would make that possibility a little more distant.

'Oh yes,' he began, and I could hear how chuffed he was. 'I started by telling them that here in Finland we have a place even warmer than your desert, and once we started talking...'

I let Erkki tell the story that I'd first heard over twenty years ago. The late summer hummed around the car on both sides. Lakes and ponds glistened through the trees as I passed. I wasn't thinking about the story but about the call itself, its timing and Erkki's suggestion. In fact, I was thinking about it so intensely that I only noticed the silence a few seconds after the end of the story.

'Yes...' I said, and was about to continue when Erkki jumped in.

'One more thing,' he said, and now his tone of voice was more formal, not quite as yarn-spinning as before. 'There's a meeting tomorrow, and I'd like you to be there.'

Erkki told me the time of the meeting, and I was about to end the call when he said: 'Thank you for this little chat. It really cheered me up.'

I managed to blurt out something like the feeling was mutual then ended the call, and Erkki disappeared from my speakers. I watched the road gently curving ahead of me, and I thought I could see the air shimmering from the heat.

Three things:

There was no doubt that, if need be, Erkki was capable of running his business with an iron fist, but for a long time now he hadn't wanted to be involved in the day-to-day minutiae; at times he was even becoming, dare I say it, a little careless. So what had changed? Finances were tight – but that was nothing new. Artisanal sauna stoves were hard to sell and didn't really excite the masses. In practice, we'd always had our backs to the wall.

My second concern was the prospect of joint sales trips. The very thought was nerve-wracking. I had done my job alone and quite successfully for twenty years – the last six months notwithstanding. I didn't think that Erkki, with his new style of bouncing from one subject to the next, would be of any use in tricky negotiations.

Finally, and strangest of all, was that he seemed to know all about my visit to Kahavuori. I hadn't told anybody that I was going to see him and I hadn't gone to the office beforehand; I'd set off from my very own driveway. And despite all his wild and gory theories, Kahavuori didn't seem like the kind of person who would first tell me of his radical change of heart, only to call Erkki a moment later, especially given that the two had never been in direct contact. For the life of me, I couldn't think how Erkki had heard about my visit, or why.

I glanced at the clock. I didn't have any meetings scheduled at the office or anything else that required my presence. I decided to take care of my remaining emails and bits and bobs remotely, at home. I drove straight back to Pilviniemi.

I noticed I was clenching the steering wheel again.

3

The yellow house glided into view from behind the birches, and for a moment it looked like it was slowly but surely sliding towards the lake opening up before me. Of course, this wasn't the case. The house was located on a gentle slope along the eastern shore of a narrow peninsula, in precisely the same place where it had been erected eighty years earlier. Its elevated granite foundations would make sure it stayed there too.

I took the final turn towards the house, heard the crunch of the gravel beneath my tyres. Again I wondered at how that perfectly mundane, everyday sound could seem so pleasantly familiar. And the thought felt a lot less nerve-wracking than my previous ones. Throughout the journey, I'd tried to get to the bottom of my problems, which seemed like a whole cluster of challenges, both new and old. I stopped the car, switched off the engine and looked, perhaps a little longer than usual, at the two-storey house, the unmown lawn and the open window, and I quickly realised that arriving home was going to help me with my thoughts no more than being on the road. I supposed I hadn't expected it to. I stepped out of the car.

The air was still, the tall birches cast just enough shade across the front garden. The lake looked as though it had been stuck onto the landscape, never to move or change again. From this place, this spot, there was no way of seeing into the neighbours' gardens, either to the right or the left. Two kilometres away, across the lake, was the national park, a distant green strip along the horizon. I'd sometimes thought that if paradise existed, or if such a thing were ever created, it needn't differ from the landscape in front of me. That being said, paradise might not *sound* quite like this.

When it came up in conversation or when people asked me, 'What's the best thing about living out by the lake?' I never said it was the silence. I certainly couldn't have said that now.

The motors wailed, almost in agony. The commentator sounded like he was about to leap out of his skin.

I looked up at the open window, where the sound was coming from, and I looked at the garden, which needed some attention. I collected my stuff from the car and took the three steps up to the front door. Once inside, I took off my shoes, walked into the kitchen, drank a glass of cold water, then another. I stood for a moment, my hip resting against the kitchen counter, and considered my options. Eventually, my eardrums made the decision for me.

I walked across the living room, my whole body feeling the wall of sound growing, both in pitch and intensity. I opened the first sliding door and arrived in the hallway that we had once intended to turn into an extension of the living room. It hadn't happened. The hall was still a hallway.

I opened the second sliding door. The noise was dizzying. It felt as though I was following the race from right next to the track.

Santeri was sitting in his armchair; the cars were whizzing around their course. The image on the large TV screen was faint and unclear. Which was understandable; manually recorded VHS tapes from the 1980s and 1990s were like that. This was one of hundreds of such tapes. Still, I was sure I'd seen – or should I say, heard – this particular tape before. I said this aloud, making sure Santeri heard me.

He flinched, fumbled for the remote control between his bare thighs.

'What?' he asked as the grainy cars froze on the screen.

'Monaco, nineteen eighty-eight,' I said, nodding at the television.

Santeri looked at me as though I were speaking a foreign language, then I saw the penny drop. A pout, a shake of the head.

'Zandvoort, Holland,' he said. 'Nineteen eighty-two.'

'Close,' I said.

'What?' he asked again; he sounded about as incredulous as if I'd just told him I'd been elected president. 'No, no, not even close, no, that's—'

'Fried sprats for dinner?' I suggested. 'I thought, if you mow the lawn, I'll heat up the sauna and fry the sprats. Or the other way around. If I mow the lawn, you could—'

'I can't,' he said, quickly glancing at the television, then at me, a deep furrow between his eyebrows. 'Haven't got time. I've got to finish watching this. There's a panel discussion on Zoom later. We're going to go through the race.'

'The race ended forty years ago,' I said without thinking.

At this, the room seemed suddenly a little darker. Or perhaps a change in Santeri caused the light to dim. I knew what I'd said. It was a touchy subject. No, not touchy; it was sacred.

And right now, we were in the inner sanctum, the Holy Church of Formula One, Santeri's very own Sagrada Familia. The room was quite large, but it was also full. The walls were lined with shelves of video tapes, all of long-gone races that played out in our house time and time again. The tables, glass cabinets, plinths and various display panels were adorned with collector's items, everything from helmets to jumpsuits, hundreds of sashes, stickers, badges and assorted paraphernalia. And on one of the tables there was a bona fide, used Formula One tyre: Mika Häkkinen's front left tyre from his world championship race. The real deal. According to Santeri, at least.

Our living room was a hub for the buying and selling of Formula One collectibles. In theory.

The Formula One collectors' club was a business idea Santeri had set up about ten years ago. It was his life, and that was why he'd left his day job as an electrician. The business wasn't exactly a roaring success. It didn't turn a profit – it never had – and as the years went by the reason for this became apparent, even to me: Santeri himself was his own business's greatest client.

'You know I don't like sprats.'

Oh, Santeri, always so boyish. I suppose that's what I'd been so taken with at first, perhaps even what I'd fallen in love with. He was boyishly handsome, even now. Which, in fact, was nothing short of a miracle given that he spent most of his time in this room, and most of that time in his armchair. Yet there he was, in his fifties, still well proportioned, still with his dimples, his big round eyes and hair that looked like it wanted to curl but couldn't quite manage it. And, of course, telling me what food was good enough for him and what was not.

'I forgot,' I said, though suddenly I wasn't so sure I had forgotten. 'But if you could tear yourself away from Nigel Mansell for a—'

'This isn't Nigel Mansell!' Santeri snapped, and I almost detected a note of hurt in his voice. 'Pironi, Piquet, Rosberg.'

It had already been a difficult, muggy day. Now I felt as though I was glued to the spot.

'Have it your way,' I said. 'Maybe one of them could cut the grass.'

Santeri leapt out of his chair. He took a few steps then spun round to look at me. I noted that he was now standing on the spot where he often stood when we talked about difficult matters: right next to Häkkinen's tyre.

He pursed his lips and exhaled slowly. 'You don't take this seriously,' he said. 'You never have.'

Of course, we'd spoken about this before, but this time Santeri looked particularly upset. As though I'd said something far worse than simply mentioning Nigel Mansell and suggesting Piquet might be a dab-hand with a lawnmower.

'How about I heat up the sauna?' I suggested, trying to sound as conciliatory as possible.

'I've already had a shower,' said Santeri.

'A shower?'

'Yes.'

'The lake's over twenty degrees today. Why didn't you just go for a swim?'

Santeri quickly glanced at the racing tyre next him, then looked up at me again. 'It was windy,' he said.

'Windy?'

'Yes, the lake ... was windy.'

'When?' I asked. I was genuinely curious. I recalled the shimmering road, the stagnant air in the garden.

I could see the agitation on his face. The redness spreading across his cheeks only seemed to heighten the impression of boyishness.

'Does it really matter when exactly it was windy?' he asked. 'I suppose it must have been when I decided not to go for a swim.'

'I just didn't notice any wind,' I said. 'And it was a hot day today.'

Santeri shook his head. 'I haven't got time for all this ... hot air,' he said. 'I'm in a hurry...'

'Where are you going?'

'Zandvoort, of course,' he said, and now he sounded distinctly agitated. 'They still haven't had the first tyre change. The race is only halfway through.'

I was about to say something, but I didn't. I looked at Santeri in his McLaren polo shirt and light-blue shorts. He could have been a surfer in an American movie. At the same time, I both understood and did not understand why I had once made the choices I'd made. Our conversation had followed the usual pattern, even beyond the details of the racing cars and teams. Santeri hadn't asked anything about my day. He never did. I used to think of this as another example of his boyish behaviour, but these days I didn't know what it meant. On top of which, I now had a sense that I'd mentioned the sprats for a reason. I thanked him for our little chat and wished him luck at Zandvoort. And I meant it.

⌇

I mowed the lawn and warmed up the sauna. By the time I sat down in the sauna, the sun had already set.

Logs crackled in the fire chamber, their glow lighting the sauna through the glass hatch. I scooped up a ladleful of water, threw it on the stove and paid close attention to every stage of the process: the sizzle, the steam, the blanket of air – just hot enough – the beads of sweat on my skin. I didn't know why I'd suggested Santeri and I have a sauna together. He didn't much care for the sauna. I, on the other hand, loved it. And I enjoyed having a sauna by myself. It had to be said that, in many ways, this was my sauna. I had taken care of the renovations, designed the interior, chosen the stove (of course) and – now that I think of it – I had always carried the logs from the woodshed and heated it myself. Naturally, I'd paid for all this myself too.

To me, these familiar benches and the familiar, soft-yet-powerful steam were a place where I could finally relax, let go of everything. Over the years, I'd become used to the idea that whenever I had problems or concerns, the sauna always helped me resolve them. The combination of sauna and lake had the power to loosen even the bonds that bound me most tightly to the world and its events and provided a much-needed sense of distance. But this time, as I threw another ladleful of water onto the stove and listened as it hissed on the hot stones, several things came into focus at once. Right now, taking a step back seemed impossible: there was no room in any direction.

Ilmo Räty, Steam Devil, Kaha Cabins, Erkki Ruusula, Santeri.

The sauna arson, the murder, a small company's quandary, a true-crime-loving chalet mogul, the looming change of CEO, and a marriage that felt like it had abandoned the race and driven back to the pit.

And though I felt the need to complain about everything piling up at once, to moan and marvel about how everything happens at the same time, I couldn't do it.

I knew better.

Nothing that had happened today had actually started today. Some of these things were probably as old as me. Even the most recent were already celebrating their anniversaries.

I cast more water on the stove.

In my heart of hearts, I couldn't say that any of these problems had come as a surprise to me. Life is like a sauna stove. When you heat it, it warms up. I was fifty-three years old. I knew it was pointless trying to pretend I'd made all the right decisions, and I knew I didn't have to look far to see where the buck stopped. There was no one else in the sauna but me.

The water in the lake felt soft – still warm from the day's heat. I swam about seven hundred metres around the dark bay. Long, calm strokes, elegant glides beneath the surface. Only once I got back to the shore and climbed onto the jetty did I truly register the strain in my muscles.

I wrapped a towel around myself and sat on the wooden chair at the end of the jetty. The house was half dark, the sauna sparsely illuminated. It didn't matter. I knew this terrain, the forms of the buildings. My eyes panned across the dips and dells, though parts of the landscape had already sunk into darkness. I remembered the location of every tree, every shrub, and I knew precisely the limits and extent of the porch, though its far end vanished into the late-evening dim. The jetty boards beneath my feet still held the last vestiges of the afternoon warmth. I sat there until my breathing steadied.

Then I walked back, washed my hair, rinsed the inside of the sauna and left my towel on the railing to dry.

In the kitchen, I coated the sprats in rye flour, fried them in butter and ate them by myself.

4

The company's three buildings formed three sides of what might otherwise be called a square. The fourth side was open, allowing people to drive into the factory, the warehouse building and the office wing standing between them. Of the three buildings, the red office building was by far the smallest, though it was the size of a largish, prefabricated bungalow. Behind it glistened the expansive, open waters of Lake Puhtijärvi.

I turned off the road from the village and into the car park, right in the middle of which stood the Stove, towering about fifteen metres tall. The Stove, with a capital S, because this was the name of the sculpture commissioned from a local artist to celebrate the company's thirtieth anniversary, a work whose maintenance had proved surprisingly demanding. Small stones kept falling off the Stove, and animals had nested in its fire chamber; mostly hares, pine martens and once even a fox. It looked like a distinctly Finnish version of the Tower of Pisa, leaning gently to one side, only unlike its Italian cousin, this leaning tower wasn't constantly surrounded by a throng of tourists.

I parked my car at the foot of the Stove and walked towards the office wing.

The small, slightly dark foyer was quiet. It was rarely anything else. As always, it smelt of the characteristic birch whisks that served as a design element along one of the walls. Erkki had come up with this idea, and he made sure someone replaced the old whisks with fresh ones at regular intervals.

The first room I walked past was that of finance manager, Susanna Luoto. I didn't know why she had specifically asked for a room *without* a view across the lake. Susanna was standing in front of a filing cabinet and noticed me in the corridor. I said good morning; she said good morning. I was almost past her door when I heard her speak:

'There was a mistake in your mileage invoice.'

I stopped and returned to the doorway. Susanna was a small, carefully groomed woman, who usually wore a thick layer of make-up, which nonetheless never crossed the boundaries of good taste and instead came across as an example of her thoroughness, her general preparedness for any situation that might come her way. She looked at me, her eyes bright and green.

'What kind of mistake?' I asked.

Susanna flicked her hair as if it was in front of her eyes. It was not. 'A discrepancy of three kilometres and four hundred metres,' she said, now a little more loudly. 'I can't just turn a blind eye.'

I thought of all the other employees whose jobs involved a lot of driving. I knew that Porkka, for instance, was almost as creative about the kilometres he drove as he was about developing new sauna stoves. Besides, I hadn't filed an incorrect invoice on purpose. I'd made a mistake, which was understandable given how many hundreds of kilometres I drove each week.

'Fine,' I said. 'Show me the mistake and I'll correct it—'

'Then there's a lunch at Ulminiemi Manor,' she added.

I had to think for a moment. Then I remembered.

'That was six months ago,' I said. 'I invited a potential client for lunch, the manor was under renovation, the bathrooms had been stripped out both in the private apartments and the hotel, and I just thought—'

'It wasn't itemised,' Susanna continued. 'So now it looks like you travel the country having fancy lunches at the company's expense.'

There were many things about this situation that I didn't understand. Susanna knew very well that Ulminiemi doesn't do fancy lunches. It was a restaurant you visited for the view, but even the bubbling rapids and majestic rock formations couldn't make up for the miserable food. But my greatest confusion was reserved for something else: the question of her volume. Why was she speaking so loudly, though I was only standing a metre and a half away from her?

'If you just send me—'

'I've already sent it to Erkki,' she said. 'But I can send you a copy.'

We looked each other in the eye. Then Susanna turned back to her wall of files and folders. It seemed the conversation was over. I continued on my way.

Among other things, Ilmo Räty's death had revealed just how little I knew about my colleagues. Or perhaps it had shown new sides to everybody. Susanna had always been pedantic, but now it seemed like she couldn't rein in that side of her personality any longer: even the smallest mistake, a form filled out incorrectly, a missing cent here or there now seemed grounds for an obsessive accounting witch hunt, the results of which still left her unsatisfied.

But this was as nothing compared to how worried Mirka Paarmajärvi had become.

I spotted her in her oblong office, where half the walls were made of glass, and thought that, should we ever need another statue to erect next to the Stove, here was the perfect candidate. Mirka looked frozen in front of her tall monitor. The thirty-six-year-old amateur bodybuilder had been the fretting type before, but during the last week and a half her muscular right arm seemed to have become attached to her copper-brown brow. I understood her pensive, presumably painful, forward-leaning posture, though. She was responsible for logistics, warehouse management, orders, deliveries – everything that came in and everything that went out. And right now our stoves weren't moving as much as we needed them to. It was as though Mirka had taken the gradual accumulation of unsold stock very personally: her blouse seemed to get tighter across her broad shoulders by the day.

After passing Mirka's room, I turned. I quickly glanced towards the so-called northern wing but didn't see any movement near Erkki's office. And I managed to avoid bumping into Kaarlo, which was a source of great relief, today just as it was every day.

My office was on the side nearest the lake. I loved the view that opened up through my floor-to-ceiling windows and filtered between the dark trunks of the tall, straight, stately pines. Between them I could see Pitkäselkä – the stretch of open water on the other side of Lake Puhtijärvi – as well as the forests, houses and cottages along the opposite shore. On this side of the lake, diagonally to my left, I could see three log cabins. Smoke rose from one of the chimneys.

I walked right up to the windows and watched the smoke more carefully. It was thick, powerful. The fire chamber had just been refilled. Just then, I saw Porkka walking between the saunas with a towel around his waist.

Porkka was a stove enthusiast through and through, a resourceful, thick-moustachioed man, passionate and even zealous when it came to his inventions, constantly carrying out new trials and experiments. His reaction to Ilmo's death had been an intensification of this behaviour. He seemed to work night and day, and this morning's sauna must be related to some new feature he wanted to test. He stopped, looked like he was listening for something, his head turning slowly from side to side. Or perhaps he was just admiring the rippling of the blue lake, taking it in from slightly different angles. Whatever it was, it didn't last long. Porkka disappeared into the steaming sauna, and I sat down at my desk.

I emailed two counteroffers, and even as I typed them out I knew that neither would lead to the desired result. After this, I combed through my inbox, without coming across any surprises, let alone happy ones. And I did not need Kaarlo's smart-arsed reminders that we didn't just manufacture sauna stoves; we were supposed to sell them too. I knew this perfectly well. I even dreamt about stoves.

Which reminded me that, yet again, I had spent the night alone. This was nothing new. Santeri had his own mattress in his Formula One museum, and it felt as though, years ago, and without ever discussing the matter, we had reached the decision that he would sleep there. What I thought about now, though, was the silence during the night. I hadn't heard Santeri. I hadn't woken up to his movements, the sound of him fetching something to eat, his heated online discussions or the roar of motors. I thought about what had happened yesterday and concluded that maybe the reason I hadn't heard anything was because I was so exhausted.

I spun around in my chair, gazed out at the lake.

Of course, Ilmo Räty's death had affected me – in ways I could never have foreseen. Initially, I'd felt almost paralysed. Ilmo was my colleague, and though I'd never known him properly – didn't know what he was *really* like – I'd spent a lot of time in his company. He was good at his job, notwithstanding a few unusual slip-ups back in the spring. I didn't know what had caused these, but Ilmo had looked like he was just getting over whatever it was when...

The consensus was that the sauna arsonist must be Ilmo's wife. Their divorce had been sudden and bitter, and it was generally felt that Saija was out for revenge. On top of that, it turned out that Ilmo had amassed quite the fortune, something he was known to feel very passionately about and wouldn't give up any part of without a fight. For many people, this created an obvious connection between Saija and the sauna. The thought had occurred to me too. I'd met Saija a few times, and it didn't surprise me that she had fallen out with almost everyone in the village. But being arrogant and always knowing best is one thing; setting a sauna ablaze is another. But it wasn't impossible.

Another popular theory was that a pyromaniac must have been responsible. Somebody wanted to set fire to something, and Ilmo's lakeside sauna had been too much to resist. This theory was supported by the recent burning-down of an old, half-collapsed barn in Sinijärvi a few months ago. At first, the fire was attributed to youngsters, maybe a drunken prank gone wrong, but now people seemed to think there was an active pyromaniac roaming the area, someone whose behaviour had now escalated. On top of this, some of the older residents recalled the mysterious island fires of two decades ago: at the height of summer, when the ground was tinder-dry, someone had built bonfires on the small islands dotted throughout Lake Puhtijärvi and set them alight, then disappeared, causing several near catastrophes, suggesting that, for some people, fire is an element that can never satiate the appetite, not even after all these years.

The third theory focussed on Ilmo's recent appointment as Steam Devil's next CEO: someone objected to the idea so much that they decided to get rid of Ilmo. This felt a little extreme, to put it mildly. Of course, Ilmo had had his own ideas about how best to develop the company, but everybody knew that Erkki planned to stay on as chairman of the board of directors for the next two years – no matter that he had already mentally checked out – and Ilmo wouldn't have had much power for a long time yet. Which in turn meant that a potential murderer wouldn't be in a hurry; there would be at least two years to burn down the sauna.

The fourth and perhaps most plausible theory was that this was about something else entirely. As it turned out, nobody knew Ilmo very well, if at all. He had arrived in the village ten years ago, and nobody really knew where he'd come from or why he'd ended up in Puhtijärvi. He had a family, but he'd made no connections with the locals, and nobody seemed to know of anybody who had ever said more than a few words to him outside of work. And at work everything about him was business-like, even his penchant for the sauna. He seemed to enjoy it, though for him that too was work. *Summa summarum*: Ilmo Räty had always been something of a mystery.

I'd decided not to discuss the subject any further with my colleagues. But that didn't mean that I didn't still have unanswered questions. But I had some new questions now. Questions that had changed focus and that I didn't ask out loud. Questions about me.

My fifty-three years, my life.

If my sauna were to burn down with me inside it, what would I think?

'Miniatures,' I heard behind me. 'Do you want to take part too?'

I knew who was speaking without having to turn around. I did though and saw Jarkko peering into my office.

'What's this about?' I asked.

'I'm selling some miniature models,' he said, taking a step closer.

This meant he was now right in the middle of my office. Jarkko Mutikallio stood almost six foot seven inches tall, and his shoes must have been a size fifteen. He was both the tallest and the largest CEO's personal assistant that I knew. I suspected he was the tallest and the largest CEO's personal assistant in general. He almost always wore enormous flannel shirts, and he had dark, naturally thick and quite long hair, and maybe this was why I often thought of an indie band consisting entirely of exceptionally large men whenever I saw him.

'The proceeds are going to the Puhtijärvi sports club,' said Jarkko. 'For the junior football team's new shirts. The old ones still have the Caravan Beer logo. The local brewery went out of business years ago, and the boys say the other teams laugh at them. I don't know why. Anyway, the new shirts are going to have the logo of Catwalk, a local modelling school that—'

'This is a lot to put together,' I said.

Jarkko seemed to have forgotten about the object in his right hand. He looked at it.

'An aircraft carrier with fighter planes on deck,' he said. 'It's a surprisingly small and nifty set, actually.'

The set was not small. Having said that, even our stoves would have looked small in the palm of Jarkko's hand. I thought about the miniature aircraft carrier and its fleet of fighters. And almost as quickly, I thought that, all things considered, it looked like one aircraft carrier and twenty fighters too many. I'd bought Jarkko's fundraising miniature models before. I still hadn't built a single one of them.

'It's a no to the aircraft carrier,' I said. 'But if there's any other way of contributing towards the new shirts, I'd be glad to help.'

At first, Jarkko looked a little disappointed, but he said it was possible. Then he said that the miniature models weren't the real reason he was here.

'I came to confirm your presence at the meeting,' he said. 'It will be starting soon. Erkki said it's of the utmost importance that you're there.'

'What does "of the utmost importance" mean?' I asked. 'In this context?'

Jarkko seemed to think about this for a moment.

'He didn't say, just that it was of the utmost importance that—'

'Fine,' I said. 'Thanks, Jarkko.'

Jarkko nodded, again looking like he was thinking about something. This time I couldn't even begin to imagine what.

'Are you sure about the models?' he asked after a pause. 'It could make a nice change for you. All you do is go to the sauna every evening.'

I stared at him. I didn't remember ever discussing my sauna habits with him. Still, it was perfectly possible that he could have been within earshot when the subject had come up. But I wasn't sure I remembered when that might have happened.

'Thank you,' I said eventually. 'I've still got last year's to keep me going.'

Jarkko reminded me about the meeting once more, then quickly turned around. With a single stride, he was out in the corridor. I knew he was nimble for a man his size, but it still took me by surprise every time. He was about to disappear from view when I remembered what he'd said before.

'Jarkko,' I called out, and he stopped. 'About that new sponsorship deal. Have you made sure that—?'

Jarkko looked like I'd asked the most obvious thing imaginable.

'Of course,' he said. 'This one isn't about to go into administration. It seems like a popular place. Everybody's talking about Catwalk. The boys are going to love it. See you in the Sauna.'

5

The Sauna (capital S) referred to the largest of our conference rooms. The sauna theme was evident in the light-coloured birch panelling on the walls, the linen seat covers and the black sauna stove permanently on display in the corner of the room. This particular model was called Steam Devil I. It was the company's very first stove model, though this was obviously not the very first unit. That had been sold by the man sitting at the head of the table, Erkki 'The Stove King' Ruusula.

If it was possible, the day beyond the windows had become brighter still. The lake was dazzling in the sunlight; it almost hurt the eyes to look at it, so I sat down with my back to the lake and glanced over to the other side of the table, where Mirka and Porkka were already sitting.

Mirka had pulled her peroxide-blonde hair into a tight ponytail; in the bright sunlight her taut, tanned face was like carefully sculpted metal. Next to her, Porkka gleamed bright red – sauna-fresh. His thick black moustache looked like a broad-headed brush that he had brought back from his sauna trip and that had for some reason been left to idle on his face. He poured a glass of sparkling water; Mirka gave a sigh.

I looked over at Erkki, who appeared to be reading a document in front of him. His overall appearance seemed to combine two men and two eras: he was still broad-shouldered with large, sturdy hands that it was easy to imagine manufacturing stoves and lugging them from one place to the next. Meanwhile, he was also a silver-haired old gentleman lurching from one topic to the next, just as he was now; judging by the movement of the frame of his glasses and the restlessness of the paper, he was reading bits of the text here and there and would probably have preferred not to have to read it at all.

Kaarlo arrived, sat down at the other end of the table and placed his hands on the tabletop. His eighty-three-year-old palms still looked surprisingly strong, their blue-and-violet veins like cables running under the skin, his fingers like ten powerful steel hooks. I still wasn't sure exactly why Erkki had hired him, or why *he* wasn't the one about to retire. In fact, Kaarlo's plans appeared quite the opposite. He had taken the race to succeed Erkki very seriously indeed. At present, his role was something between an internal consultant and an advisor whose job it was to use his fifty-year career in the bathing business to help us in our work. But my experience of Kaarlo told a different story. He suggested the impossible and almost always knew better than everybody else – specifically with the benefit of hindsight. For a long time now, I'd suspected there must be something else between him and Erkki, something more than just sauna stoves.

Kaarlo glanced up at me; then, just as quickly, glanced away again.

Susanna came into the room, more floating than walking. She passed behind me, sat down next to Erkki, placed some papers on the table in front of her, divided them into two piles, held a ballpoint pen above the right-hand pile and clicked it into action. This all happened very smoothly, in one and the same movement.

The last to arrive was Jarkko, who somehow managed to sit down both next to Erkki and at the head of the table. In practice, this meant he was sitting against the corner of the tabletop, which I imagined he probably thought made him look like Erkki's right-hand man. His voice all but confirmed this as he told Erkki that everyone was now present and we could begin the meeting.

Erkki looked up from the papers, allowed his blue eyes to pan across the room, then cleared his throat into his clenched fist.

'Good,' he said. 'Two things: the first is regarding these recent ... events.'

Erkki looked at each of us in turn, presumably to check we all knew what he was talking about. To me, it was clear that we did.

'A police officer contacted me this morning and told me that the investigation has progressed a little and—'

'Who was it?' asked Kaarlo.

'The officer?' asked Erkki.

'The murderer,' said Kaarlo.

'I don't know,' said Erkki.

'Okay,' said Kaarlo.

Both men fell silent. If all their communication was this effectual, I thought, then our company really was in dire need of new leadership.

'Right, so,' Erkki continued, though now he looked as though the matter was causing him considerable anguish, 'the investigation has progressed and ... Now, we've all been speculating about different possible scenarios, but it would appear that ... as curious as it sounds ... well ... if I've understood correctly, the evidence points to ... well...'

'Would you like me to chair this meeting?' asked Kaarlo.

'Did the police call you too?' asked Erkki. He looked genuinely confused.

'No,' said Kaarlo.

'Well, then you don't know what this is about.'

'No,' said Kaarlo. 'I don't know anything about anything.'

The two men looked at each other. I had to think about it for a moment, but then I remembered which actor Kaarlo looked like right now, as the sun gleamed against his bony profile: the baddie in those Clint Eastwood Westerns I'd watched all those years ago – Lee Van Cleef.

'Right,' Erkki continued once again. 'So, the evidence seems to suggest that the perpetrator might be someone from around here.'

If anything had been flying through that suddenly chilly room, it would have stopped in mid-air. And if someone had had a knife or a spade, for instance, not only could they have cut the air; they could have shovelled great chunks of it.

'What's more,' Erkki continued, and by now his voice sounded like the only voice in the world, 'they want to talk to all of us. And they've asked me to give them a little hand coordinating everything. Timetables and the like. And to remind you all that nobody should leave the village.'

Again, silence. Only now it felt all the more crushing.

'Are we suspects?' asked Porkka, though it sounded more like a statement than a question. His skin was still red and flushed. 'That's what it means.'

'Brilliant,' said Mirka, then sighed and rolled her rounded, muscular shoulders. 'Here we go. This is it. I'll be the first to have the finger pointed at me.'

'This is just awful,' said Susanna. 'First our beloved colleague dies, and now we're the suspects. This can't be happening.'

'But it is,' said Kaarlo. 'A man burned to a crisp. All that's left of him is ash.'

'That's not what I meant,' said Susanna. 'Which of us would ever think of—?'

'Let's speak one at a time, okay?' said Jarkko. He was sitting with his back straight as a ruler against the corner of the table, looking even more like an enormous singer-songwriter. 'I've made an agenda, and you'll all be allowed to speak in due course...'

'What else did the police say?' I asked.

I hadn't meant to raise my voice quite as much as I did. I noticed heads turning to look at me. I had a good reason to ask. Having known Erkki for over twenty years, I was sure he hadn't told us everything.

'Right,' he began again. 'Of course, they asked this and that about the company and ... as I'm sure you can imagine ... about all of you too ... as these things are all linked, naturally ... and seeing as I'm about to step down ... at the end of the year, as per the original schedule...'

When people say the air felt electric – I felt something along those lines right now.

'So I told the police about this ... process, in which you were all involved, as candidates, and to which, in a way, we should return, seeing as Ilmo ... So, with that in mind, I'm still, or should I say, again or once more ... I still need to appoint one of you to take over from me, and they – that is, the police – were very interested in both the timetable and the identity of my successor.'

Erkki again looked at each of us in turn, but this round was considerably quicker than the previous one.

'And so, I told them,' he continued, 'that I will inform them of my decision at the beginning of the week of Steam Fest, at Saturday's closing ceremony ... in good time before Marko Tapulinen's concert ... I do like his Dean Martin renditions ... *That's amore...*'

Perhaps Erkki, like us, realised he had slightly veered away from the matter at hand. He peered out towards the lake, and when his eyes returned to the table, his gaze was sharper, more focussed.

'And then, the police,' he continued, 'asked which of you is the strongest candidate. And I thought, well ... even if the matter doesn't come up during your interrogations ... informal chats, I believe they're called ... under the circumstances I think it's best to get it all out in the open ... to lay it on the table, as it were.'

I might have been mistaken, but it felt as though most of those present glanced down at the birch table in front of them. There was nothing on it.

'And so, I explained to them,' said Erkki, 'that I've been thinking about Anni ... our master saleswoman ... for years, in fact ... and she's about to seal our biggest deal for years ... sixty-four stoves...'

The room felt painfully bright. It was as though the chair I was sitting on was being winched upwards, most unpleasantly, as though I was a statue about to be unveiled – a statue that would bitterly disappoint those gathered to witness its unveiling. I looked over at Erkki, and I saw his eyes. Perhaps it was the brightness in the room, perhaps the sparkle from the lake. Or maybe his eyes always shimmered in a way that I'd never paid attention to before. And perhaps Erkki noticed this too, as he lowered those eyes and looked as though he was concentrating again.

'However, I would like to stress,' he began, and to some degree he sounded almost like the old, decisive Erkki of many years ago, 'that the competition is now open ... and that each of you has the opportunity to demonstrate the ... skills ... that will settle the matter ... which is a hard decision in the sense that you are all ... masters in your own fields ... and in that sense the decision will be both hard and easy ... and naturally the honour could fall to anyone in this room.'

I was sure that, with these last words, Erkki was aiming for a sense of gravitas. But his intention seemed to be the very reason his words had almost the opposite effect. I didn't think I was the only one who thought so. I noticed my colleagues' quick glances in my direction.

'After all,' Erkki said, now almost with a touch of urgency, 'at the end of the day we are all Steam Devils to our core.'

He held a brief pause, then added:

'And looking at you all now, I'd say that steam ... well, it's in our blood.'

6

The shop was situated on top of a hill on the eastern edge of the village. I drove to the furthest end of the car park and took the last in an empty row of spaces. I stopped, switched off the engine, but didn't get out of the car. The sun had lowered in the sky, changed timbre, and I could already make out a faint red glow along the horizon. Though the difference in altitude was slim, I could still see the entire village and the lake beyond it. The longer I looked out across the village, the smaller it seemed. Of course, some of the reasons for this could be found within me.

As soon as Erkki had informed us about the upcoming interviews and my position in the race to succeed him, the meeting had come to an end. But this did not mean that we all went back to business as usual.

Throughout the afternoon, I'd noticed dozens of furtive glances in my direction and had also been forced to acknowledge that the way people behaved around me had suddenly changed. When I wanted to discuss things with Erkki in greater detail, he had already disappeared, and Jarkko wasn't any help either. Quite the opposite. His behaviour was now even more formal than usual. He had asked me to dictate a message that he would forward to Erkki as soon as he had turned it from the handwritten version into a more formal report, a process that knowing him might take two to three working days. I thanked him and said I would return to the matter later. Via me, please, Jarkko had commented to my back as I walked away.

What about the sales? Kaarlo had asked at my office door, but without waiting to hear my answer. Two and a half hours later, he was back at my door again. What about the sales? he asked once more, again disappearing before I had a chance to respond. I'd seen him by the photocopier, where he was printing off something he clearly didn't want me to see. This I deduced from the way he was hovering around the large machine, making sure to keep his back to me at all times.

After the meeting, it looked like Susanna had touched up her eyeliner – either that or her gaze had been more intense and direct than usual when she popped in to check on the sales figures for the stoves' spare parts. We checked the sums, literally down to the last cent, and I thought I even caught a hint of disappointment when the figures turned out to be correct after all.

And when I'd stood up from my chair and looked out of the window towards the lake, I'd seen Porkka outside, looking right at me. He stared at me for a moment, a glowing-red, moustachioed man with a towel round his hips, then he turned and went back into the sauna, which sputtered thick smoke from its chimney.

Last of all, I had bumped into Mirka in the staffroom. She was eating a pot of Icelandic sour yoghurt – a second pot, it seemed, as there was an empty pot on the table. She didn't interrupt her eating even to give a sigh or to have a quick chat about our swimming trips around the lake, as we often did. She continued eating her synthetic, pineapple-scented yoghurt, her expression stony and impassive. Her silence said more than a thousand words.

And then, one after the other, my colleagues had left the building.

Eventually, I'd found myself alone in the stove factory, and one thing was absolutely clear: from now on, everything would be different. What's more, I was going to need a little time and space to think about everything. And with that, I'd gathered my things and left the deathly silence of the factory behind me.

I gazed at the distant horizon, its redness gradually deepening, and the motionless village, and all this made me think of Ilmo Räty's death. Erkki had told us that the police suspected the murderer must be someone associated with the stove factory. But the more I thought about this, the harder I found it to believe. I simply couldn't think of anyone who objected to Ilmo Räty's plans to sell off and relocate Steam Devil quite as fervently as I did. And I knew I hadn't killed him. Everyone else in the succession race was somewhere between Ilmo's position and mine. In a way, this was good news. It meant that to find a stronger motive and the eventual perpetrator, I'd have to look further afield.

Furthermore:

If the police, or anyone else for that matter, had spent so much as a day in our business, they would have noticed right away that nobody was behaving towards me, the person who had just been named first in the line of succession, the way a cunning, calculating killer would behave.

Would Kaarlo have continued his ranting and his curious behaviour at the photocopier; would Mirka have sulked behind her yoghurt pot; would Porkka have stared at me, his whole body bright red; would Susanna have been on my tail, hunting down missing pennies; would Jarkko have come up with the most convoluted ways of passing on a simple message?

Of course not.

A cunning, calculating murderer would have behaved very differently. That person would want to get close to me. They would have been friendly, helpful, polite. And if not that, then certainly neutral, their behaviour unchanged.

Therefore:

Whoever Ilmo Räty's murderer was, that person was not from Steam Devil.

This realisation made me feel a little better. But only a little.

I got out of the car and filled my lungs with the chilled, early-evening air, hoping this might release some of the tension in my body and calm the faint tingling at my fingertips. But the tension and tingling were here for the long haul. And the village still seemed to be shrinking. Maybe breathing wasn't enough. Maybe the wisest thing I could do was resort to what had always helped me in the past.

I would go to the shop. I would buy something nice for dinner – maybe some fresh liver that I could cook on the griddle and serve with crushed lingonberries that I'd picked by myself. And I would have a sauna and take a long swim in the moonlit lake.

Then I would think about things. And I would find balance.

7

Blue flashing lights filled my car, and I instinctively glanced down at the speedometer before looking in the mirror.

Yes, I was over the speed limit.

Yes, there was a police car behind me.

I slowed down, looked for a suitable place to pull over and found one a short distance ahead. I glanced at the dashboard again. Half an hour had passed since I had decided to seek that all-too elusive balance.

The road ran along the top of a ridge; Lake Puhtijärvi opened out on both sides in the dark blue of early evening. The lay-by was popular with tourists in July, and a steep path with gnarled roots and undergrowth led down to the sandy shores and a small public barbecue.

Right now, there was nobody else in the lay-by, and when I rolled down the window and switched off the motor, I couldn't even hear the wind in the boughs of the trees. The police car had switched off its engine too; I heard the driver open the door, then footsteps against the gravel, and my eyes immediately turned to the side mirror. Did I recognise those footsteps? Surely not. Maybe I just knew who was going to step out of the squad car. It was a small village with two policemen.

'Just a touch over the limit,' said Janne Piirto, leaning close to the window, 'but for quite a long stretch. All the way from the Haukkakoski crossing, actually. I had the lights on for quite a while before you noticed me.'

I looked up and was about to reply when the setting sun shone right in my eyes. It felt disturbing and unpleasant, and I decided to step out of the car. I opened the door, pushed myself out. But the sun's sharp beams caught me in the eyes again, and I stumbled. I quickly shifted position, trying to regain my balance, and as a result ended up closer to Janne than I had planned. I told myself this was all because of the August sunlight, its position in the sky, Puhtijärvi's current position in the universe, and nothing more.

'Are you alright?' asked Janne.

I squinted, and only then did Janne properly come into focus. I told him I was alright.

He looked at me. 'Very well,' he said, and then I saw his brown eyes. 'But given how you stumbled just now, I'm going to have to breathalyse you. You won't drive off while I fetch the meter now, will you?'

'I won't drive off,' I said. 'I'll be waiting right here. I'm not going anywhere.'

He stared at me, hard. I thought about what I'd said, and wanted to blame my words on the sun, again, or the universe, or maybe even Erkki and the sauna stoves. Naturally, I knew better than to say this out loud. Janne turned, strode off towards his car.

I watched him go. Those same slender hips, the broad shoulders, the sinewy arms. He still had his own hair, perhaps a little thinner now, a third of it speckled with grey. Fifty-three years old, but from behind he looked surprisingly like he did long, long ago. From the front, his dimpled cheeks, the wrinkles on his face and the slightly darkened bags under his eyes revealed that he was precisely the age that he was.

I only turned my head away once Janne had taken the meter from inside the police car and was walking back towards my car. Yes, I did recognise his footsteps.

'If you could just blow in there for me,' he said.

I took the straw between my lips and exhaled. We waited for a moment.

'Zero,' he said.

'I haven't been on the booze today,' I said. 'Not much, anyway.'

Janne smiled. That same smile, right from the deepest muscles in his face. Then the smile disappeared.

'I'll be coming over to see you soon, actually,' he said. 'A few things have come up.'

'Indeed,' I said. 'Erkki told us that the police want to talk to everybody.'

Janne didn't answer right away.

'Yes,' he said. 'We do. But we've recently learnt that you're the prime candidate to succeed him as CEO of Steam Devil. Which is why I was going to head over to your place. I was going to tell you this at home ... but you are a person of particular interest in the case. That's not to say that we suspect you of anything, though. Not at this stage, at least.'

I was certain that the sunbeams had suddenly become sharper still. They pierced my eyes like spikes coated with salt.

'I don't understand,' I said, honestly, but I managed to avoid rounding off with the word 'anything'.

'If it's not too much trouble,' Janne went on, 'perhaps you could come by the station, maybe the day after tomorrow, and give us some samples. Fingerprints, DNA, that sort of thing. It will take half an hour at most. It's just routine stuff.'

'I did not murder Ilmo Räty,' I said, and even I was surprised at the speed of my words, and especially at their tone. As though I had to convince Janne Piirto, of all people, that there was nothing suspicious about me.

Janne stared at me. The evening light was flickering from behind him, highlighting his dimples. They were deeper than before, accentuating the lines at the corners of his mouth.

'Right,' he said. 'That's exactly what we want to get to the bottom of. And we're not calling it a murder yet either.'

His brown eyes now looked at me meaningfully, and I felt the urge to glance away. But that would have suggested I had something to hide. I didn't. Except, of course…

I tried to stop my thoughts, but it was pointless. Events from thirty years ago flooded my mind. At first I saw us together, me and Janne, then I saw myself alone, that fateful evening on the lake.

The moonlight.

The glint of steel.

The quick thrust.

But none of that was something I was trying to hide, I thought. I reminded myself that what had happened was something that had protected us both, and, more importantly, it had no place in this conversation.

'No,' I said. 'Of course not. I just assumed, based on—'

'Naturally,' said Janne. 'And you're right, of course. But we have to be absolutely sure of things and everything has to be in order before we make a public statement.'

'Quite.'

'But it was murder.'

'Right.'

'Right.'

A loon squawked somewhere across the lake; the sound was exceptionally loud, there was almost a sharpness to it, as though the bird was trying to tell us something. We both heard the loon, I thought, just as clearly and just as brightly. And for some reason the thought felt a little disquieting.

'How are you doing otherwise?' Janne asked.

The question took me by surprise. In a flash, I thought this must be either a complete and sincere change of direction or a police interrogation technique, or both. Did it matter? I knew I wasn't a murderer. I knew only that … Well, what *did* I know?

'Fine, thanks,' I said. 'You've already heard about the work situation. Apart from that ... same old. Nothing new.'

Even to my own ears, that last sentence sounded odd. The events of the last few days had been nothing but new.

'How about you?' I asked. 'How have you been?'

Janne hesitated. It lasted less than the blink of an eye, but I noticed it all the same.

'Same here, mostly,' he said. 'Work, as usual. Otherwise, everything's fine. Just like before.'

'Great,' I nodded.

The loon gave another squawk. It was starting to feel like harassment. I imagined that while going about its evening business out on the lake, it must have noticed us standing on the ridge. And now it was laughing, mocking these silly people and their stiff conversation, trying to melt decades of ice with meaningless small talk. On the lake, everything was simpler: swoop, dive, take food to the nest, sleep; at daybreak fly off and do it all over again.

The silence following the loon's laughter was short, perhaps only a second, one and a half at most, but it felt all the more uncomfortable. I wondered whether we both wanted to make sure that the bird really had fallen silent.

'So...' Janne began. 'You don't mind ... coming down to the station...'

'I'm happy to get things sorted,' I said, truthfully, then thought of something I'd noticed earlier. 'But why the day after tomorrow? Why not tomorrow?'

Janne briefly glanced out towards the lake, adjusted his posture, though I didn't think there was anything wrong with it.

'Tomorrow's busy,' he said.

He didn't continue, and I concluded that this was his last word on the matter. I nodded and said I would be there.

'Excellent,' he said and now seemed more than a little relieved. 'Then we can take care of your interview. Kiimalainen and I, that is.'

This time, my answer didn't come quite as quickly.

'Of course,' I stammered.

We stood there on top of the ridge a moment longer. The sunbeams continued stabbing at me, unrelenting. We each said an awkward 'bye' and turned towards our respective cars. Before getting in, I listened out in case the loon might give us its final judgement.

It did.

Laughter echoed across the open waters.

8

The morning was nothing but a faint glimmer somewhere at the edge of the earth as I walked into the kitchen – and was completely taken aback.

I'd slept unexpectedly well, thanks, obviously, to the sauna and a swim in the lake. However, the sauna hadn't helped me unravel my problems to the extent I'd hoped, and now I was lost in thought once again. So lost that my shock was sudden and profound. I let out a shout and jumped backwards. Something similar happened on the other side of the kitchen too, by the toaster.

The slices of bread that Santeri was about to place in it flew from his hands, rising vertically into the air, while Santeri himself spun around 180 degrees, then looked at me as though *I* was the one whose behaviour was somehow out of the ordinary.

'What is it?' he asked as the bread fell to the floor with a slap.

The rush of adrenaline was still hanging in my body, and I thought, exactly: what *is* it now? It was early in the morning, and Santeri was in the kitchen before me. He was even dressed. I couldn't remember the last time such a thing had happened. And besides...

'You weren't home last night,' I said. 'So I just assumed that if you were out late, you'd want to sleep late too. I wasn't expecting to see you. But ... here you are.'

Santeri crouched down. 'I got back from Jyväskylä quite late,' he said, gathering the slices of bread. 'And now I'm heading off to Helsinki.'

'Oh?' I asked. 'What's happening there?'

Santeri scrutinised the bread. He turned it in his hands, held it closer to his face, as if to examine it in more detail, then dropped the slices into the compost bin. He looked up at me again, his gaze almost a little accusatory now.

'What?' he asked.

'What's in Jyväskylä?' I said. 'What's in Helsinki?'

'You're not really interested,' he said. 'But if you must know, I went to Jyväskylä to pick up Michele Alboreto's jumpsuit.'

'And now you're taking it to Helsinki?' I asked.

Santeri shook his head. 'You can't give up something like that once you've got your hands on it,' he said. 'Alboreto was legendary on the bends. Nobody could come out of the chicanes the way he did.'

I said nothing. I worried that he'd see anything I said as evidence I didn't understand quite how important all this was.

'I'm going to Helsinki to fetch more items to sell,' Santeri continued. 'There's a pair of driving socks signed by Mika Häkkinen. I've already got a pair, and they could be sent by post, but I want to compare the socks in my collection to the socks on sale, to check the quality and make sure the signature is genuine.'

I didn't ask how you could tell the scribbles on textiles apart or what point there was in acquiring a pair of Mika Häkkinen's old socks. I wanted some coffee. Santeri was wrestling with the loaf of bread and eventually managed to get a few slices in the toaster. I switched on the coffee maker, took a yoghurt from the fridge and glanced out of the window. I saw the sunrise, the first beams of light on the horizon. Something about it reminded me of yesterday, the meeting in the conference room. I never talked about work matters with Santeri, but now I decided to make an exception. The matter was important enough, I reasoned.

'Erkki Ruusula,' I began, 'told us yesterday that he's planning to retire. And he told us there's a race on to succeed him.

Apparently I'm the front runner, his favourite candidate for Steam Devil's next CEO.'

The slices of bread popped up; Santeri looked like he was afraid of them. The empty plate in his right hand wobbled, so he steadied it with his left hand too. For a moment he stood there holding the small plate with both hands, then he released his right hand and began placing his toast on the plate.

'That's ... really...' he stammered. 'Er ... congratulations.'

I thanked him. He began opening a packet of sliced chicken, which looked like it was putting up a fight.

'Is it ... you know ... official?' he asked eventually.

'Is what official?'

'Right,' he said, still shaking the packet of chicken slices. 'I mean, is this the same as when ... back when ... you know, when—'

I was beginning to understand what he meant.

'Nobody has been anointed, if that's what you mean,' I said. 'The way Ilmo Räty was. But someone asked Erkki if he had a favourite, and he answered. The race is on.'

Santeri finally managed to open the packet and began placing slices of chicken on his toast. The procedure seemed to require a degree of concentration. The coffee maker was gurgling and sputtering. I sat at the table and ate my yoghurt. Santeri carried his plate of toast to the table, sat down opposite me and took a bite. He kept his eyes fixed on the window, on the morning burgeoning beyond it.

'But I suppose it's possible,' I said, 'that eventually I'll be selected.'

'Right,' he said, his mouth full of toast. 'But do you think it's worth it? Erkki's job ... it's quite different from what you've been doing all these years. You've been able to come and go as you please, quite freely.'

I swallowed the last of my yoghurt, licked the spoon clean.

'Maybe I don't want to come and go anymore,' I said. 'Maybe I want something else.'

I didn't know where these words had come from. Of course, I'd thought about this in the sauna, considered it very carefully, but hadn't drawn any conclusions one way or the other. It felt as though I'd just said aloud thoughts I'd been keeping secret – even from myself.

Santeri swallowed, audibly. 'That's...' he began. 'That's what I thought you liked about the job.'

The coffee maker had stopped sputtering. Now it was giving long, satisfied sighs.

'I used to like that,' I said, and even I could hear the way I stressed the past tense. 'But maybe it's time for me to do something else. Run the company, for instance.'

Again, Santeri looked over at the window. I stood up, fetched myself a coffee cup from the kitchen cupboard and returned to the coffee maker. I filled the cup with black coffee; it smelt more alluring than usual. Something had happened just now. It was as though the events of the last few days had suddenly condensed, making my thoughts instantly clearer.

And what was I thinking?

Distinctly simple, straightforward thoughts.

I really was the best candidate to run the company, and what's more, I *wanted* to run the company. These were the sorts of things it was inappropriate to say out loud; for me to say out loud, that is; for a woman of my age to say out loud. I had turned my thoughts over, twisted them around and around, all in an attempt to shift the responsibility for this decision onto someone else. But as my thoughts came into focus, like the day brightening outside, things looked unexpectedly clear, irresistible. Things were just things: they were simply one thing, or they were another thing, and that was that.

I noticed I was breathing more easily; even my shoulders had suddenly relaxed. I turned and looked across the table at Santeri. I was about to say something about how talking has a strange way of helping us, but I'd missed my chance.

'I might spend the night in Helsinki,' he said. 'At the sock trader's place, the one with Häkkinen's gear. He's got plenty of other stuff. He's been acquiring paraphernalia from the Silverstone Grand Prix. I want to look at his collection in peace. Thousands of items, all top-notch.'

I was standing behind Santeri, and all I could see was a thin strip of his profile, a little of his cheekbone and his munching jawline. I realised it was perfectly possible that he hadn't actually heard everything I'd told him. But the thought didn't seem so bad. I was happy that I'd heard myself.

'Silverstone ... That sounds nice,' I said, and meant it too. 'I hope things in Helsinki go well for you.'

I didn't hear Santeri's reply. I was already on my way out to the patio, coffee cup in hand. I wanted to see the sunrise.

9

I turned off the main road and into the car park and pulled into my own space. I gathered my things, stepped out of the car and walked towards the main entrance to the office wing. The morning was pleasant and warm, not at all hot or muggy, a kind of blink-and-you-miss-it day between two seasons in which the lingering warmth of summer and the freshness of autumn come together in perfect harmony. The gravel crunched beneath my trainers, I felt the sun on my face and bare arms. I was nearly at the door when I spun around. I had noticed something as I'd arrived but for some reason had only just registered it.

The Stove was wonky.

Well, of course it was wonky; it was famously wonky. But now there was something different about its wonkiness. It was wonkier than it had been yesterday. I was sure of it. The shift wasn't big, but if you looked closely you could see it, plain as day. If the Stove continued listing to the southeast, before long it would topple over. To be precise, it would fall right on top of my car.

I wondered who was responsible for the Stove's care and maintenance. It probably wasn't anybody in particular. Porkka might know something about it. He knew everything there was to know about the construction and technical design of sauna stoves.

Speaking of Porkka...

He was just stepping out of the factory building and took a few hurried steps towards his car, which was parked in a rather curious place. He'd parked it almost behind the building, while his allocated space stood empty. His body language was pure Porkka: quick, frantic, almost jittery. He didn't appear to have noticed me. I called out a hello, and he stopped and turned.

'Morning,' I said for a second time. 'Could you come over here for a sec?'

There were perhaps thirty metres between us, and Porkka was wearing his trademark black baseball cap, so it was impossible to make out his expression. But something about his body language told me that he would rather continue towards his car than stop for a chat with me. Eventually he began walking in my direction. His gait wasn't quite as brisk and efficient as a moment ago.

'I hope I didn't interrupt anything important,' I said, then I pointed up at the Stove. 'I wanted to ask your opinion. Do you think the Stove is wonkier than usual?'

Porkka had come to a halt a metre and a half in front of me. He was distinctly shorter than me, and the peak of his baseball cap hid his eyes from view.

'I don't suppose.'

'You don't *suppose*?'

'It's always been wonky,' he said. 'It's famous for being wonky.'

He turned a little, and the peak of his cap rose just enough that I saw his eyes. It was brief – the peak lowered again almost immediately and I could only see the lower half of his face: his ruddy skin, his thick, black moustache. I hadn't actually seen any expression in his face.

'Is there any way we can measure it?' I asked. 'The tilt, I mean, so we can see if it really has moved. As you can see, if the Stove were to topple over, it would fall pretty squarely on my parking spot.'

Again, Porkka didn't answer right away.

'It doesn't look like it's about to topple over,' he said at last.

'I'm not sure,' I began. 'I don't mean we should stand around waiting for it to fall over. I'm just wondering whether we should try to ascertain whether or not it's—'

'I'm actually in a bit of a hurry,' Porkka butted in. 'I'm testing a new flue system later today, and I need a few special gaskets.'

I knew I wasn't going to get anything else out of him. We stood there for a moment longer, almost side by side, scrutinising the Stove, or at least I did; under the lip of his cap, Porkka might have been thinking about his gaskets. Then we said goodbye, and Porkka marched off to his car with a renewed air of determination, the gravel crunching underfoot. I went back to my car and moved it closer to the edge of the woods, further away from the Stove.

Inside the office wing, things were quieter than usual. I knew it was vain to imagine this had something to do with me, but what else could I think? Nothing else had changed – only people's behaviour towards me.

I walked through the foyer and saw Susanna in her office. She was sitting with her back to the door, hunched over her desk. For some reason, I wondered whether she was yet again scouring my reports and invoices. Her hair was gleaming, but it still looked natural. I said good morning, and she responded without turning around. I continued on my way and glanced towards Mirka's office, but it seemed she hadn't arrived yet.

In my own office, I switched on my computer, looked out at the lake and decided to adjust my offer to Kahavuori one more time. I couldn't lower the price, but my encounter with Porkka a moment ago had given me another thought. We could expedite the delivery. Porkka wouldn't like it, but he could meet the deadline; I knew it. My fingers were just about to touch the keyboard when my phone rang. It was Erkki.

'Good morning,' I said. 'Could I ring you back in a—'

'Would you come to my office, please?'

'Your office?' I asked, confused. Erkki's office was on the other side of the building, and usually, whenever he wanted to speak to someone, he either sent Jarkko to fetch the person in question or walked to that person's office himself. I had never received an invitation by phone like this, let alone from Erkki himself.

'And if possible,' he continued, 'as ... discreetly as possible.'

I couldn't tell whether Erkki sounded like himself or not. Still, I recovered from my surprise enough to say I would come down as soon as I'd sent a revised offer.

'We can talk about that too,' said Erkki, and hung up.

On my way to Erkki's office, I walked past the large windows giving a panoramic view of the lake and slowed my step as I reached the final window. At the end of the long jetty, I saw two people whom I had never seen together, suddenly together.

Mirka and Kaarlo were standing on the jetty, and for a moment it looked as though Kaarlo was performing some kind of mating dance for Mirka to assess – her nose was literally in the air. Then I realised what all this was about. Kaarlo was taking pictures of Mirka on his phone as she posed in various positions that accentuated the musculature of her upper body. For Mirka, this all looked perfectly routine, but Kaarlo was clearly having difficulties. He was obviously new to the art of photography and couldn't seem to find the right angles. However, none of this was as curious as the fact that the pair were together in the first place.

Mirka had vented her frustration with Kaarlo to me in the past. To put it bluntly and concisely, she thought he was a 'wanker'. Kaarlo, meanwhile, had publicly declared that he thought Mirka was a female Schwarzenegger who didn't use her muscles for any practical purpose, though I had to admit I'd never seen Kaarlo doing anything practical either. Yet here they were, cavorting on the jetty like BFFs, as the kids say: *best friends forever*. Obviously, I couldn't hear their conversation, but as I watched, Kaarlo said something that made Mirka laugh. It looked to me as though Mirka was exaggerating her laughter. I carried on, passing Jarkko's empty office on the way.

Erkki was sitting behind his desk and didn't get up when I stepped into the room.

I closed the door behind me, walked to the armchair on the other side of the desk and sat down. Erkki's office provided a vista as magnificent as anything in the National Gallery. The windows took up two walls, one facing the lake and the other the pine-covered ridge. By turning your chair slightly, you could gaze from the sparkling waters of the lake, up into the boughs of the tall pine trees and all the way to the blue sky. Right now, however, it felt as though any admiration of the landscape was out of the question. Erkki's expression was serious, and his first question touched on the wishes he had expressed on the phone. No, I told him, I had not noticed anybody following me.

'Good,' he said, then leant back in his chair, looking as though he had to force himself into a more comfortable position. 'So, our offer to Kahavuori. You'd like to talk about that?'

Of course I didn't. This was typical of the new Erkki: he was trying to make it seem as though I had asked for this audience with him myself. I decided to proceed as diplomatically as possible.

'I've adjusted the offer,' I said. 'Everything is in hand and we are moving forwards. If I need any help, I'll ask.'

'Well then,' said Erkki. 'That's ... excellent.'

For a moment he was silent.

'There are a few things I'd like to talk about – about yesterday,' he said. 'Because, you see, I really meant it: you are my firm favourite to take over the company.'

'Thank you,' I said. 'That's—'

'Very firm indeed,' he interrupted. 'By a country mile.'

I examined Erkki more closely. He was sitting in a position that, though trying to exude relaxation still gave off a sense of tension. For a moment, everything in the room felt frozen.

Then Erkki quickly leant forwards, placed his elbows on the desk. 'I just have one question,' he said. 'Then we can move on.'

'Very well,' I said.

He looked like he was checking the position of both his glasses and his head to ensure uninterrupted eye contact with me.

'Did you murder Ilmo Räty?' he asked.

He was serious; I could see it. A brief thought crossed my mind: what would happen if I said yes? Would we still, as Erkki had put it, move on?

'No,' I said eventually, aiming for the same sense of gravitas as Erkki. 'I did not.'

Erkki was silent for a moment, perhaps mulling over my answer.

'Good,' he said. 'I just wanted to be sure.'

It seemed Erkki's murder investigation was now over. If I were a psychopathic serial killer, I thought, I would just have got away with one murder, and would be free to move on to the next.

'I must admit,' said Erkki, 'I'm relieved. To be candid, I don't know quite what I would have done if you'd told me that you were the one who burned poor old Ilmo. That would have been ... quite the ... turn of events. You, a murderess.'

Erkki did appear genuinely relieved. To such an extent that I was beginning to think our little conversation might be drawing to a close.

'Anni,' he continued, now sounding like a different person altogether. 'May I be frank?'

I was starting to appreciate how Erkki had constructed the

trajectory of our meeting. First the mandatory questions, presented in the manner of a police interview, then the real matter at hand, leaving me with no idea what to expect. I told him that being frank was always a good idea.

'What do you think of me?' asked Erkki.

I had been preparing for all kinds of questions, but not this. I tried to focus, to see more clearly, but it was impossible. We were already looking each other in the eye, there in the soft, bright, late-summer-morning light that filled the office.

'Well,' I said, drawing out my words in the hope I'd come up with something to say. 'You and Steam Devil, you're like the—'

'Do you know?' Erkki interrupted again. 'I'm sick to the back teeth of these stoves.' His voice had risen slightly. 'Or, well...' he said, rowing back. 'Not so much the stoves ... They are the foundation upon which everything else is built. But I don't...'

He held a brief pause, then continued.

'I'm more than just stoves,' he said, looking me right in the eyes.

I didn't know how to respond. What could anyone say to that? Especially as this was the Stove King himself.

'Well,' I began. 'I don't suppose anybody is *just*—'

'Life's over before you know it,' he said.

'True,' I conceded.

'You're fifty years old,' he said. 'So you know what I'm talking about.'

I strongly suspected I didn't have the foggiest what he was talking about. Of course, I understood the words, the sentences, but not why we were having this conversation.

'I'm fifty-three,' I said, just for something to say.

'And I am seventy-two,' he said.

I know, I told him.

Erkki looked as though he was making a choice, deciding between two options.

'When Mirja died four years ago,' he said eventually, 'I rather went off the rails, so to speak. You could say it was my way of dealing with the depression. In Spain, mostly. Dancing, every evening. But you can't do that forever.'

He looked like he was waiting for a reply.

'That's probably right,' I said.

Erkki nodded. 'And now I don't feel depressed anymore,' he said.

'That's nice to hear,' I said, pulling myself closer to the edge of the seat so I could spring to my feet as quickly as possible.

'It's good talking to you,' said Erkki. 'I knew it would be.'

I said nothing.

'Time passes faster and faster,' he said. 'As a child, when someone said you had to wait for something until after the weekend, it felt like an impossibly long time. Now the seasons fly past, they fall like newspapers through the letterbox, and there isn't even time to open them. If newspapers still existed, that is...'

Again, he waited for an answer.

'I read the newspaper every day...'

'I knew you would have noticed the same thing,' he said with a smile.

There was something unpleasant about that smile, the way it related to what he had just said and the tone of his voice. As though we had been travelling together, arrived at our destination and were now staring longingly into the same sunset. But that wasn't what had happened. It would be more appropriate to say that I'd been ambushed and now somebody was firing arrows in my direction. I was about to say that I should be getting back to my office when Erkki spoke.

'It doesn't have to be so mournful, you know,' he said, 'the passing of time.'

'I suppose not,' I said, and I could hear how uncertain I sounded.

'Some things cheer us up whenever they happen.'

'That's—'

'And it's only one day,' he continued. 'Isn't that what they say? Every day is a new beginning.'

'Yes...'

'Besides,' he said. 'One of the upsides of growing old is that you don't have to care about what other people think. You can make some daring decisions, go out on a limb.'

He smiled again. It felt every bit as unpleasant as his previous smile. But I believed I understood what he meant, at least in rough, broad terms. I too had found myself pondering my age and my life, where I was, where I was going and, as was always the case in ponderings like this, what I ultimately wanted. And what other people wanted or expected from me. As time went by, the latter held less and less significance. But I didn't plan to encourage Erkki any further in his own ponderings.

'I've just remembered,' I said, standing up as quickly yet as politely as possible. 'I've got to reply to a smaller counteroffer by...' I glanced up at the clock on the wall: the small clockface looked like a sauna stove and its hands resembled ladles '... eleven-fifteen. It looks like I've got two minutes.'

Erkki's smile disappeared, and he looked like he had been roused from a dream. 'Of course,' he said. 'That's ... important.'

I thanked him for our little meeting, and I was already at the door when I heard his voice again. I turned.

'Don't get me wrong,' he said. 'But maybe there's a meaning to all this. Ilmo getting himself ... killed like that.'

Erkki smiled.

This smile was new, one I had never seen before.

10

A handful of newspaper scrunched at the bottom of the fire chamber, on top of that some thin birch strips, sliced from the timber logs with an axe and placed horizontally, another layer of paper, then more birch strips to form a lattice, a third layer of newspaper, then another layer of strips. To finish off, two average-sized logs, then light it at the bottom with a match. I watched as the flames licked from the paper to the birch strips and eventually caught the tinder-dry bark of last year's logs. The flue hungrily sucked up the smoke, the sauna began to warm. I closed the hatch, left the sauna via the changing room and stepped out into the August late afternoon.

I walked down to the shore, only stopping when the toes of my trainers were about to touch the rippling water. The day's events were swirling through my mind.

I hadn't seen Erkki all afternoon. Not that I was especially keen to continue our surreal conversation, but at the same time I found it odd the way he had simply disappeared from the building. I knew this because I'd heard Jarkko in the corridor, wandering from one office to the next asking if anyone had seen Erkki, with whom he had some important business. I'd heard Susanna reply that she had been sitting in her office all day and hadn't seen Erkki at any point and that she would certainly have noticed him as she too had some important business to sort out with him. Eventually Mirka had joined the conversation and commented that she hadn't seen Erkki either, and that she too had some important business...

And so on and so forth.

Interaction with my colleagues had followed the same curious format as the day before. If I said hello to someone or approached them on work matters, they behaved as though I'd come to drill their teeth: some fled the scene right away, some answered my questions reluctantly, and as monosyllabically as possible. I had sent Kahavuori our new counteroffer, but he hadn't even acknowledged receipt of it, let alone responded.

And as for Santeri: he was in Helsinki chasing socks. (I didn't know what to make of the fact that this did *not* appear to bother me in the least.)

I'd always enjoyed being by myself. But right now it seemed to combine with a sense of loneliness, which was altogether different, and probably had something to do with the fact that everything in my life was suddenly in motion – nothing felt particularly stable or permanent. Not even sauna stoves, because my conversation with Erkki had cast them in a new light too, a light that seemed to suggest he had come to regard the whole stove business with a certain doubt. It was a crisis of faith. He hadn't said it in as many words, but to my mind his frustration with the stoves felt deeper and more profound and perhaps wasn't entirely to do with Spain, dancing and death. It was as though he knew something, as if he'd seen something that made sauna stoves take a back seat. Or maybe I was reading too much into it. I was a little off kilter by the time I had left Erkki's office. I wasn't prepared for, or indeed used to, Erkki's new perspectives and new smiles, especially as we were talking about death and the inevitable passing of life and of time.

Which took my thoughts back to yesterday – and tomorrow.

Yes, my encounter with Janne had been unexpected, but more unexpected still was my own reaction to it. It was hard to believe, and even harder to admit, that he still had an effect on me. An effect that felt like my whole body was possessed: talking became fumbling for words, a sensation like a mixture of cold and tingling spread around my diaphragm, and upon my shoulders came that same, familiar weight of guilt, which of course over the years had changed form but which still felt both solid and impossible to shrug off, as though I were carrying on my shoulders a long length of two-by-four that dug deeper into my muscles with every metre.

How long had it been?

Almost thirty years had passed since I'd broken off our engagement without any explanation. It didn't help that I told myself I was young then and I'd only been doing what I thought was right, given the circumstances. This didn't alleviate my guilt, but it gave me a rational explanation, which, at least in theory, ought to have offered some level of comfort. Now I wasn't so sure.

Time did not seem to pass at the same speed in all places and at all moments. This unevenness and disproportionality in my sense of time intensified those flashbacks to the autumnal evening all those decades ago that were now popping into my mind at an increasing rate, thoughts cold as lake water and stained with droplets of blood, fragments that only a moment ago were nothing but snatches, dream-like and quickly evaporating. They had clearly grown in power, and they now left physical symptoms behind too: shivering, adrenaline, a weight on my heart.

At the same time, I realised how well I had hidden from myself the fact that I had been avoiding Janne all these years, these decades. I hadn't even given it a second thought all those times I'd caught a glimpse of him and walked the other way – I'd simply switched direction so that I wouldn't bump into him, doing so on autopilot, without my noticing it. I'd even managed to tell myself the lie that neither he nor the events of thirty years ago had anything to do with my life anymore. They didn't bother me. The truth was, they hadn't bothered me because I'd never faced up to them. But I did yesterday. And I would again tomorrow.

Maybe this was simply the nature of things – everything eventually wound its way back to the beginning – or perhaps sprung back from wherever I thought I'd stuffed it away, out of sight. Just like trying to forget something was a sure-fire way of remembering it.

I listened to the lake's repetitive lapping against the rocks along the shoreline, gazed along the shore opposite, its bays and peninsulas, and my eyes came to rest upon the wooden bench and railings at the end of the jetty.

And only then did I realise what I'd seen.

Not here, not out on the lake, but...

I backed away from the shore, turned, briskly walked back to the sauna, took the steps up to the porch and stepped into the building.

What had I seen but not registered?

I'd been lost in thought, my mind still so occupied with the day's events that I hadn't even paid attention to what my own eyes were telling me. But now I was certain that something was different from before. Naturally, it wasn't a big change; I wouldn't have ignored something like that. This was something subtle, and yet crucial.

I took a deep breath, concentrated, and started with the dressing room.

The window on the back wall opened out towards the yard. In front of that stood a dark-brown, wooden coffee table that I'd found in a second-hand store. On the table was an empty light-green vase and two coasters. Along the left-hand wall was a long, light-coloured Ikea sofa, and over the arm nearest me was the dark-red blanket I'd folded and left there the last time I'd bathed here. Then a small 1950s bookcase, with all the books in their rightful places. Then there was the other window in the room, which opened out towards the lake. And here, near the doorway, a coat stand with my two dressing gowns – a lighter one for the summer months, a warmer one for winter. I took two steps forwards, stood in the middle of the space, turned to look at the wall opposite the sauna. The fireplace and its slabbed edging was tidy; to its right was the basket I used to carry firewood; it was still full, just as it should be. Left of the fireplace stood a shelving unit as tall as me, this too from a second-hand store and this too made of dark wood. On the shelves were the paraphernalia one would expect in any sauna: soaps and shampoos, towels, on the lower shelf two pairs of bathing sandals and warm slippers.

I turned again. I was beginning to think that either I'd been mistaken or the change was so miniscule that you couldn't see it with the naked eye ... but then I knew where to look. I turned once more, and though part of me wondered whether all this turning might be reaching neurotic heights, now I was certain. I'd glanced at the right-hand side of the shelving unit when I'd been fetching tinder for the fire chamber, and somehow I'd saved the image in my mind.

There they were.

The 'bumlets' – the squares of linen to keep the benches clean and stop your bum being singed by the hot wood.

As I'd suspected, the change was miniscule. The pile was lower than it should have been. I took a step forwards, counted the bumlets. There were two missing. I looked at the bumlets in my hand, at my name embroidered on their surface (a nice little touch provided by one of our suppliers). I placed the bumlets back on the shelf and felt first relieved then ridiculous.

I'd solved the mystery – but what now? What might the disappearance of two bumlets mean? Yet, as I began to suspect almost straight away, had they actually disappeared at all? Had I perhaps forgotten about some of the bumlets – washed them and left them on the clothes horse or somewhere else? It wasn't unheard of for me to leave things where they didn't belong.

I sighed.

Middle age.

Nobody had told me it would be like this: constant second-guessing, a lonely hunt for two mislaid bumlets.

11

There were two routes to the police station: through the village or by taking a slight detour across the bridge at Peurasalmi. I plumped for the scenic route. The road curved and swerved through the late-summer morning, which was like a carbon copy of the last few mornings: bright, almost cloudless, sunny and warm. At the bridge, I slowed a little, glanced over at the marina and the open lake. I clearly wasn't the only one to have noticed the string of sweltering days that showed no sign of abating. White, slowly moving dots speckled the lake's gleaming, dark-blue waters. After the momentary expanse of the views from the bridge and out across the narrow sound, the terrain on both sides turned to thick woodland and the road became windier. This suited me fine; I was a little early, and besides, I felt no inclination to hurry. The slower speed felt good in all respects.

The police station had been built in the early 1970s, when the primary aim of local town planning was to grow Puhtijärvi, which included the eventual construction of a new road between the village and what was to become a western district where, in addition to the new police and fire stations, the original scheme was to build the first suburb of modern high-rise flats in the area. Of course, none of this had ever come to fruition. The main road was never built, and the villagers' grassroots movement opposing the suburb – *Puhtijärvi, bright and fair / Hands off our village, don't you dare!* – disbanded after a single, rancorous meeting.

The police station was a product of its time: it looked like a small and shoddily constructed shopping centre. The building was low and narrow, and the entrance was surprisingly hard to locate. It was in an alcove at the northern end of the building, and you couldn't really distinguish it from the rest of the wall until you were standing right in front of it. I pulled the handle and stepped inside.

The entrance foyer was basically the end of a corridor that stretched all the way to the other end of the building, office doors standing along it at regular intervals. It looked like an old leisure centre or an abandoned motel. I knew that there were currently only three people working at the station, and at a quick count there were a total of twelve faded, yellowing doors, six on each side of the corridor. The employees have their pick of offices, I thought at first, but a second or so later I realised that some of these doors must be to the cells where the local drunks could sleep off the liquor. The nearest door along the right-hand wall opened just as I was about to call out and ask whether I'd come at the wrong time.

Janne Piirto asked me to step inside.

The room was windowless, like a sealed silo. A pallid, steel-legged table was positioned across the room. The plastic chair I sat down on was uncomfortable, like sitting in a saucer, and the lampshades on the ceiling were so retro they were probably original fixtures.

The same could be said of one of the men sitting opposite me.

Janne was sitting diagonally to my left. Next to him, diagonally to my right, was one Reijo Kiimalainen. Kiimalainen was Janne's superior, and he had been the village's senior constable (senior in every sense of the word) back when I'd got my driving licence, which I had picked up from this very same police station and from none other than Kiimalainen himself ... thirty-five years ago.

I wondered whether Kiimalainen might be breaking the law himself right now by continuing to work so long after reaching retirement age. Perhaps, at some point, time had stopped and let him step off for a while, all so that he could continue to serve as the village's senior constable. Kiimalainen was a stubborn know-it-all who still managed to win the senior category in all the lake-swimming competitions across central Finland. Yet there was nothing about his general appearance that suggested a suitability for open-water swimming, let alone taking the podium. His movements weren't especially sporty, and the coordination of his arms and legs wasn't exactly smooth. Moreover, he couldn't see very well. And despite this impairment he seemed to spend a great deal of time and effort positioning and maintaining the right-side parting in his grey and still thick hair. I knew Kiimalainen after a fashion; I'd run into him at many meetings of the Beach Preservation Association over the years. To this day, he had opposed every motion I had ever put to the committee.

Janne began. He told me that this was a preliminary interview regarding a matter that all those present in the room were well acquainted with, that the interview was intended to be general and exploratory and that, at this point, I was not under any suspicion. He also reiterated that I had come in for interview voluntarily, that we all agreed on this, and he then asked whether I needed a glass of water. I didn't have a chance to answer.

'Thank you, Janne,' said Kiimalainen. 'Your summary of the situation isn't quite up to date, but it'll get us started.'

Janne's expression remained unchanged. Kiimalainen was moving a plastic sleeve containing some papers around in front of him; once he had got them into what I assumed must have been the desired position, he clasped his hands together on top of them. He began with questions that all sounded distinctly general and exploratory, just as Janne had promised. Then, Kiimalainen took a bunch of papers from the plastic sleeve and a ballpoint pen from his jacket pocket.

He raised his unfocussed eyes to me. 'How exactly did you know Ilmo Räty?' he asked.

I told him that we had been colleagues for around ten years, but that more recently I'd come to think that perhaps I didn't know him all that well after all, so it would be reasonable to say that we were only work colleagues and in all other respects simply passing acquaintances.

'Were you familiar with his sauna?'

'Pardon me?'

'His lakeside sauna,' said Kiimalainen. 'The one that burned down.'

'I don't quite—'

'Have you ever been there?'

I was about to say 'of course not', but then I remembered something.

'Actually,' I began. 'I once went there very briefly. About a year ago, Porkka installed Ilmo's new sauna stove, and I visited at Ilmo's behest to check it had been installed properly. He appeared to trust my judgement.'

Kiimalainen was silent for a moment, scrawled something on his papers.

'What was this trust based on, in your estimation?' he asked. 'How did it develop?'

I glanced at Janne, who still had the same, unchanged expression on his face.

'I can only think it was because of my job,' I said. 'And I suppose it must have grown over time. I've worked with sauna stoves for a long time and—'

'So, in your estimation,' Kiimalainen interrupted, 'you'd say that you were acquainted both with the sauna *and* the stove. And that Ilmo Räty had learnt to trust you?'

I didn't like Kiimalainen's tone of voice, but I had to admit that everything he said was correct. At least, in theory.

'If you want to put it like that then—'

'And now you are Erkki Ruusula's favourite to succeed him as CEO,' he continued.

This was true, I conceded. It was pointless trying to think how Janne or Kiimalainen had come by this last piece of information. Everything that happened in the village or at the stove factory was common knowledge within a matter of minutes. And something like this, which seemed to excite everyone, spread even quicker than standard gossip about marriage or divorce, money problems or drink-driving.

'So it would appear,' I said. 'But I'm innocent—'

'Oh, you Korpinens are always innocent, aren't you? Pure as the driven snow,' said Kiimalainen, and now he sounded agitated. His flabby cheeks were red and blotchy.

It took a full second of silence for me to understand what this was really about.

'You've got to be kidding,' I said. 'I know what's eating you. What's always eaten you. For crying out loud, it was over twenty years ago.'

Kiimalainen was about to say something, but this time I didn't even let him begin.

'Has it ever occurred to you,' I said, 'that the reason my father managed to fell the Great Elk before you is because he was the better hunter?'

'It was my elk.'

'It was *an* elk,' I said. 'That lived in the woods. It wasn't yours and it wasn't—'

'Your father,' Kiimalainen interrupted, 'didn't wait for—'

'Who was he supposed to wait for?' I asked. 'The hunting season started at six a.m., and he shot the elk at one minute past.'

'But how?' said Kiimalainen. 'How did he know exactly where it was? How did he find its tracks so quickly? There's something deceitful about the whole—'

'Ingenuity can feel like deceit,' I said, 'to someone who doesn't have any.'

Right away, I realised I shouldn't have said that. But I couldn't back down. Kiimalainen's cheeks were a deep red now. I knew I'd done something very short-sighted and, at the same time, contradictory. Though I appreciated the need to keep the elk population under control, I didn't really care for hunting. But now here I was defending my long-dead father for his resourcefulness.

'Let the transcript reflect,' said Kiimalainen, 'that the respondent is deliberately trying to slow down the investigation.'

Neither of the men sitting across the table made the slightest move to let the transcript reflect anything at all. In fact, I hadn't seen anything that looked remotely like a transcript. I said nothing. There was a curious gleam in Kiimalainen's eyes.

'You have a reputation as a very keen sauna-goer,' he said. 'Would you agree?'

'I suppose so,' I admitted. 'But what has that—'

'An *experienced* sauna-goer?'

'You could say that...'

'You can withstand very hot steam,' he stated more than asked, 'and your ability to function would not be impaired, even if the temperature were to rise considerably?'

'Was that a question?' I asked. It felt somehow necessary to do so.

Kiimalainen's eyes were still gleaming. The ruddiness of his face had risen from his cheeks to his hairline, and maybe even beyond.

'Your engineer, Porkka,' he said, 'who installed the stove in Ilmo Räty's sauna, told me over the telephone that this stove model is very middle of the road, the kind of stove that's suitable for the average sauna-goer. And it wouldn't necessarily be able to withstand very high temperatures, certainly not for an extended period of time. And definitely not very hot steam, the kind that requires you to refill the fire chamber several times over. And this is the very stove that you yourself inspected and that you know so well.'

'I still don't know how this—'

'It would appear that the fire started in the stove,' said Kiimalainen. 'Therefore, someone knew exactly how to heat it and how much heat it could take. That someone must presumably have enjoyed hot steam too, at least to some degree. But if you're an experienced sauna-goer whose skin is used to it, well...'

I shook my head. I was about to say that this conversation, or interview or whatever it was, was in danger of veering into unfathomable territory. But Kiimalainen didn't wait for my comments.

'Furthermore,' he continued, 'there would have been plenty of room on the benches.'

'Meaning?'

'Ilmo Räty had recently divorced.'

I looked at Kiimalainen. I looked at Janne. Then I looked at Kiimalainen again.

'I have never saunaed in Ilmo Räty's sauna,' I said. 'Let alone saunaed with him. And I have never heated Ilmo Räty's sauna stove. I performed what is called a cold inspection a year ago, that's it. I don't know how you've got into your head that—'

'Would you be willing to give us a DNA sample?' asked Kiimalainen.

I kept my eyes fixed upon him. 'By all means,' I said. 'But, before that, may I ask a question?'

Neither of the men responded. They didn't even flinch.

'Am I a suspect in the murder of Ilmo Räty?' I asked.

Still, neither man said a word.

'Because it's starting to sound like it,' I said. 'And it goes without saying that it's completely absurd. You know that perfectly well.'

'Perhaps,' said Kiimalainen, and again he looked agitated, 'we know something that you don't know we know ... So ... Perhaps you Korpinens aren't as smart as you think you are. Perhaps your scheming doesn't always turn out the way you'd like.'

Kiimalainen took a breath; he seemed to have realised what he'd just said.

'An old grudge is hardly proof of my guilt,' I said. 'And if the only evidence you've got is that my father managed to fell the largest elk in local history before you did, I don't think that's going to cut it in court. Not that I've murdered anybody, but for want of any evidence I—'

I interrupted myself. As I said the word, I saw this was the crux of the problem. It was this that made Kiimalainen behave so arrogantly, it was this that allowed him to cross a line, to let out all that pent-up anger and avenge the wrongs he felt had been done him.

Evidence.

A chill spread through my body. The realisation came a hundredth of a second later. Evidence. But of course.

'Someone stole the bumlets,' I said. 'I don't know when. I noticed two had gone when I had a sauna yesterday evening. And what could a clean bumlet tell us about—'

'A used one,' said Kiimalainen, and smiled as though he had tasted something exceedingly sweet. 'A used one can be a real treasure trove.'

'In any case,' I said, 'it was stolen.'

'Of course it was,' he said, now sounding particularly pleased with himself. 'Puhtijärvi is full of bumlet pinchers. They're a real scourge. There's nothing they want more than other people's bumlets. Especially the kind with someone else's name embroidered on them. And used ones, at that. They're the most sought after – among bumlet pilferers, that is. But unlike your average knicker nickers, these bumlet purloiners are so eager to get their hands on other people's sweaty bumlets that they abandon them right beside recently burned-down saunas...'

'So, you agree to a DNA test?' asked Janne. This was the first time he had spoken, and I was grateful.

'Right away, if you like,' I said, though even I could hear that I didn't sound quite as certain anymore.

Kiimalainen was about to say something when Janne stood up, his chair legs scraping across the floor. I stood up too. For all his smugness, Kiimalainen looked a little disappointed; he would clearly have enjoyed savouring his surprise win a while longer. I was happy to let him have the last word. For now.

I followed Janne out into the corridor, we turned right, passed two closed doors, Janne opened a third and gestured for me to step inside.

The room was bleak. Along one wall there was a countertop with all kinds of supplies and equipment. In the other half of the room was the kind of table you might see in a doctor's surgery and an angular metallic chair. Janne showed me to the chair; I sat down. We didn't speak. This did not mean that I'd run out of things to say. On the contrary, it felt as though my head was whirring with several hundred chains of thought. None of which seemed to produce favourable outcomes.

Janne had his back to me while he got things ready on the worktop. Then he turned, a surgical mask over his mouth and a pair of latex gloves on his hands, and asked me to open my mouth. I stretched my jaws, Janne crouched closer to me, asked me to lower my tongue. I felt his fingers gently touch my lips.

Just then, we looked each other in the eye. It was a brief moment, then I turned my attention to the 1970s ceiling, and Janne appeared to focus on the inside of my mouth with renewed concentration.

I had to admit, I was outside my comfort zone, both physically and mentally. Janne ran the swab along the inside of both my cheeks, took it out and turned to the worktop. He pottered with the equipment for some time, closed the various boxes and resealable bags, took the mask from his face and turned back around. He looked the same as he had during my interrogation a moment ago, though somehow more serious now.

'What I can tell you,' he began, pulling the gloves from his hands, 'is we don't ask everybody to provide a DNA sample.'

'That doesn't sound good,' I said.

'On the other hand, if you're innocent, there's nothing to worry about.'

How well do we know a person, I wondered, if you know them from almost thirty years back?

Janne's expression gave nothing away. I was about to ask him directly what he thought of the matter – Kiimalainen had made his own stance pretty clear – but just then there came a knock at the door and it opened right away. I saw a woman's face in the doorway; it seemed detached from the rest of her body.

'Senior Constable Kiimalainen,' said the woman, presumably an office secretary, 'doesn't want you to spend any extra time with the suspect.'

12

Though it was filled with light, the morning suddenly felt cold and overcast. As I drove along the road leading back to the village and the stove factory, a single phrase echoed through my mind.

The *suspect*.

I realised that if the police used such a term, they must have good, clear reasons for doing so. And Kiimalainen, for all his ancient grudges, wouldn't have behaved the way he did – as though he were finally about to fell the elk that he'd set out to hunt twenty years ago – unless the matter was beyond all reasonable doubt.

I was driving along a road lined with tall, thick clusters of trees, trying to organise the questions in my mind.

How had my bumlet – a used one, at that – ended up in the vicinity of Ilmo Räty's sauna?

Stealing it would have been easy: my sauna was never locked. But in that case, the bench napkin would have been dry, unused. I always put the bumlets straight into the washing machine after use and switched the machine on. Without exception. Nothing and nobody ever got in the way. Not even Santeri. The very thought of Santeri anywhere near the washing machine was as ridiculous as the thought of him in the sauna. And even if Santeri had managed to strike at the optimal moment and carried out the linen theft through some nefarious skulduggery – which, objectively speaking, he was incapable of – what could possibly have been his motivation?

Santeri's passion, to the extent that it ever manifested itself, was for motor races that had already been raced. But perhaps more importantly, how would he have known what to do and when? He only knew the details of Steam Devil's business when I made a point of telling him, and even then he only seemed to remember a tiny fraction of what I'd said. No. Quite simply: no. Santeri lacked the ability and wherewithal to carry out the deed, and I didn't mean that in a bad way.

But, in that case, what did all this mean? The answer was so obvious that I felt icy nails running the length of my back before I'd even got to the end of that thought. The theft of my bumlet must have taken place while I was bathing; this was the only way the cloth could be a DNA *treasure trove*.

But how...?

My thoughts were scrambling around when my phone rang. The number was withheld. I pressed the button on the steering wheel, and a dull hum filled the car. A few seconds later, I realised this wasn't the typical humming sound that comes with any phone call. This was breathing.

'Hello?' I said. 'Who is this?'

'What if I'm the murderer everyone's looking for?'

The voice sounded like a man's, but it had been modified somehow. Just then, I remembered something and waited a moment.

'Are you?' I asked after a pause.

'I might be.'

'You sound unsure.'

'Maybe I don't want to reveal myself.'

I took a deep breath, slowly exhaled.

'Lauri Kahavuori,' I said. 'Now isn't a good time to—'

I heard a click, then a more familiar voice. 'To talk about sauna stoves?' asked Kahavuori. 'I thought we could talk about your most recent offer. I might have come up with a solution. I'll be on site all day, if you've got a moment to pop round.'

I looked at the time, then the road.

'I'll be there in an hour,' I said.

))

Kahavuori was nowhere to be seen in the car park, and I couldn't
see him in the spaces between the chalets along the hillside either.
The sun on my back felt warm as I looked around for him. Here
and there I saw workmen in bright-orange jackets. I heard
hammering and the faint sound of drilling. I was walking towards
the cottage where there seemed to be the most activity when I
heard Kahavuori's voice somewhere to my right.

'Over here,' he shouted, but I still couldn't see him anywhere.
Then I looked up at the chalets themselves, their walls.
Kahavuori's face was framed in the small window of one of the
saunas as he peered out.

'Through the porch,' he said. 'The door's open.'

I stepped inside the new-smelling building, found the sauna
and, in the steam room, Kahavuori himself. He looked excited,
a fact that seemed to have sharpened his facial features all the
more.

'We live in interesting times,' he said. He sounded sincere.

I agreed this was true and tried to steady my breathing.

'And that offer of yours,' he continued, 'it really got me thinking.
I mean, for that price, with that delivery time, and all the extras
thrown in, I can't see any reason we shouldn't strike a deal.'

'That's great to hear—'

'And, as I said on the phone, I think I might just have thought
of a way we can both achieve our desired outcome. You see, I've
got a theory.'

'Excellent,' I said. 'Naturally, the offer was just a suggestion.
We can take a look at it now if—'

'There's nothing to look at,' Kahavuori interrupted me. 'And my theory has nothing to do with that. It's about how we resolve another matter.'

The small window above his left shoulder was still open, revealing a shoebox's worth of blue sky.

'I've been doing some background research,' he said. 'A spot of criminal profiling, you might say. Have you ever watched *Mindhunters*? It's my favourite show. It's very informative and, I've noticed, surprisingly practical.'

'I haven't had a chance to watch—'

'Once you start, you'll get through it in one sitting,' he nodded. 'But that's not the point.'

'That's good, because—'

'The police over in Puhtijärvi haven't even got a suspect yet, right?'

The question stopped me in my tracks. By now, Kahavuori was standing very close to me indeed. His body language had gone from enthusiastic to intense, almost insistent. My whole morning had already been stressful before this episode, but now it had suddenly developed new layers of stress. I tried to steady my breathing. And was trying to form some semblance of an answer – I didn't want to lie – when Kahavuori edged another few centimetres closer.

'But I do,' he said.

Kahavuori's eyes and the areas around his eyes were dark as night. This was presumably because we were standing in a sauna, I thought, though the little air vent was open and outside it was still August.

'Really?' I asked.

'Oh yes,' he said. 'This is someone who knows Puhtijärvi and its surroundings inside out, someone who is at home out on the lake, rowing and swimming, and either lives alone or in a relationship where neither party ever asks what the other is up to. In his or her youth, this person has perpetrated an amateurish crime or misdemeanour, but has found their true calling, if we can call it that, later in life. The perpetrator has planned the crime with meticulous attention to detail, and there might be several reasons for this. They probably hold some kind of generalised grudge against the village and the community, and perhaps they've only started behaving in a threatening or semi-threatening manner quite recently. This person likely has a strong financial motive for the crime. And, it goes without saying, he or she knows saunas and sauna stoves like the back of their murderous hand. To be perfectly honest, it wouldn't surprise me if this person really loved saunas and going to saunas. It might just be their most cherished way of relaxing.'

Kahavuori straightened his back slightly, which seemed to make him grow in stature, commanding the small room.

'How does that sound?' he asked, managing to look both demanding and a little smug.

I assumed he wasn't thinking the same things I was thinking right now: that he had basically just described me, and that he and Kiimalainen could quite easily join forces and pin Ilmo Räty's murder on me. And that if that were to happen – and I really didn't know where this particular thought had come from – I probably wouldn't care much about my unsold stoves. That wasn't especially comforting.

'Mmmhmm,' was all I could say.

'You're right,' Kahavuori nodded. 'It could do with a bit of tweaking – it needs a proper focus. But I've got a good hunch I'm pretty close to the essence of whoever this is and, therefore, his or her identity. Very close, I'd say.'

'Quite,' I agreed. I heard Kahavuori take a breath.

'And there's something else too,' he said, now lowering his voice. 'Something that's every bit as important.'

'Really?' I asked in as neutral a voice as possible.

'Yes,' he said, then held a brief pause before continuing. 'People like this – they don't stop. And I've got a theory about how this is going to go from here.'

I said nothing.

'Next time,' he continued, 'the modus operandi could be quite different. The tools and tactics, I mean, the time and place. But the end result will always be the same. The perpetrator will do it again. I've been trying to think how regularly this person might feel the need to satisfy their urges, but based on this solitary crime I'm not yet able to form an overall picture. But it'll happen again soon. The fact that this first act was so powerful speaks for itself. This was carried out with a lot of passion, a lot of gusto.'

Kahavuori took a breath, calm and careful. After filling his lungs, he looked more emboldened still.

'But we'll get to the bottom of it one way or another,' he said. 'We'll sort out the matter of the stoves, and we'll sort this out too.'

Once again, Kahavuori escorted me back to my car. I could tell that he thought everything was all but wrapped up. I could feel it in his handshake – *as far as Kaha Cabins is concerned, the deal is done bar this one little detail* – and it was apparent in the kind of contact he suggested we keep, reporting back to each other at regular intervals. I took part in the conversation just positively enough and just monosyllabically enough to keep him happy, and it was a relief when my car door finally closed.

I waved a hand at him and managed to muster a smile until I could see him in my rear-view mirror.

And at that, my smile evaporated.

13

The Scots pines outside my office no longer balanced the landscape. Naturally, they were all still standing in exactly the same places, and the lake between and behind them gleamed blue, as it had done on previous days, but I felt as though everything I was looking at – the trees, the lake, the sky – had set off on a journey, moving inexorable, without knowing quite where it was heading. A storm seemed to be simmering beneath the calm surface of the lake, and the pines, which I'd considered almost eternal, impossible to fell, now resembled matchsticks. The sky looked like it might lose its grip at any moment and come crashing down on my shoulders.

I got up from my desk, walked to the right-hand side of the window, gripped the gauze curtain and dragged it to the other side of the wall. The room was dimmed but not entirely darkened. I returned to my desk and sat down.

My head had started to ache as soon as I'd left Kaha Cabins, and I'd only eaten half of my lunch at Leila's Tavern before I'd had no choice but to put down my cutlery and leave. I'd taken a painkiller an hour ago, but it still didn't feel as though it had kicked in. And now I was convinced I'd thought myself into a headache.

With my left hand, I rubbed the area where my neck joined the back of my head and wondered how paradoxical it was that Kahavuori of all people should be the one to make me realise how precarious my situation was. I didn't know quite what to make of his true-crime hobby, though. It felt completely overblown, and at worst downright paranoid, but despite this he seemed to be on the right track, in his own way, at least.

With my right hand, I clicked the mouse. Neither action – rubbing my muscles nor using the computer – brought about the desired result. In fact, my headache only got worse the more my online searches drew a blank or gave me results that I knew already.

Of course, I wasn't expecting to find a website explaining that Kaarlo Suomi was a bloodthirsty murderer long before he took up a position at Steam Devil, or that, before becoming the company secretary, Jarkko Mutikallio had had a healthy fascination for arson. But I hadn't given up hope of finding something and somehow putting together the various bits of information I managed to pull up.

Because there had to be a connection. Somewhere.

And that connection must be near at hand.

Someone had murdered Ilmo Räty and was now trying to frame me as the culprit. But who? Because there was no immediate answer to this question, I had to approach it from a different angle: the sauna, the stoves, Steam Devil. In fact, I agreed with many of the conclusions Kahavuori had listed about the qualities that the potential killer needed to have. But this didn't help whittle down the list of suspects at all. One way or another, everyone with a passion for saunas, stoves and Steam Devil similar to mine and Ilmo's possessed the very same character traits.

Everyone knew Puhtijärvi and the surrounding area through and through; everyone knew how and where Ilmo used his sauna, how and where I used mine. Every one of them would have known how to gain access to my sauna changing room; everyone would have known how and for how long to mistreat Ilmo's stove by adding too many logs. To my knowledge, every one of them in recent years had had their own marital and relationship struggles. And every one of them wanted to become

Steam Devil's new CEO, which meant that every one of them had a financial motive for the crime. Every one of them, as it were, fitted the bill.

But, as curious as it sounded, none of *them* was under suspicion.

I was.

And what's more, I was the only one who knew, quite definitively, that I had not killed Ilmo Räty.

Which made the situation an enormous jigsaw puzzle that I had to put together one piece at a time. That was what it felt like right now. My headache appeared to be on the move. Either that, or it was growing, spreading.

I closed my eyes, then opened them again.

I didn't exactly see the light, but something akin to that occurred. It didn't matter where I started. What was most important was that I started. Somewhere.

Mirka Paarmajärvi was clearly straining. Her eyes were glued to her computer screen, and whatever it was she was looking at apparently wasn't doing her bidding. Her bare, bronzed arms were impressive; her biceps looked like rubber balls covered in veins. I thought her general appearance had stiffened and tightened a bit over the last few days, which suggested she was getting ready for a competition or some other trial.

'Got a moment?' I asked, and stepped into her office.

Mirka quickly turned her head – almost a flinch.

'I need some help,' I said.

Mirka glanced towards the corridor, perhaps in the hope of seeing other colleagues, anyone who might come to her aid. The corridor was empty.

'What's this about?'

'I've got a headache,' I said. 'And the quickest way to get rid of it is to find something else to think about. I thought we could go through the warehouse inventory together. Maybe we could come up with a promotional campaign, something to cheer us up and make someone's day when they find out we've got just the stove they need.'

'I don't know...'

I reminded Mirka of how last year we'd discovered eight of our XL stoves lying around in the warehouse. Too big for home saunas but too small for public swimming pools. Together we'd hit upon the perfect buyer for them: a bowling centre that was just about to renovate its facilities. And I reminded her that we only managed to do this by putting our heads together.

Mirka looked as though she was weighing this up. We both knew that the warehouse was more than overstocked. The muscles of her upper body tightened further, then relaxed.

'Alright then,' she said, then turned back to her computer and started typing away. 'How about I list them starting from the oldest models and you shout out when you hear something that rings a bell?'

I watched her typing and thought that she must get through several keyboards a year. Each clack of the keys was like a hammer blow; each *enter* like a rock cracking in two.

'Besides,' I began, once I was sure she had got into such a rhythm that she wouldn't stop. 'Clearing out the warehouse will strengthen your position in the race to succeed Erkki, because—'

Mirka stopped in her tracks. 'You're never going to be chosen,' she said. 'You know it yourself. You've made sure of it.'

There was something very hard to read in Mirka's eyes. But I was used to that; her expressions never gave anything away. But

the one thing that most caught my attention was the confidence
with which she stated her position.

'How exactly have I made sure of anything of the sort?' I
asked, sincerely.

'Oh, come on,' she said. 'Everyone knows.'

'Knows what?'

'About you,' she said. 'And ... Erkki.'

Mirka looked deadly serious. She *was* deadly serious. It was all
I could do to maintain a calm exterior. This explained my
colleagues' sudden change in behaviour. It explained a lot more
too.

'That's not true,' I said.

'We all guessed you'd say that.'

I was about to protest, to stress even more emphatically that
the mere suggestion of such a thing was absurd, a lie through and
through. Then I stopped myself, reminded myself of what had
brought me here in the first place. Mirka might be the murderer.
Of the two of us, she was certainly the more likely candidate –
because it wasn't me. Very well, I thought, I'll approach this from
another angle.

'It's really not true,' I said, now a little less emphatically.
'Where on earth did you hear something like that?'

Again, Mirka snuck a look towards the corridor. When she
looked back at me, her eyes had chilled.

'Lost interest in the warehouse?' she asked. 'All those
forgotten stoves, that untapped potential?'

Her voice was neutral, but it seemed to be hiding something,
and in it I sensed the same kind of danger I saw in the muscles
rippling beneath her skin. I said I was still ready to go through
the warehouse.

'In a way, I get it,' she said after a moment. 'We all do what
we've got to do, right?'

Again, the same neutrality, the same barely concealed threat. Even before this conversation, I'd wondered whether, at the end of the day, I didn't know my colleagues very well at all. Now I was ready to admit that I knew Mirka particularly badly.

'Ultimately,' she continued, 'it's all about how much you want something. Isn't that right?'

'What else have you heard?' I asked.

The question clearly took her by surprise. It was supposed to. And though it wasn't exactly a crack that appeared in her hard, bronzed exterior, it was at least a hairline fracture. She had to fumble for words.

'What else...? What else should I have heard? Isn't it enough that you and—'

'Whoever has been spreading rumours must have told other stories too,' I said. 'Such as when this supposed affair started, how serious it is and, above all, who saw what and where.'

Mirka had regained control of her exterior; now there were no hairline fractures in sight.

'You'd know best about that, I'm sure,' she said.

'Would I?' I asked, and looked her right in the eyes.

We sat in silence, staring at each other. I thought back to the Westerns I'd watched with my father. Clint Eastwood and some other guy staring each other down. Maybe this little episode was the Puhtijärvi version of that same scenario: two middle-aged women in a sauna-stove company seeing who blinks first.

She eventually broke the stalemate. 'Maybe we can go through the warehouse another time.'

'I'll be back soon,' I said, but still didn't get up from my chair.

'Sounds good,' said Mirka, and I could hear in her voice that she meant something completely different. 'Anytime.'

'What's most important is Steam Devil,' I said, 'and its

continued success. For the common good. Individual success can wait.'

'Of course,' said Mirka. 'This is a team sport. There's plenty of wood to go around.'

I stood up and made my way towards the door. I waited for Mirka to say something else, but I heard nothing.

14

The police car looked like it had been sitting outside for a while. I don't know why I thought this; maybe because I couldn't see a driver anywhere. I steered my own vehicle past the police car, pulled up in front of the house, switched off the motor and opened the door. I heard a blackbird, nothing more. The garden was already a little dusky, the shadows growing all the while, but a bright sunbeam cut across the darkness here and there, and light was still filtering through the boughs of the tall birches. It shone from behind them and far out across the lake, which sparkled and glimmered invitingly. In truth, the sunlight only warmed the surface of the water, perhaps only to the depth of a forearm or so, and after that it was cool and, eventually, cold. I listened for any sounds coming from inside the house, but everything was silent. Santeri's car was under the carport, which meant he was at home, which in usual circumstances would mean some kind of noise would be coming from somewhere. I could think of only one reason why everything was silent: the presence of the police car. A presence that I hoped would be explained soon. I took the steps up to the porch, opened the door and stepped inside.

I stopped in the hallway, and just as I had heard the silence, now I felt it too. Silence in your own home is like that: it's somehow physical and concrete, familiar. Anywhere else, silence is just a kind of quietude. I waited for a moment, went back outside. And just as my mind was beginning to conjure up wild theories about the cars parked in the drive and their missing drivers, I heard the rapidly growing sound of conversation. I walked between the cars to the edge of the gravel path and looked down towards the sauna.

And saw Santeri and Janne.

They were standing at the corner of the sauna, talking about something; I couldn't make out the words. They took a few steps towards me, lazily walking up the gently sloped garden, looking for suitable footholds, as though the garden was significantly steeper than it really was. Janne noticed me before Santeri did.

'Hi,' he said, and raised a hand.

'Hi,' I replied.

'We were looking at the sauna,' said Janne.

'Right,' said Santeri, followed by something I couldn't quite make out.

Both Janne and Santeri had stopped halfway up the slope.

'And what did it look like?' I asked.

'Everything looks fine,' said Janne.

I stepped off the gravel and onto the lawn, walked around the currant bushes and came to a halt a few metres away from the two men. Right away, I noticed how uncomfortable I felt. I looked at Santeri and could see how awkward he felt too. Only Janne didn't seem to have noticed how odd the situation was. He was gazing around, continuously; anyone who didn't know him better might mistake him for a carefree summer tourist.

'Just popping by?' I asked, though I knew it wasn't the case. 'Or did Santeri invite you for a sauna?'

'What?' asked Santeri, and now he seemed a little panicked too.

Janne shook his head. 'No, this is strictly business,' he said. 'We're investigating the ... incident over at Koivulahti, so let's say we're getting the lie of the land.'

Santeri looked like he wanted nothing more than to extricate himself from the situation – fast. I hadn't told him that I'd been down to the police station for an informal chat; it wasn't something I especially wanted him to know.

'Santeri and I talked about other things too,' Janne continued. 'Mostly motor sports. Seeing as he's the local expert on the subject.'

Santeri was blushing, and I saw his Adam's apple bob, first up, then down.

'But now that you're here,' Janne went on, addressing me, 'and if you've got a moment, there are a few questions I'd like to ask you. I understand the sauna and the shore are your domain, so to speak?'

Santeri had turned towards the woods, away from Janne, away from me. The shift in his position wasn't big, but it spoke volumes about his levels of discomfort. I told Janne I'd be happy to answer his questions.

'Let's go down to the shore,' he suggested, then turned to Santeri. 'Thank you, Santeri. I'll be in touch if the need arises.'

'Right,' Santeri said and started making to leave. 'Of course ... but how ... right ... my phone number ... over there...'

As he spoke, Santeri moved away from us but didn't quite turn his back. His gait looked cumbersome, as though he were trying to walk up the hill sideways. Eventually he seemed to realise how hard this was, turned and walked off towards the house.

Janne gestured towards the sauna building. I led the way.

'I see you haven't told Santeri about our little chat this morning,' he said.

I wasn't surprised that Janne had picked up on this. But I didn't want to discuss my husband with Janne. The situation felt uncomfortable enough as it was. Janne was a policeman. And the police thought I was a murderer.

'I noticed,' he continued, 'that the sauna door wasn't locked. Is it always unlocked?'

'Yes,' I said. 'Of course. I wasn't expecting anyone to steal my bumlets. I doubt anybody does.'

Janne said nothing. I turned. We were standing at the corner of the sauna.

'Kiimalainen's theory is barking mad,' I said. 'And he's wrong. Let me say this once and for all: I did not burn down Ilmo's sauna.'

Janne gazed out towards the lake. The evening was beautiful, almost still. The blackbird was singing again.

'From here, it's only a short boat ride to Ilmo Räty's sauna,' he said. 'Especially if you know the short cut through the narrow, reedy strait, whose name I can't remember. The one that looks like it's completely overgrown but isn't. In a good boat, a quick rower could cover the journey in under half an hour.'

So, he *did* remember. I had always liked rowing. He and I had rowed out on the lake together long ago. Which sounds a lot more romantic than it actually was. The rowing had been hard going, demanded a surprising amount of concentration. But if you knew what you were doing, it was a quick, quiet way of travelling, especially when the lake was still, and especially in weather like there was that evening a week and a half ago. I looked at my rowing boat, tethered to the end of the jetty. I kept it in good shape, just the way I kept everything else. The boat was also, as Janne had put it, my domain.

'Kivisalmi,' I said. 'That's the name of the strait. And no, I did not row over to Ilmo Räty's sauna. Because I did not—'

'At this stage, we're looking into all possible theories,' said Janne. 'We're keeping everything on the table.'

'Do you mean we or you?' I asked. 'Kiimalainen has already decided I'm guilty. He won't listen to a word I say. He's got an explanation for everything – even that missing bumlet.'

Janne turned to me. 'For everything?' he asked. Maybe it wasn't a question.

I don't know what went through me. The intervening decades, perhaps. Something great and heavy hummed within me; it whooshed and gusted through me, leaving me with the sensation that I'd been standing in a biting wind for hours without any skin. There was a minute change in Janne's expression too, in his whole posture: a loss of focus, a softening. Something that had made him suddenly speak in a different tone, with a different manner. But he began correcting it right away. I decided to speak before he could take back his words.

'I'm sorry,' I said. 'For what happened. Back then. All those years ago. It wasn't right. I was so young; I didn't know how to behave. I made a mistake. I made lots of mistakes.'

There, I thought. I'd made the start I knew I had to make. I didn't know what I felt though. Not liberation, nor even relief. I certainly didn't feel as though a rock that had long been weighing down my shoulders had suddenly been rolled away. It was still there. But maybe – just maybe – I'd made a move in the right direction. I'd done something important. At the same time, it felt like I'd dived right into the cold lake. Not this one, glimmering and shimmering in thousands of rippling currents around us, but another lake, somewhere else.

Janne didn't respond. I saw him slowly exhale. I didn't hear the sigh, but I saw it.

'You weren't the only one,' he said after a pause. 'To make mistakes. Then or now.'

We looked each other in the eyes. I felt neither the desire nor the need to look away.

I decided to be honest. 'I don't know why it's taken me so long to say it.'

'Time has that effect,' said Janne. 'Sometimes thirty years feels like it was yesterday. For better or worse.'

'Do you ever wonder…?' I began, then realised something. 'Are you a cop right now or … I don't know, just Janne?'

'I'm always a cop, just like I'm always … me,' he said, but still with a smile. It was a cautious smile, a familiar one. 'But I've never arrested anyone for an overdue conversation.'

He shifted his bodyweight to his right leg. His posture was somehow more relaxed now.

'Do you ever find yourself thinking you got to fifty-three years old before you even knew it?' I asked.

'No so much that,' he said. 'More that there are only a finite number of, shall we say, useful years left, even if everything goes as well as it possibly can.'

'Isn't that the same thing?'

'In the former scenario, you're looking back in time,' he said. 'In the latter, you're looking ahead.'

'And you look ahead?'

'I try to,' he said. 'But it doesn't always work.'

'What happens when it doesn't work?'

'I remember that I really am fifty-three years old.'

We stood for a moment in silence. The blackbird reminded us of its presence.

'I didn't tell Santeri I was at the police station,' I said, 'or that I was interviewed. Or that Kiimalainen suspects me of murder.'

'I understand,' said Janne. He glanced at the lake then turned back to me. 'At least, I think I do.'

'How is Emma keeping?'

'She's in Helsinki,' he said. 'For good.'

'I'm sorry…'

'It was an easy decision,' he said. 'A relief, actually. We spent six years in a kind of limbo. Emma working in Helsinki, me out here, neither wanting to resettle permanently in the other place. I filed the divorce papers, told her about it, she thanked me, and we haven't spoken since.'

'You sound happy.'

'I'm looking ahead,' said Janne.

The evening sun flickered from behind the birches, casting shadows on Janne's face, highlighting his dips and furrows, but somehow softening his features. Just then I heard a familiar sound coming from the direction of the house. Formula One. I saw that Janne too had heard the screech of racing cars cutting through the lakeside idyll.

'I'm really sorry,' I said.

Janne looked up at the house. 'No need to apologise,' he replied. 'I watch the odd race too, every now and then. The new ones, though. The ones where you don't already know the result.'

I couldn't help myself; the laughter burst out before I was able to stop it. Janne smiled, but it quickly faded.

'Sorry,' he said, and now he sounded like he really *was* sorry. 'It's none of my business.'

'No need to apologise,' I said. 'I needed a little light relief. Let's just say it's been a long day.'

'I can imagine,' he said.

'After all, I've never been a murder suspect before,' I said, and realised that my exhaustion combined with the laughter, and the instant sense of spontaneity it created, made me a bit too relaxed. 'Sorry, now it's my turn to apologise—'

'I think we've both apologised quite enough,' he said.

We stood there, barely a metre and a half away from each other, but the distance felt smaller still. Perhaps it was the vastness of the landscape that made it feel so small, the distant shore across the lake, the tall, dark-blue dome of the sky above us. Or maybe it was shrunk by the fact that thirty years seemed to have vanished into thin air.

For a moment, at least.

Because the thoughts and memories that followed this brief repose were far less pleasant, and I wasn't prepared for them.

The October darkness.
The feel of hard metal.
The man in the rowing boat rising to his feet.

I wanted to shake my head. I had to return to the here and now, this evening, this conversation. It was easier said than done, but I got there in the end.

'Despite everything,' I said, 'it was nice of you to pop round.'

Janne smiled, clearly more relaxed. 'This went better than I'd expected,' he said, but then looked as though he'd remembered something and suddenly became serious. 'Considering, of course...'

'Of course,' I conceded.

'The investigation is ongoing.'

'Quite.'

We stood in silence again.

'I know I'm repeating myself,' I said. 'But I'm not a murderer.'

Janne didn't answer at first. He was gazing out across the lake, and it felt as though he moved a millimetre or two further away from me.

'I assume you won't mind,' he said and looked me once more in the eyes, 'if I come round again – if something comes up?'

I didn't look away or glance to the side. I said that would be fine and did my best to hide my disappointment that he had completely ignored what I'd said. We then said a few words about the exceptional August evening around us, and this we did in a manner that felt safe: we each stammered, the gaps between our utterances getting longer as though by mutual agreement.

And with the last ellipsis seemingly hanging in the air, we began walking – again as if by agreement – towards the house, until we reached Janne's squad car. Janne got in, reversed to the place where the driveway widened, then calmly turned the car.

The police car disappeared into the distance.

And despite everything...

...This might have been the first time in my life when I wished the police would come back.

15

I filled the fire chamber. The sauna was already warm and ready to use, but I wanted a good soak, some decent steam. I needed it. I sat down on the upper bench and listened to the growing hum of the stove. I dipped the ladle into the pail, scooped up some water and threw it on the stove, which spat angrily, then sizzled, and finally hissed. I felt the hot steam around my shoulders, on my back, my arms, my earlobes. I peered at the thermometer. Ninety. I put the ladle back into the pail and did what I often did in the sauna.

I sat there thinking.

And no matter how fast recent events, encounters and conversations raced through my mind, and although gripping at one loose end revealed another five, the conclusion was clearer and brighter than at any point before.

I needed to hurry.

If even Janne didn't believe I was innocent, I couldn't just wait around for the results of the police investigation. To be frank, I didn't trust the impartiality of the investigation. It appeared highly likely that Kiimalainen had already decided the exact day he was going to arrest me. He clearly had his own theory, and I doubted very much that he would entertain any evidence that might disprove it. And it was clear I couldn't count on Janne. His reference to the short row across the lake and his retreat at the end of the conversation told me he had strong suspicions, still, despite everything we'd talked about.

I really was alone. And there was even less time to prove my innocence than I'd imagined.

I threw another ladle of water on the stones.

It was a good thing I'd already begun my own investigation, although it had got off to a jittery start. But I was a middle-aged stove retailer, not Sherlock Holmes.

The water sizzled on the stones, instantly turning into steam, which clenched me in its arms, its teeth gently biting my skin.

My thoughts jumped here and there.

As the steam continued to pinch and squeeze me, more positive things occurred to me. I'd started one conversation at the stove factory, and now I would start some more. Mirka was just the first of many. And now I saw something new to consider in what Erkki had said, and, above all, in *how* he had worded it. I didn't think Erkki was a murderer, but one way or another he was the key to getting to the bottom of the matter, of that I was certain. But I wasn't excluding anyone else. Even Santeri was on my list, though I knew he was in Vaasa on the night of the fire – this time chasing after a clutch that had come off Gerhard Berger's practice car and that had suddenly turned up for sale – and whom I found it extremely hard to imagine voluntarily rowing anywhere.

No, they were all on my list.

Mirka, Erkki, Porkka, Kaarlo, Susanna. Even Kiimalainen. How much did the elk that my father had killed still gnaw away at him? Or maybe it was someone else from the village. Someone who happened to have a disagreement with Ilmo's wife and wanted to take revenge on her but ended up incinerating her husband instead?

As I've said, I wasn't going to dismiss anyone. But I needed to act quickly.

I threw more water on the stove, sat there until the cloud of steam had dissipated, then stepped outside. Dusk was gradually falling. The lake water looked cool, velveteen.

My swim was a little shorter than usual.

16

The remains of Ilmo Räty's sauna were still cordoned off with police tape. They hadn't scrimped on the tape, and I couldn't help wondering whether the police department had been trying to clear out their own warehouse too. The tape ran around the crime scene, stretching from the edge of the woods to the other side of the garden before turning and running deep into the woods, curling thick spruces and large boulders into its embrace, then returning to the sauna. There wasn't much left of it now, and I couldn't keep my eyes on it for long. Part of Ilmo was still there, and I didn't want to imagine what form it took or how much of it there was.

This was the second time I'd paid a visit here.

On the first occasion, both the sauna and Ilmo were still here, on the long and narrow strip of land, and I hadn't paid attention to anything else. I was there at Ilmo's invitation to assess the sauna and its stove, so obviously these were the things I focussed on. This time I looked at the surroundings with fresh eyes. First of all, I walked down to the shore.

As I came to a stop by the foot of the jetty, I thought I understood the rationale behind Janne's rowing-boat theory. The jetty was at the end of a tapered channel of water. On either side of the jetty, the channel was thick with clusters of reeds, which meant the end of the channel and the jetty were hidden from view from almost every direction. The only place from which you'd be able to spot a boat tethered at the end of the jetty was further out on the lake, and someone out there was unlikely to stop halfway through their journey to case out Ilmo Räty's jetty without a good reason.

But Janne had been right about the length of the row. By

turning west directly after the channel through the reeds, the rower would reach the protection of a peninsula thick with birches in a matter of minutes, and from there continue along the undulating shores of the national park and past the countless tiny islands, all the way to Tiirislahti, and from there it was only a further twenty minutes to my jetty.

Half an hour from jetty to jetty, just as Janne had said.

I stood there a moment longer, staring at the channel and the reeds, the narrow opening leading out into the lake. At the end of the jetty was a ladder that looked as though it might lead somewhere other than into the lake, somewhere far deeper.

I turned around.

The garden currently looked like a construction site. But that was because of the tyre tracks the heavy vehicles had churned into the earth. If you forgot about those and squinted a little in the morning light, the garden looked very well cared for. Naturally, the lawn was somewhat overgrown and some of the shrubs had suffered in the exceptional August heat, but still, this was a place that had been well looked after.

I let my eyes pan across the entire garden: up towards the house, back to the sauna, the shore, along the other side of the garden, across the garden to the woods and from there back to the sauna. I felt a bit silly. I had no idea what I was supposed to be looking for. And what exactly did I think I would find that the police hadn't already? Was I here simply because I'd read and seen in films how detectives visited the scene of the crime one last time and only then discovered a business card that the murderer had accidentally left behind or a pair of glasses they wore, then sped off in an attempt to prevent the next homicide?

No, maybe not. I didn't expect to find a matchbox from the killer's favourite bar or a laundrette receipt that had fallen from their pocket as it was pulled open by a rogue branch.

What I wanted was to understand how this deed had been carried out, step by step. How far was it from the sauna to the jetty, from the woods to the sauna, from the sauna to the driveway? What were the most logical routes from the perspective of someone about to take a sauna? Because the one thing I understood better than most people was the sauna, and as far as I saw it, this was the key to finding a solution.

It was to this thought that I'd woken up before sunrise.

That word...

The SAUNA...

I'd seen the word in tall letters, screaming in front of me even before I'd opened my eyes. I wasn't sure whether I'd said it out loud while in the borderlands of the dreamworld, but that's what it felt like.

Though I didn't like the idea of the sauna being used as a murder weapon, I knew only too well how easily it could turn into one. A few years ago, I'd sat in a client's sauna at 110°C a little too long, and even I'd been forced to admit that enough was enough. I became painfully aware of the cigarette paper's difference between a really hot but still enjoyable sauna and one in which you could potentially lose your life.

I faced Ilmo's sauna and forced myself to look at what was left of it. I tried to place everything: the dressing room and the washing facilities, the steam room and its interior. The benches used to be over there, the stove over there. I stood staring at the latter. As Kiimalainen had mentioned, it was one of our basic models. However, a number of small, precise adjustments had been made to it. In particular I remembered its rather intense fire chamber, which meant that it heated up more quickly than many other stoves. If you knew what you were doing.

I stared at the spot where the stove had once stood for a while. But then my gaze shifted. Though I couldn't see anything even remotely resembling sauna benches, I thought I must be looking at where they'd been located. First I thought about the distances between them, then everything else. Assuming I had understood correctly, Ilmo Räty had been sitting on his bench right till the bitter end. The thought made me shudder. I recalled what 110°C had felt like. Yet something had kept Ilmo on the upper bench. There were multiple possible explanations for this.

Whoever had heated this sauna up to ignition point might first have rendered Ilmo unconscious then sat him on the bench. If Ilmo had indeed been unconscious, burning down the sauna might have been an attempt to destroy the evidence of a blow to the head, for instance, or of knock-out drops or poison administered earlier that evening.

But in that case, why couldn't the killer have simply drowned Ilmo in the lake? The deepest point wasn't very far away. Or why not bury him out in the woods, which started right at the corner of the sauna? Or transport him in any direction at all – all around there was nothing but woodland, lakes, marshes, fields and thousands of boulders, places where nobody would ever look.

With this in mind, a loss of consciousness – however it was brought about – seemed an unlikely option. As I saw it, heating the sauna up to a critical mass was a unique act, an act that was meant to say something. But if nobody was there to hear or witness it, the whole operation – the sweat and physical exertion of carrying all those logs and keeping the fire chamber stocked – would have been a pointless exercise. The perpetrator must have needed someone to witness the chain of events and all the effort they had gone to.

In other words, they needed someone to be taking a sauna.

To my mind, the most plausible yet grizzly explanation was that Ilmo had in fact been conscious, that he had been sitting on the bench and for some reason stayed there as the temperature rose and the fire chamber was refilled time and again, as the police had said. So, the real question was: what had kept Ilmo on the bench from one refill to the next, and why hadn't he tried to stop it? The answer to this was both simple and complicated. Something had prevented him. But what?

The screech of a seagull brought me back to the here and now. I glanced at my watch.

I wasn't where I was supposed to be.

17

Erkki probably wasn't aiming for a look of sphinx-like mystery, but that was the impression he was giving. I was happy that we'd been able to arrange a meeting at such short notice. But now I was late for the time we'd agreed – according to the ladles of the sauna clock, by exactly six minutes – and I apologised as I sat down.

'Not at all,' said Erkki from behind his desk. 'This has been, one might say, rather ... pleasant waiting – comfortable, what with everything. Your message really cheered me up.'

I tried to look at him more closely, but it quickly started to feel like staring. On the one hand, it looked as though Erkki might be smiling, perhaps even simpering, while on the other he appeared very sombre and serious about something. Or maybe he was just concentrating hard. This happens sometimes: when you concentrate, you forget what you look like and end up looking like yourself.

'There's something I'd like to talk to you about,' I began. 'Something that's come to my attention. It's to do with the race to succeed you.'

Erkki nodded. A little more enthusiastically than I'd expected. And the whole situation began to feel more awkward.

'The matter is a bit delicate,' I went on, 'and I'm not sure how to approach it. There's a rumour. One involving you and me.'

I couldn't be sure, but something seemed to ripple across Erkki's face – around his mouth particularly – something between a smile and a sigh.

'You and me?' he asked.

'Yes,' I said. 'There seems to be this idea going around that we are—'

'People like to talk,' he interrupted. 'They say all sorts. There's no need to pay it any attention. I don't.' Another mysterious ripple.

'That's ... easier said than done...' I said.

'Are you absolutely sure this rumour is specifically about you and me?'

'Pardon?'

'Is the rumour you've heard about the two of us? You see, I've heard a rumour, or perhaps I should say it was my understanding that you and Ilmo were...'

He paused; I waited. Perhaps he was looking out of the window, perhaps at the sauna clock.

'...sauna companions ... before...' he continued before trailing away.

All at once I felt like a passenger in a car that suddenly had no driver. I had to grab the steering wheel.

'I haven't heard any rumours like that,' I said. 'And it's not true. At all.'

Erkki looked at me again. He seemed to be weighing up my answer.

'Well, I wouldn't worry about it,' he said eventually. 'After all, that situation is in the past now.'

'What situation?' I asked.

'Quite,' said Erkki, scanning the floor for something to focus on. 'The situation between you two, now that Ilmo has tragically passed away...'

I was getting agitated, but I couldn't help myself. 'I want to make it absolutely clear that there is and never was any *situation* between me and Ilmo. We were never sauna companions or anything else like that. We were colleagues. Here at Steam Devil. That's it. And whoever is spreading—'

Something stopped me in mid-flow.

'Have you…?' I began. '…Have you talked to the police again?'

Erkki hesitated a moment. I took this as an answer in the affirmative.

'And in that conversation,' I continued, keeping my hands firmly on the steering wheel of this car, 'did you get a sense of where they had heard this rumour?'

Erkki shook his head. 'No,' he said. 'And I'm not sure I could tell you even if I had.' His expression was hard to read. Either he really meant what he'd just said, or he did not.

'So, you did *not* get that sense?'

'No,' he said, now sounding about sixty years younger, like a little boy who'd been caught red-handed. 'And I made sure to say only good things about you. I wanted to give them the best possible impression.'

'Thank you,' I said, then asked: 'But what do you think about the sauna being burned down – and Ilmo's death, and the possible culprit? Did you share your thoughts with the police? You've been in the sauna-stove business for decades, and you know more about it than all the rest of us put together. They must have listened to what you had to say.'

At first I thought that flattering him like this might have been pointless, but then he leant a fraction forwards and nodded.

'Naturally, I can't tell you everything at this stage,' he said.

'Of course not,' I replied.

'But when I heard their thoughts on the matter,' he continued, 'I thought it was my responsibility to express my concerns about the stoves, and even to steer their investigation in that direction.'

I tried to conceal my surprise. I think I managed it.

'What kind of concerns?' I asked. 'About the stoves?'

'Well,' said Erkki, and I could see he was choosing his words very carefully. 'Obviously, this is all confidential.'

'Obviously,' I agreed.

'I suspect,' he began, 'that someone has been leaking information about our new fire-chamber locking system to our competitors.'

I said nothing.

'We were the real pioneers of pump-lock technology,' Erkki continued. 'The small ventilation mechanism in the fire-chamber handle that makes sure the handle never heats up too much, no matter how hot you like the sauna. It was one of our trump cards – especially among hardened sauna connoisseurs. But then, only last week, I heard that the boys from Log Standard Ltd have released a new signature stove that has a very similar, dare I say identical, mechanism as the one in our catalogue. I told the police all about it,' Erkki rounded off. He looked almost offended.

'How did they react?' I asked.

'They said it didn't sound like industrial espionage,' said Erkki, and now he really did sound offended.

'May I ask who you had this conversation with?'

'It's not a secret,' said Erkki. 'Senior Constable Kiimalainen. But that's all I can tell you about our conversation.'

I now suspected Erkki knew more about Ilmo Räty's death than I did, and he might even know something of the utmost importance. And I also imagined, as I looked at the king of artisanal sauna stoves, that his words had probably had no impact on Kiimalainen or his suspicions. Which only served to confirm what I was expecting Kiimalainen to do in the very near future. I was about to add something about being grateful to Erkki for defending me when he spoke.

'In any case,' he said. 'I'm glad you suggested we have this con-versation. That we were able to talk things through and ... yes ... clear the obstacles from our path. These matters have been bothering me too.'

I didn't quite know what Erkki was talking about, so kept my mouth closed.

'And as for the matter of the new CEO,' he said, 'I don't want there to be any of the uncertainties that we saw around Ilmo's case.'

I still kept my mouth shut, deciding to let him speak for as long as he had something to say.

'It's perfectly obvious to me that you're no more a murderer than a special sauna companion,' said Erkki. 'I take you at your word.'

Upon hearing this, dozens of questions popped into my mind, but Erkki had reverted to his sphinx-like manner, so I decided to return to the beginning of our conversation.

'About that rumour,' I said. 'I think it would be a good idea to correct that misunderstanding as soon as possible.'

'As soon as possible,' said Erkki. 'That sounds excellent.'

Just then, someone knocked at the door. I looked behind me and immediately had to adjust my gaze upwards. Jarkko's head appeared, slightly askew, right up against the top of the doorframe, as though he were standing on a stool hidden behind the door and awkwardly peering through the gap. Of course, Jarkko didn't need a stool.

'Marko Tapulinen has been waiting here for a while,' he said. 'You wanted to talk to him about performing at Steam Fest. The Dean Martin act and your special requirements.'

I turned to Erkki.

'*That's amore*,' he said.

18

It seemed as if the lake outside burst into flame just as I stepped back into my office. Of course, I realised this was just the sun making an appearance, having been hidden behind an unusually dark cloud for some time.

I forced myself to stop before sitting down and switching on my computer. I took a deep breath, tried to put my thoughts in order.

I thought hard to make sure I could remember everything I'd just heard in my conversation with Erkki – and in my previous conversations with him too – as many details as possible without leaving out anything important. Only then did I roll my chair under my desk and switch on the computer.

It took about thirty seconds for it to boot up, and during that time I stared out of the window. By now, the brightness felt appropriate.

I signed into the company's internal server and opened windows for the company's finances, the warehouse stock and the staff's shared diary. I went through all the statements from the last month, cross-referenced everything, then examined my findings. Then I worked backwards, one month at a time. After that, I searched the internet, using dozens of keywords, and, about an hour later, came back to where I had started and asked myself whether I had done everything thoroughly, checked everything twice, sometimes even three times.

Yes, I had.

The connections were all there.

Most of them were strong and clear, some more flimsy, and

some of them required more than a leap of faith, but the overall picture they formed was perfectly logical and plausible and seemed to provide at least some kind of explanation for what had happened.

Ilmo Räty, who had seemed to appear in Puhtijärvi and at his job at Steam Devil out of nowhere, had once been a keen diver, something I'd never heard mentioned before. The diving club's website contained updates over a period of two decades. The young Ilmo Räty used to go diving in Finland and Thailand. Judging by the photos uploaded to the website, a man by the name of Jalmari Heinonen appeared to have done the same near the island of Koh Samui.

And, what do you know? This very same Jalmari Heinonen was the director of Log Standard Ltd – the company competing with Steam Devil in the world of artisanal sauna stoves that Erkki claimed had copied our technology. Given everything Ilmo Räty had said about fusions, mergers and moving our operations to another part of the country, it wasn't impossible to imagine that he and Jalmari might have had some preliminary talks about collaboration between the two companies and off-the-record conversations in which he had divulged classified information about technical innovations in stove design, in particular about the aforementioned fire-chamber handle.

A device that, naturally, Porkka had designed, developed and ultimately built. I remember well the pride with which he had presented the handle to us. What's more – and in hindsight, this now seemed especially important – Porkka had considered his invention one reason among many why he should become Steam Devil's next CEO. He had brought this up on numerous occasions, reminding us about it at virtually every meeting. It wasn't an exaggeration to say that Porkka's handle had the same significance to him as a crown to a king: it was to be the final seal on his meteoric rise to the Steam Devil throne. This had not happened, and his disappointment had been, objectively speaking, immeasurable.

Of course, Porkka himself hadn't talked about the matter, but I'd noticed at the time that his sauna sessions had become more frequent and his general ruddiness had increased exponentially. For a few weeks, he'd looked like a fusion of red light and stewed meat. What if, after all this, Porkka had found out that Ilmo, who had just been named the new CEO (unfairly, if you asked Porkka), had also been leaking information to the company's competitor about *Porkka's* invention? He would have taken the matter both seriously and very personally, and I couldn't imagine what a hot-headed sauna enthusiast like Porkka, who would stand or fall by his principles, might have done in such a situation.

Perhaps I could imagine it. I'd visited the scene of the fire that morning.

More links then appeared, both in the financial statements and the shared diary.

Porkka had been away on business both on the day of the fire and the following day. But away on business *where*? There was no mention of a destination in any of the documentation. Furthermore, he hadn't submitted his kilometres or petrol bill for the dates in question. Simply put, it looked like he had disappeared for two days. This was exceptional. In normal circumstances, he was the most efficient member of the team, especially when it came to filing expenses; he billed for every metre, every minute. Now he appeared to have discarded a full forty-eight-hour period and who knows how many kilometres, just like that.

Ilmo Räty, meanwhile, had demonstrated both conscientious-ness and doubtless unintentional carelessness by indicating the destination of his trip on an expenses claim from three months ago. By sheer coincidence, this was the same location as the factory belonging to Log Standard Ltd. And it appeared that one visit hadn't been enough. Though Ilmo hadn't specified the destination of subsequent expenses claims (perhaps he had realised his mistake), a month later he had filled up his tank at the petrol station in that same town and, again conscientiously, attached a photograph of a petrol receipt to his claim. Most notably, he had claimed he was visiting a town that was in the opposite direction. I still wasn't Sherlock Holmes, but it wasn't hard to conclude that he must have been in the town where he filled up his car.

But as I came up with connections and a picture began to emerge, I came to realise that understanding that picture required a very specific set of skills. You had to believe that the connections were real. You had to know the people in question and their idiosyncrasies. And you had to recognise the principles of the sauna and stove business and its innumerable unwritten rules. If you didn't believe, know and recognise these things, everything looked random, and there was no meaning to any of the apparent coincidences. So I knew very well what would happen if I were to drive to the police station and present my theory to Kiimalainen. From his perspective, it would all be further evidence that I was the guilty party; I was simply trying to come up with wild and wacky explanations for other people's guilt.

It was clear I would need something more, something tangible.

I needed Porkka.

19

It goes without saying that middle age doesn't make you a better detective – at least not automatically – but I suspected it would be to my advantage right now. I knew who I was; I understood my own limitations.

I couldn't grab Porkka by the scruff of his checked flannel shirt and demand an explanation, like the hero of an action film might have done, and I couldn't load all my guns (not least because I didn't have any) and dash towards him and his test saunas like Rambo. And this was probably for the best. At the end of the day, there were only a very limited number of options available to me, and after looking at things head-on, there was really only one.

Porkka lived by himself; he had divorced a few years ago. I remembered him once saying that his ex-wife used to constantly complain about two things: mosquitoes and the sauna. And because Porkka had built his house by the edge of a marsh, there were millions of mosquitoes most of the year, except in the dead of winter, when he spent most of his time in the roasting-hot sauna in the garden. As such, time spent together and any shared interests were in rather short supply for the couple, and when it finally came the divorce was a relief to both of them. According to Porkka, that is. I couldn't recall ever having met his wife, and I wasn't even sure of her name, but she had a point about the mosquitoes. I'd spent the last few hours being eaten alive, and the incessant buzzing – not to mention the continual attempts to suck my blood – had me thinking of murder, and not just in an investigative sense.

I'd made my decision a few hours ago, popped home, changed my clothes, eaten a banana and a tub of fat-free blueberry quark, taken the hilly, roundabout route to the road through the forest that came to an end about a kilometre away from Porkka's house, left the car and walked the rest of the way.

The house stood right at the edge of the woods; the marshland started behind it and continued far into the distance. I looked at the time. It was almost eight. I'd been waiting in the woods for ages now. The sun would set in about an hour. It had already dyed the horizon a deep red, spreading a soft, dreamlike haze across the marsh.

My original idea had involved Porkka's house, particularly his home workshop, which was the size of a barn and was, he'd often said, the key to all his inventions. This was the place where, in his words, he 'built and tested everything' before introducing it to us. The word 'everything' had caught my attention, because the way he enunciated it said something about how important and profoundly personal this was to him. I'd imagined I would have a look around the workshop, and even if I couldn't find anything directly linked to Ilmo Räty or paraphernalia suggesting a connection to the sauna fire, knowing Porkka as I did, I would doubtless find *something*. And it would mean my investigation could take a few steps forwards.

It turned out my idea wasn't very sensible, and that was because of Porkka. He had got home before I arrived, despite the fact that I'd seen him talking to Kaarlo and Mirka – together, *again* – in front of the Steam Devil test saunas as I'd hurried to my own car. And now I'd been waiting hours for him to leave his house, even for a moment. But his car was still parked out front, Porkka was inside the house, and I hid among the spruces, at the mercy of the mosquitoes.

But I had no intention of giving up. Perhaps this was another benefit of middle age: I had a thorough understanding of discomfort and how to deal with it.

I'd just wiped another mosquito from my cheek when I heard a sound from the house, and my first thought was that I'd been seen.

Porkka shot like a bullet into the garden, coming to a halt in the middle of the drive. 'What are you doing over there?' he shouted. 'Come here...'

I wondered whether I should turn and run, or fall to the ground and take cover, but then I realised he wasn't talking to me; he was on the phone, which I hadn't seen because he was holding it to the ear facing away from me.

'If anyone should be going anywhere, *you* should be coming to *me*. And why Aurinkoniemi? That's no longer—'

Porkka listened. I was standing behind a large spruce approximately twenty metres away from him, and I could see him surprisingly clearly. The evening sunlight was shining into the garden from just the right angle to make his thick, black moustache gleam and to intensify his usual ruddiness. Set against the backdrop of the marsh, which was now bathed in the last rays of sunlight, he looked braced and alert, like an ancient hunter. Porkka and the landscape seemed perfect for each other.

'And you guys have got it with you...?' he said eventually. Then: 'Fifteen minutes.'

Porkka lowered his phone then gazed out at the marsh for a moment. The mosquitoes didn't seem to bother him. He stood perfectly still. When he finally moved, he did so in typical Porkka style: brisk and angular. He plonked himself on his quadbike, started the engine and careered down the driveway. I, too, made up my mind.

I started running.

〰

Aurinkoniemi was an unfinished lakeside village that at one point was supposed to become the main draw for tourists to Puhtijärvi. Building work had begun with great ceremony about ten years ago, but was quickly interrupted, and from then on construction had been more or less at a standstill – notwithstanding a few bursts of activity here and there. The reason for the constant interruptions was the main building contractor's financial quandary, to which there seemed to be no solution in sight. Or rather, as local supporters of the venture always put it, the solution hadn't *yet* been found.

Aurinkoniemi was situated on a long peninsula stretching out into the lake. Standing out on the peninsula were the structure for the new spa centre, a long pier leading into the water and a giant lakeside sauna that was, astonishingly, almost complete and which people knew was in use, despite the security risks and the fact that it wasn't officially open. The sauna had been designed to fit around three hundred bathers: the length of the benches guaranteed that this sauna could accommodate several busloads of the long-awaited tourists.

I proceeded cautiously; while I was familiar with the terrain, I was taking a shortcut. But I did need to get a move on. I had lost sight of Porkka for the moment, and if I didn't find the murderer soon, I would be the one accused of the crime. So the clock was ticking. I could see and hear it in my mind. And it didn't help that its hands looked like sauna ladles and it sounded like an old-fashioned grandfather clock.

On a bright, sunny summer's day, Aurinkoniemi lived up to its name – Sunny Cape – but the dwindling daylight and the long shadows of the August evening made the whole place, especially the unfinished, abandoned buildings, look like pieces of a theatre set. Or maybe even the location for a horror film. I stopped at the edge of the area, crouched down behind a pile of gravel, caught my breath and looked for movement, either around the main building or the sauna. By the shore, a goldeneye duck flapped in the water a few times, rose into flight, disappeared behind the trees. I couldn't hear Porkka's quadbike, or anything else.

I thought of the quick decision I'd just made. And concluded that running through the woods for fifteen minutes still seemed reasonable. The phone call Porkka had taken was clearly about something very important to him. So it might be important to me too. There would be time to visit his workshop later; now I just had to find...

...Porkka. Who just then I saw descending the stone steps of the main building into the yard and continuing towards the sauna. His footsteps were familiar – heavy and purposeful. He walked around in an arc, approached my hiding place, then turned back and headed towards the sauna and the concreted patio area. Porkka came to a stop, looked in both directions, then out towards the lake, before finally turning to face the sauna. A few seconds passed, then a sound came from inside the building and Porkka set off, approaching the main entrance to the sauna. He waited again, glanced around, leant his head to the side, stepped closer still, stretched his neck as though he was listening carefully, then finally stepped inside.

What now?

I stepped out from behind the gravel pile, hurried across the yard to the side of the sauna and waited. I couldn't hear anything, so I made my way along the side, to the corner, stopped and looked towards the patio. The evening was darkening quickly and the far end of the patio seemed further away than it had only a moment ago, and I knew that in half an hour the woodland waiting behind it would swallow it whole.

I moved onto the patio, making sure my steps were silent all the while. I reached the entrance, stopped again and listened, trying to locate Porkka using sound alone. But all I could locate was my own heart, thumping in my chest, pounding in my ears. The effect was like a washing machine. And the difference between a detective and a stove retailer was very clear. I had no prior experience of such a situation.

I peered in – then stepped inside. The setting sun shining in through the enormous windows cast everything in a soft, crimson light, but this didn't make the place any cosier. The concrete interior and the general desolation gave me symptoms of agoraphobia and, simultaneously, claustrophobia. A sign on the wall told me that this was the men's side, but right now I didn't think my presence here was the worst of my offences. My biggest mistake was coming here in the first place.

I was about to turn, and most probably run out of the building, heading anywhere else but here, when I heard something. Porkka was speaking; I couldn't make out the words. The voice was coming from the direction of the steam room.

I walked through the hall and into the shadows, constantly ready to retreat to the darkest corner. Eventually, after walking for what seemed like a long while, I reached the doorway leading to the washing facilities and the gigantic steam room. I cautiously stepped into the men's showers – ignoring a second sign – and now Porkka's voice was louder. But I still couldn't make out the individual words.

I snuck towards the doorway and peered into the sauna.

The space looked like a sports arena where people could sit in the steam. The benches were long and even, there were five or six rows of them, and in front of the benches was the largest stove that Steam Devil had ever manufactured. During the production phase, it had been nicknamed the Quarry because of the extraordinary volume of stones it held. From the benches there was a direct view of the lake and the sunset – when such a thing was on offer. It no longer was.

Dusk had descended more quickly than I'd thought.

My eyes had gradually become accustomed to the diminishing light and had tricked me into assuming I'd be able to see much better than I actually could. So it took a moment before I spied two figures at the other end of the steam room; and what happened next took another two or three seconds for me to decipher.

Porkka stepped away from the other figure, turned and immediately began to wobble. At the same time, the other figure retreated behind a large door. Now Porkka was approaching me – staggering, as though he was looking at the floor to find a suitable place for each step.

There was something in his forehead, something shiny. At first I thought he must have attached a headlamp, the kind people used when orienteering, but I soon realised that what I'd seen was not a light but a reflection.

One step at a time, he came closer to me, and just then the reason for the unexpected dusk became clear. There must have been a cloud in front of the evening sun. For now the light from outside intensified, the wood of the benches and wall panels started glowing a deep red.

Porkka had almost reached my hiding place. Not that there was any need to hide anymore.

A sauna ladle was jutting from his forehead. He looked as though he was examining it. Upon closer inspection, it was the handle of a sauna ladle that was protruding from his forehead, and unfortunately I was able to inspect his red face, his expression of irritation and his black, imposing moustache much more closely than I would have liked. The reflection was coming from the metal ring attached to the end of the handle. It wasn't hard to imagine that someone must have removed the ladle bowl and used the handle and the metallic shaft as a sharp weapon.

Porkka was only about four metres in front of me when he finally stopped, his eyes still fixed on the handle. Then he slowly turned towards the setting sun, swayed back and forth, ruddy and teddy-bear-like, and finally toppled over like an ancient, noble tree.

20

The Steam Devil flag was flying at half-mast. I stood in the forecourt outside the factory with my colleagues and Erkki 'The Stove King' Ruusula as we all took part in a minute's silence. Thirty-six hours had passed since I'd fled Aurinkoniemi, and thirty-five hours since Porkka – perhaps by chance, perhaps not – had been found in a hundred-seater sauna with a ladle handle sticking out of his forehead.

The storm inside me was still raging, almost as much as when I had run through the woods and back to my car. The storm was understandable, and I didn't blame myself for not seeing recent events or the present moment in a particularly positive way or viewing my current situation as a marvellous opportunity or a new and interesting bonus challenge.

It was a warm, windless day, so the flag wasn't fluttering as it should but looked more as if it was hugging the flagpole in order to take some comfort or perhaps to extract a little extra power so it could flutter again at some point in the future. Erkki had prefaced our minute's silence with a speech in which he had listed all of Porkka's stove innovations from the oldest to the newest, then explained how Porkka had first come to work for Steam Devil. I hadn't heard this story before so had learnt a small but interesting detail: it was Kaarlo who had originally told Erkki about Porkka's expertise in this field.

When Erkki mentioned this, I looked over at Kaarlo, and in his taut, angular face I saw a shudder I'd never seen before. It might have been grief or some other emotion associated with Porkka – or something else, about which I knew nothing.

I had to admit that, yet again, I was seeing my remaining colleagues with fresh eyes. And my thoughts kept returning, again and again, to the other figure I'd seen in the dusky sauna. But the more I tried to bring that figure into focus, the more evident it was that I'd seen very little and had registered very few of the details. I couldn't even say what size this person might have been.

At first, I'd imagined that the person in question must have had considerable muscle strength in their arms, but now I'd begun to doubt this too. There was a rumour that the end of the ladle's shaft had been filed to a point until it was as sharp as an ice pick, so using it might have required more skill than brute force. And I couldn't help thinking that the murderer must have been well acquainted both with Aurinkoniemi and Porkka. All of which meant that suspicion fell on each of those gathered here today as equally as it had previously.

The flag continued hugging the pole, and my eyes moved from the flag to the people standing around it. Erkki looked sad, but also as though all this was taking a considerable toll on him. Which it was, of course. If he carried on losing his staff at this rate, he would soon have to go back to building, selling and transporting the stoves by himself, just as he'd done in the early days of the business. I didn't doubt for a minute that his grief was genuine. He and Porkka had spent a lot of time together; they even went fishing together every autumn, and by all accounts they got along rather well.

Next, my eyes rested on Mirka, who had been very quiet since hearing the news. Of course, she was always worried about something, but now her seriousness and distressed sighs were particularly noticeable, as was the way she tensed her muscles, especially her biceps, as she adjusted a wisp of hair. As if, in addition to all her other concerns, she was preparing to lift a particularly heavy barbell.

Jarkko always seemed to follow Erkki in all respects, and that
was the case now too: he looked sad and overwrought, though
he didn't own a stove factory and hadn't really known Porkka.
He held his hands in front of his body just as Erkki did: arms
straight, the fingers of his left hand slightly inside those of his
right. He glanced over at Erkki more often than anyone else,
probably waiting for further instructions.

And then, of course, there was Kaarlo. I was used to his general
stiffness, his wiry, bony figure, but now he looked starved, like a
panther tensed and showing its ribs. His facial features appeared
to have sharpened too – his high cheekbones now looked as
though they could have cut through sheets of metal. His steel-
cable arms with their wire-like veins looked as though they were
waiting for an opportunity to strangle a railway track to death.

Then I noticed I wasn't the only one observing their
colleagues. Everybody else was doing so too, and in basically the
same way as I was – as covertly and discreetly as possible. This
strongly suggested that we all suspected one another of being the
murderer. Except, that is, for the person who actually *was* the
murderer and who would be observing the others to see whether
anyone suspected anything, or perhaps in order to decide who
to kill next.

The storm inside me showed no signs of abating. I had no
intention of getting myself killed; I intended to find the killer.

For me, there was an important aspect to what had taken place
a day and a half earlier: the killer almost definitely hadn't seen
me there, so even though I didn't know who the murderer was,
in all likelihood that person didn't know that I had seen them in
the act, albeit fleetingly.

I tried to breathe as calmly as possible then returned my eyes
to the flag.

'Thank you,' Erkki said eventually, and this seemed to release those present, who began to relax and stretch their limbs. 'I'm sure Porkka is looking down on us from the great sauna in the sky, enjoying some heavenly steam and whacking himself with an Almighty whisk.'

Erkki looked at the flag or perhaps the great expanse of blue opening up behind it for a further second or two, then lowered his eyes and shifted position.

'That being said,' he continued, looking each of us in the eye, 'this obviously leaves us with certain ... well ... challenges. Both in the short and the long term. We'll have to think about who is going to assemble the stoves that have already been ordered and—'

'I will,' said Kaarlo.

Everybody turned to look at him.

'I didn't know you could assemble the stoves,' said Mirka, sounding perhaps a little too impressed. I recalled their little photo session on the jetty. 'But ... well, I'm not exactly surprised.'

'Dreadful, thinking about stoves,' said Susanna, looking over at Mirka and Kaarlo and flicking her thick hair. 'Under such circumstances.'

'We've got to,' said Kaarlo. 'Blood may spill and flesh may singe, but stoves are eternal.'

'Nobody...' Erkki interjected. He looked a little out of breath; I think I knew why. 'None of us is only thinking about stoves. But we are in a very ... precarious situation. We have to divide up Ilmo and Porkka's tasks and responsibilities and be ready to help the police—'

'Do you want me to start chairing this meeting?' Jarkko interrupted. He was standing next to Erkki and had, if possible, moved even closer to him.

'What's the latest news?' Kaarlo said.

'News?' asked Erkki.

'When were you last in touch with the police?' asked Kaarlo. 'Or when were they in touch with you?'

'This morning,' said Erkki, his voice deadly serious. 'And the news was rather worse than I had hoped.'

'Oh God,' Mirka sighed. 'I'll get the longest sentence, of course.'

'How could the news possibly be any worse?' asked Susanna.

'Things can always be worse,' said Kaarlo. 'The factory could burn down, someone could lose a limb...'

Erkki raised his hand in what looked like a stop sign. 'Nobody,' he said, 'is being charged with anything yet. But what I was hoping for most of all ... is that the culprit might not be one of us here at Steam Devil ... and, well, that's starting to look ... rather unlikely. Evidence was found at Aurinkoniemi that points to us directly.'

I had never been struck by lightning or spent any length of time at the centre of a hurricane, but it had to feel like this. It was all I could do to keep my expression and posture impassive, my eyes where they had been before Erkki's announcement. A thousand urgent questions were spinning through my head. The most acute of them was, of course, about the object or objects the police had found at the scene. I hadn't dropped anything, hadn't touched anything. I was absolutely certain of it. Therefore, these items couldn't belong to me but to the killer.

I didn't want to start casting long, quizzical looks here and there but I managed to catch a glimpse of Kaarlo's right hand as it quickly tapped his jacket pocket, and I saw Susanna lower her gaze to her shoes, the faint shift of her foot suggesting she was examining the inner side of her shoe. I didn't know whether these gestures meant anything, but they were certainly interesting. All this happened in a few fractions of a second.

'Do they want a list?' asked Jarkko.

Erkki turned slightly; he looked startled. I assumed he'd only just noticed how close to him Jarkko was standing.

'What list?' he asked.

'A list of missing items,' Jarkko replied. 'Items that might be missing from here.'

Again, Erkki looked a little out of breath. He might have been about to respond but didn't get a chance.

'One of my axes has gone missing,' said Mirka, sounding utterly deflated.

'You're joking?' Susanna gasped. 'An axe ... I can't begin to imagine—'

'I can,' said Kaarlo. 'A quick flick of the wrist and off with his head—'

'I truly hope,' Erkki interrupted, 'that we can focus on helping and supporting one another—'

'I'm happy to listen to anyone,' said Kaarlo. 'I've seen worse; this is nothing.'

I heard Mirka give another sigh, but this time it wasn't a sigh of despair but something else.

'Well,' Erkki continued, gazing now across the lake. 'I still want to believe that the culprit is from somewhere other than—'

'Is Anni still the favourite to replace you?' asked Susanna.

The question sounded completely neutral, as if she were asking the time. Everybody turned to look at me – even Erkki.

'What would we do without Anni?' he said.

I didn't think I was the only one who was expecting him to continue in some way, but he did not. The silence that followed was short but all the more excruciating. The sun suddenly made my skin tingle, the quiet of the lake and the forest felt particularly ponderous.

Eventually, Erkki spoke again. 'The race is still ongoing,' he said. 'Despite everything.'

This announcement was followed by two things: my colleagues seemed surprisingly happy, and now there was a new cast to the way Erkki studied me. And I realised I hadn't said a word throughout this conversation and that his expression was in fact inquisitive and appraising. Perhaps, despite his previous insistences to the contrary, Erkki really had started to suspect me.

As I had fled from Aurinkoniemi – my legs stiff with lactic acid, my lungs about to burst – my decision had only become stronger. Once this was over I would be Steam Devil's next CEO. I didn't intend to come second best to a murderer or anyone else. And so, despite all the storms raging inside me, I nodded.

'I'll do my best,' I said, honestly. 'And I wish everybody good luck with the competition.'

I looked at each of my colleagues – each in turn, each in the eye – and thought that one of them must be the killer and that to get through all this I needed, immediately and without delay, to go to the person with the most information. And get my hands on that information.

I needed a policeman.

21

*Hi, it's me. I was wondering if we could forget about the murders –
and about the thirty years that have passed since ... and maybe we
could...*

Hi, this is the murder suspect who made your life...

*Hi, how are things with the murder investigation? Just calling
to ask...*

My hands were trembling, the phone felt both light and
heavy – as if it was about to fly off somewhere and drag me
deep into the earth, all at once. And that didn't seem at all
contradictory.

I stood at the edge of the car park, glanced up at the Stove.
It was hard to prove, especially from this angle, when behind
it was nothing but the blue August sky, but I was convinced the
angle of its tilt had increased again. I recalled the conversation
I'd had with Porkka, which wasn't so much a conversation as a
wall of words that I'd crashed into. I also recalled his assessment
of the situation, which, at least for the time being, had proved
correct: the Stove still hadn't toppled over.

I filled my lungs, slowly exhaled then returned my thoughts
to what I was doing. How long had I been standing at the edge
of the forest, gripping my phone? Twenty minutes, maybe. My
working day had ended, the car park was empty, my colleagues
had all gone. *This is ridiculous*, I thought. I was caught up in a
series of murders, I'd seen a man with a sauna ladle in his head,
I'd been interviewed by the police, and all of a sudden I seemed
unable to make a simple phone call. Where had my courage
gone? I suspected I already knew the answer.

◊

Janne arrived at the Ulminiemi Manor quite late. He apologised; it sounded genuine, but he didn't give an explanation.

I decided not to say what I was thinking: that while I was waiting I'd been watching the rushing waters of the rapids through the windows and come to the conclusion that I'd never appreciated how hard it was to admire the white water after watching it for more than five seconds: first your heart and brain almost burst from the beauty of the bubbling waters, their fast-flowing movements, but very quickly you realised that beneath that churning surface, rapids were actually just scenery, a static phenomenon. In reality, nothing ever changed, no matter how much the waters rushed and bubbled. In this respect, rapids were the perfect metaphor for our times: despite all the loud-mouthed social-media influencers and all the other white noise around us, nothing ever really happened, nothing changed, no matter that everything was constantly in a froth. You might be able to observe changes in the rapids if you watched them for five hundred thousand years, paying attention to the ways the water wore new channels into the rock, smoothed the boulders, experienced an ice age or two, then...

I knew I was nervous but hadn't realised quite how powerful and all-encompassing the feeling was.

Janne didn't look like he was spending too much energy thinking about the water rushing past beside us, let alone its allegorical implications. He sat down on the other side of the table, moved his napkin to the side and looked at me. He was wearing a black Oasis T-shirt and dark-blue jeans, a pair of Aviators pushed up over his forehead. His T-shirt was tight-fitting, revealing his arms in all their musculature. Part of me thought I'd found my way into some kind of time machine; part of me knew only too well that that wasn't the case.

'Thanks for coming,' I said.

'Your message was a nice surprise,' he said. 'Thanks for the invitation.'

'After your visit,' I began, 'I thought it would be good to meet up and talk some more.'

This was true. Of course, there was more to it, but I meant every word.

'Right,' said Janne.

Okay, I thought. The small talk was going well enough. I hesitated before making my next move, which allowed Janne to get in first:

'Speaking of my visit, can I ask something personal?'

I was about to answer, probably in the affirmative, but right then the waiter arrived at our table. Janne ordered a beer, I took a glass of wine. Neither of us ordered food, though the waiter insisted we should. Catch of the day was whitefish, we heard, and the sauce was as good as anything you'd get in France. This was the problem with eating at Ulminiemi: the staff were always of the opinion that the food was excellent, but nobody else shared this opinion, and as a result there weren't nearly as many orders as the staff hoped. Over the years this had led to a number of awkward situations. Even now, the waiter's cheeks began to redden, and I was worried this might escalate into a full-blown confrontation, but eventually he gave up trying to push the whitefish and sauce on us and promised to return with our drinks. For some reason, I watched him as he walked away, maybe just to make sure it really happened.

When I turned back to Janne he seemed a little uneasy.

'I don't really know how ... Well, when I was at your place...'

At first, I didn't get why Janne was so hesitant, then I understood.

'You're talking about Santeri?'

'Right,' Janne nodded, and seemed perhaps a little relieved. 'Have you noticed anything odd or out of the ordinary about him recently? Shall we say, in the last year?'

'Is Santeri the killer?' I asked, and even I could hear the bewilderment in my voice.

Janne looked me right in the eyes. 'To be honest, I don't know,' he said. 'This is about something else.'

He paused, then asked:

'Have you ever looked into what Santeri really does for a living?'

The way Janne asked this question told me that he already knew something, probably quite a lot, so I might as well be totally honest.

'I know what he sells, roughly,' I said. 'And I know the business isn't a business in the traditional sense. It doesn't produce anything. On the contrary, it guzzles our money. And the truth is, I pay for everything from food, heating and electricity to repairs to the house and both cars. I have done for years.'

I couldn't read Janne's expression. He gave a 'hmmm'.

'Whatever it is, you can tell me straight,' I said, after a silence that had lasted for several seconds.

Now he looked as though he was making up his mind. 'Alright then,' he began. 'What you just told me doesn't quite match what I've found out. As far as I can see, he makes quite a lot of money. Are you quite sure he doesn't have any?'

I was about to answer when the waiter arrived, placed our drinks in front of us and lingered for a moment, presumably expecting us to order food, which we did not. Again, I watched him disappear, then said:

'I'm absolutely certain of it. Santeri never pays for anything. And when it comes to our shared finances ... I don't know about you, but I'd certainly notice if there was more money than expected in my account.'

Janne gave another 'hmmm'.

'What makes you think he's suddenly rolling in money, after all these years?' I asked.

'I can't tell you everything,' he said. 'But in the course of another investigation, I was in touch with some amateur collectors, and Santeri's name came up – by chance. I started following their deals, looked at the prices they were asking, and spoke to them again, and it's starting to look like not everything he sells is actually for sale and sometimes hasn't been acquired – how should I put this? – with the previous owner's full consent.'

Suddenly the white wine in my mouth tasted like vinegar. I swallowed – first the wine, then a second time, for another reason.

'For goodness' sake,' I said.

'What's more, in a couple of instances, it looks like Santeri has received more money than a seller like him normally would. As I've understood it, auction houses and individual vendors usually get much less than he seems to have received – anywhere between five and ten percent less, in fact. On top of that, in the last year Santeri has sold some very expensive items. He's earned a significant sum of money. Very significant. For instance, the dislodged clutch from Gerhard Berger's qualifying round in—'

'No need to tell me,' I interrupted, raising my hand. 'I know all about that clutch.'

Janne glanced out towards the rapids, took a sip of his pint.

'Jesus,' I said. 'I don't know which feels worse: the fact that he's wheeling and dealing in stolen goods, the fact that he doesn't pay his way at home, or the fact that you know almost everything – and I mean everything – there is to know about the state of my marriage.'

'Well,' said Janne. 'You know everything about my marriage too.' He paused. 'You know, it's been bothering me: I can't quite picture you as an accomplice, trafficking Nigel Mansell's stolen overalls all the way from Milan to Jurva.'

The sun glinted on the rapids outside, making its bubbles look like crystal. The rocks and the pines above them looked gilded. August at its most resplendent.

'I don't know if I'm that surprised, to be honest,' I said.

'You looked surprised,' said Janne.

I stared at him as it dawned on me what he was doing by telling me about Santeri. As he said himself, he was a policeman. Always, no matter what happened.

'You were testing me,' I said. 'You wanted to see how I'd react, what I'd say ... And in case you're wondering, I'm still not a murderer.'

Janne's answer was the same one he'd given me by the lakeside sauna: he said nothing. He turned his pint glass around on the tabletop. I concluded that arguing the point wouldn't get me any further than it had the last time I'd tried it.

'Now it's my turn to make a few assumptions,' I said. 'And maybe ask a few questions too.'

Still Janne remained silent.

'The perpetrator must be the same in both murders,' I said. 'And both murders took place in a sauna. I don't think that's a coincidence. But neither is it as simple as Kiimalainen seems to think – that this is all about ambition or something like that, that someone is simply so desperate to succeed Erkki Ruusula that they'll do anything. I think this is about something else entirely, and the sauna only features because the perpetrator is familiar with it and is using it as a weapon. Yes – I think someone is using the sauna as a lethal weapon. And I don't mean the film.'

Janne's expression was impossible to read. 'Have you got any evidence of this?' he asked.

'Why would anybody heat up Ilmo's sauna until it exploded?' I asked. 'Who would want to see the whole place go up in flames? And was there supposed to be an audience – namely, Ilmo?'

'Interesting,' said Janne, though given his tone of voice I couldn't work out whether he really meant it.

'And there are similar questions about the case at Aurinkoniemi too,' I continued. 'Such as, why was the crime committed there specifically? Puhtijärvi is a pretty sparsely populated place. If you really want to kill someone, it's easy round here, no matter how bungling a killer you are. There are quite literally a million better places to do it than at Aurinkoniemi, and in the sauna of all places.'

Again, Janne waited before responding.

'So, what am I supposed to make of all this?' I still wasn't sure of his tone of voice. It might just have been his way of having polite conversation.

I continued.

'Why weaponise the sauna? And how exactly has it been used in each case? For instance, what kept Ilmo Räty sitting on the bench the whole time after someone turned up in his sauna and started heating it and refilling the fire chamber again and again?'

Janne continued turning his pint glass. 'Why *turned up*?' he asked. 'Couldn't Ilmo have invited this person himself?'

I'd thought about this, and I believed I had an answer.

'Think about your own sauna habits,' I said. 'If you were taking a sauna with someone else, and that person started piling logs into the fire chamber when the temperature was already 120°C, what would you do?'

'I'd get out,' said Janne. 'I'm a ninety-degree man myself.'

'That's my temperature too,' I agreed. Then continued: 'Or, rather than leave, if there's nothing else for it, you'd try and stop your companion from adding more logs.'

'That could turn into a fight,' said Janne.

'In which case, the end result would be unpredictable. A person carefully planning a murder wouldn't leave things to chance. The plan would have to optimise the likelihood of achieving the desired result; *how* you achieve it and how everything would, as it were, look from the victim's perspective. I think whoever committed this wanted the victim to be a witness to their own demise. Ilmo Räty sat on his sauna bench and watched this piece of theatre play out. As terrible as it sounds.'

'And what about Aurinkoniemi?'

My theory about Aurinkoniemi was more complicated. Naturally, I couldn't tell the police that I was there at the time. For Kiimalainen, that would be the final piece of evidence he needed. After that, nothing would save me. So I couldn't say anything that even hinted I was present.

'Again,' I said, 'the sauna. Why there? I'm sure you know where Porkka lives — or lived. If I were a murderer, I'd carry out all my murders on Porkka's land. There's nobody wandering around the marshes, there are mosquitoes everywhere – they buzz but they don't talk. Why kill Porkka in an infamous sauna where, as everybody knows, you might stumble upon some clandestine bathers? And, perhaps more importantly, what significance did Aurinkoniemi have for Porkka? I'm quite sure that the choice of location was supposed to send him a message, just as the culprit wanted Ilmo to witness his stove warming up.'

Janne took a gulp of beer – almost as though he were gasping with thirst. Of the two of us, though, I was the one who had been talking so much that my mouth was dry.

He placed his pint on the table, pursed his lips. 'I'm going to have to ask again: do you have any evidence to back up these theories?'

'No,' I admitted.

'The police work with facts,' he said. 'What we can deduce, what we can prove to be true.'

I still couldn't read his expression.

'Do you mean the police,' I asked. 'Or Kiimalainen? Or you?'

Janne glanced outside. I was beginning to understand that he wouldn't react to certain subjects. I took a sip of wine; by now it had permanently turned to vinegar. Maybe it tasted corked because I'd started this conversation as a murder suspect and, by the looks of it, I was going to end it as a murder suspect too. The last few days had taught me that being suspected of homicide without any justification spoiled a good many things.

During the course of our conversation, the sun had started to set. The rockfaces had taken on a reddish hue, the water had darkened. Beside us the rush of almost-black water was weaving through rainbows, the boughs of the pine trees were still glowing, but further down, the trunks were beginning to blend into one another. A question I had already asked myself returned to my mind: how well can you know a person you knew thirty years ago? And does it help if you once knew that person better than anyone else, or does that make the current assessment even more biased? I could see that Janne didn't intend to continue the conversation – at least, not by answering my last question. And I had nothing more to add on the subject. There were other questions playing on my mind, questions that made me just as agitated as the ongoing murder investigation.

'What if...' I began. 'What if things were different?'

Janne seemed to snap out of his thoughts; he looked as though he was only too happy with the change of subject.

'Different how?'

'If there hadn't been any murders,' I said. 'And you weren't investigating them and didn't suspect me?'

'In that case, we wouldn't have met again, and we wouldn't be sitting here right now, having a drink together.'

'Does that mean you're glad that—?'

'It means it's nice to be here with you,' he said.

We sat in silence for a moment. The restaurant was half full. The tables by the windows were all occupied, but nobody appeared to be eating anything.

'You didn't really answer my question – about things being different,' I said.

'I did in a way,' he said, and I thought I heard a gentle sigh. 'And in another way I can't really answer it. When I was twenty, I thought I knew everything about everything. But these days I often think I know nothing at all. Maybe things went the way they were supposed to. Maybe we wouldn't be sitting here now if *things were different*. But, actually, it's worked out, because I want to be sitting here, with you, right now, this evening, at this age, looking like this.'

He paused for a moment, then gave a smile.

'With certain reservations, of course,' he continued. 'It took me ages to choose this shirt.'

I told him I thought it was a very suitable shirt for the occasion.

'One thing about you has definitely changed,' I said. 'You sound a lot more like a *carpe diem* type of guy than you did all those years ago.'

'Maybe it's age,' he said. 'A year or two ago I realised that I don't think about the past or the future all that much, and I don't want to either. Having said that, I haven't gone as far as a certain senior constable I know. He says he's stopped buying green bananas. But you could say that's my general direction of travel.'

'You mean, you're living like there's no tomorrow?'

'Maybe we should ask a different question: would I rather be somewhere else, at some other time, than right here right now?' he said. 'Or would I like to be younger, or older or something else? And the answer to all of that is no. And maybe that's the question you should ask yourself too.'

'I think I've already done so,' I said.

'There you go,' said Janne. 'And here we are, finally.'

'Here we are,' I said.

22

Was Janne on my side? The question wouldn't give me any peace, even as I walked through the still, quiet evening towards the sauna. I hadn't had a sauna for two days, which felt like a lifetime. The lake was resting, carrying the long final beams of light across to the other shore.

According to Santeri, he was in Stockholm, his missed call and the text message that followed had arrived while I'd been talking to Janne in Ulminiemi. I considered Santeri's absence a good thing. Right now, I didn't have the strength to have a conversation we really should have had about three or four years ago. A few days' wait wasn't going to change matters. What I needed was a soothing, relaxing sauna and the clearer thoughts it would give me, and above all I needed a quiet house without the sound of racing cars, or anything else, to disturb my concentration.

I stepped onto the porch, walked over to the box of firewood and picked up as many logs as I could carry. In the sauna, I filled the fire chamber and lit the fire with the first match. I'd just closed the hatch when I heard a sound outside. I thought it came from the porch. I thought it was the sound of a footstep.

I waited.

I heard a creak, as though one of the wooden boards had sighed with relief.

I recognised the sound. Someone had stepped off the veranda. I tapped my pockets, though I knew it was pointless. My phone was in the house, on the kitchen table. I imagined the sight of the blood-red tomatoes I'd just bought, the phone in its light-blue cover next to the tomatoes: both equally far away.

I looked around, and on the lowest bench I saw the log that I couldn't fit in the fire chamber. I picked it up; it was heavy, sharp around the edges. I hadn't heard of many struggles that had been won with the help of a birch log, but there was nothing else around, so I gripped the log as tightly as I could and took a deep breath.

I opened the sauna door, stepped into the washroom. The door into the changing room was open, as was the door out to the porch. I saw a strip of the dusky porch and again wondered at how quickly August evenings glided from sunset into a darkness that seemed to herald the coming of autumn, and I berated myself for not remembering to switch on the lights. Now it was too late to switch them on; it would give me away.

Slowly and silently, I walked into the changing room and waited again. I heard something; I didn't know what. I placed the sound at the corner of the sauna facing the house and the shore, perhaps a little behind the corner. I peered out into the porch; it was empty. I managed to place my steps very deliberately and moved slowly, making sure the floorboards didn't creak. I reached the corner of the sauna and listened. I still wasn't sure what I'd heard, but it sounded like someone trying to catch their breath.

At first, the heavy breathing sounded like it was coming from the distance, then suddenly it was closer. Whoever was standing round the corner was either just arriving on the porch or, given what I had heard, was likely returning to it. I couldn't move quickly; the intruder would hear my footsteps on the creaking floorboards. I was trembling with fear, shock and adrenaline. I instinctively raised the log, then acted at the very moment the dark-capped figure appeared in front of me.

I struck as hard as I could.

The log made a sound – the kind of sound it must have made

the very first time it was thrown on a pile of other logs, the
hollow clunk of wood on wood. Under the cap, the heavy
breathing stopped, replaced now with a shout, a yelp and a
longer, lower moaning sound. At the same moment, the intruder
fell backwards from the porch and landed on the ground. The
scenario wasn't very advantageous to me, because I knew I'd have
to run past the intruder to get back to the house and my phone.

I was about to leap off the porch when I heard a voice from
beneath the intruder's dark cap; it was still a moaning sound, but
now it was beginning to approach speech.

'Zodiac,' came the whisper. 'Zodiac.'

The voice was familiar, but at first I couldn't quite work out
where from, or why.

'Zodiac,' said the voice again, this time decidedly louder.

Zodiac, I repeated to myself. The log was trembling in my
hand, my heart rate must have been up to around two hundred
beats a minute.

'Kahavuori?' I said, and even to my own ears it sounded like I
was swearing. 'What...? I don't understand...'

'The element of surprise,' he said, now holding his head in
both hands. 'That's all I wanted ... a reconstruction ... it can ...
help us get to the bottom of...'

I stepped off the porch and stared at the holiday-chalet
magnate lying on the ground. My eyes had become accustomed
to the dusk now, and Kahavuori looked like a child who had
become too excited about a game, run right into a wall and now
needed to calm down.

He wouldn't have made a very good murderer. I saw that now
as he tried to clamber to his feet. I hadn't previously paid much
attention to his frankly dreadful physical condition, but now I
remembered him being out of breath when we'd visited the
chalets. He couldn't have been capable of the kind of physical

exertion I'd witnessed at Aurinkoniemi, or what it would have taken to heat up a sauna until it burst into flame.

Kahavuori was on his feet now – just about. 'The thing is, nobody knows who the Zodiac was ... even though he kept sending the police letters – like a madman. Which he was, of course. I just wanted to highlight the fact that the killer might make himself known to you, might be hiding in plain sight, as it were, then take everybody by surprise, and this combination of...'

Kahavuori sounded like someone who had just been clobbered round the head. It was understandable. The adrenaline was still coursing through my body, still keeping my heart rate elevated. I could hear it in my ears now, as though somewhere nearby was a large factory at full capacity, emitting a steady hum. I was about to tell Kahavuori what I thought of his little experiment and didn't plan to mince my words, when something else occurred to me.

'How did you get here?' I asked.

Kahavuori staggered a little, then managed to turn himself around and point towards the woods behind the sauna.

'I left my car out on the peninsula,' he said. 'On the uninhabited side, then walked through the woods. It took a while. I've been in better shape. But I think it was worth it. I mean ... this bump hurts like nobody's business ... feels like someone's been spinning me around in a barrel...'

'So, you stood at the edge of the woods, waiting for me to go into the sauna?'

'Correct,' he said. 'From there you can see the garden, the house, the sauna – everything.'

'And in the woods?'

'What about the woods?'

'Did anything catch your eye – down at the car park, in the woods on the way here, or at the edge?'

'Catch my eye?'

I wondered whether I might have struck him harder than I'd thought.

'Did you see any footprints?' I asked. 'Anything to suggest someone had been walking that way? Or did you come across anything that seemed strange or out of place?'

Kahavuori appeared to perk up, or at least as if he was trying to. He adjusted his cap, which clearly caused him some pain, and eventually settled for placing it loosely on his crown. He looked like underneath it he had an extremely high forehead.

'Are you thinking of the Zodiac?' he asked.

I'm thinking about my missing bumlet. I didn't intend to tell Kahavuori about the stolen linen. This would only have brought an unwanted dimension to the conversation.

'In a way,' I said eventually.

'That's it,' he nodded. 'Back at the lay-by, I thought this was far too busy a place for any self-respecting serial killer. The Zodiac wouldn't have selected it and besides—'

'Did you see anybody there?'

'Not a soul,' he said.

I waited, again restraining myself. It was hard. I was still agitated, still angry, still shocked that I'd thumped someone on the head with a log, even though that person had turned up at my sauna uninvited then hidden in the darkness, panting.

'But,' said Kahavuori, apparently chuffed at the dramatic pause in our conversation. 'I did note that someone appeared to have visited the place by bike – a few times, actually. Which is mad, because the lay-by takes you right into the woods, and the ground is so uneven it would be no fun cycling; even a car would be thrown around for a good while. Yet someone seemed to have turned up there by bike. Quite recently. Several times.'

'Are you sure about this?' I asked.

'Absolutely,' he said and gave a serious nod. 'I know how to read tracks. You see, I'm...'

While Kahavuori gave me an exhaustive commentary on all the true-crime series he'd watched, I turned my attention to the sauna. The chain of events was straightforward – which made everything even more unpleasant. Hidden in the woods, someone had watched me bathing, then visited my sauna while I was swimming in the lake. That person had taken the bumlet I'd been using, put another one down in its place and made it look like the one I'd been sitting on, assuming I wouldn't notice that the pile in the changing room had lowered slightly. And then, my used bumlet had been deliberately left at the scene of the first murder.

All this had required a great deal of planning, and must have taken place before Ilmo Räty's sauna was burned down. But why me and why then? At the time, nobody knew I was Erkki's favourite to succeed him as CEO. Framing me for the murder would only make sense after Erkki had told everybody about his decision. At the time of the sauna burning, I was just another employee like everybody else. Having said that, after the announcement, so was Porkka. And when Porkka was murdered, nobody thought he was about to start running the company. Apart from Porkka himself, that is.

My thoughts, these leaps of logic, were just getting me somewhere when something Kahavuori was saying caught my attention.

'If I were the killer, I'd try to get closer to the officer investigating this case,' he said. 'It's very common for someone like this – someone methodical and pathological – to do just that. There are countless examples of it. Often, this person might even try to help the police, or pretend to, presenting their suspicions to an officer and trying to learn how the police are progressing with the investigation, how much they know.'

I thought of Janne, whom I had just been with. Whom I had tried to probe for information, and to whom I had presented my own theories.

'This person,' Kahavuori continued, 'might be really convincing, charming even. There might even be romance in the air, assuming certain basic conditions are met. The person we're looking for might have previous emotional ties to the officer in question, which would make things much easier. Of course, all this might be a bit far-fetched, but I've even considered the possibility that this person, who's now cosying up to the police officer, might think they're doing the right thing, in a way making amends for some previous infraction.'

The evening was dusky, Kahavuori's excited eyes were flickering like lights beneath his apparently enlarged forehead.

'So,' he nodded, 'alongside my other lines of investigation, I would keep an eye on the investigating officer, and I would pay particular attention to any person or persons who have suddenly turned up in their life, maybe even in the most intimate way.'

Kahavuori fell silent, finally. It was a relief, in more ways than one.

'Thanks for your help,' I said. 'I'm actually in—'

'Of course,' he said. 'I should be getting home too. Back to the car, through the woods, and with this bump on my head, and then...'

He added that he understood my reaction, but said he was surprised at its power and determination. I had no intention of telling him what was flashing through my head right then: a perfectly normal moonlit night, almost as real as the night around us now; the droplets of blood that, instead of fading, glowed redder and more intense than ever. I knew that these flashes and repeating images were like a flooding river that would only grow in strength, and that if I wanted to avoid drowning, I only really had one option. Whatever the repercussions.

Naturally, I didn't tell Kahavuori any of this, or anything else for that matter. With all the stress and activity, I was tired. I needed peace and quiet – to be alone with my thoughts.

Kahavuori finally walked off.

I watched him until he had completely disappeared into the darkening woods. I stood on the spot for a moment longer, watching smoke billow from the chimney stack into the quiet evening, and decided to have a sauna.

Serial killers or no serial killers.

23

The lack of wind wasn't helping matters. The patio was large – perhaps twenty metres wide and about five metres deep, but it still felt cramped. I was sitting opposite Erkki, and the full glare of the sun, bright as the lights in an operating theatre, felt both revealing and exceptionally hard to comprehend: the long table was equipped with a sunshade, but it was at the other end of the table from where we were sitting and eating. This bugged me, but I couldn't think of a polite way to ask if we could move.

Moreover, the midday sunshine kept my pike oven-warm and guaranteed me a direct view of the lake, and what can only be described as a dentist's view of Erkki's mouth (upper right, eleven: dill; lower left, thirty-five and thirty-six: a piece of pike, a smattering of creamy mashed potato) as he explained why he had invited me out to his villa.

'I don't want this gossip to cause you any problems,' he said. 'But you and I have to talk about the matter. And when I pulled this pike out of my net this morning, well, it felt like a sign. While I was gutting it, I thought of you...'

'Thank you,' I said. I pronged a piece of pike with my fork but didn't lift it from the plate. 'For the invitation.'

When Erkki called me, I was heading somewhere very different from the patio at Villa Löyly. But that other meeting would now have to wait. Erkki was still my boss and he was still the Stove King himself, the owner of Steam Devil, so his invitation had to be taken with due respect. However, that wasn't the only reason I had come here, and in something of a hurry too.

The very moment I'd answered the telephone to him, I'd

realised something I ought to have realised a little earlier. (As I've already mentioned, I am very much a middle-aged sales executive, not a master sleuth or Mata Hari.) Nobody knew the company better than Erkki; including how each member of staff had ended up there, and what our respective backgrounds were. And though Erkki wasn't exactly up to speed about recent events, he knew the company's history. He *was* the history of Steam Devil.

'And I agree,' I went on. 'It's important to talk about the future of Steam Devil.'

'Quite,' he said. At first he looked confused, then a little disappointed. 'Right, the future ... of Steam Devil... I've been thinking—'

'We're in exceptional circumstances right now,' I interrupted before, one way or another, he could steer the conversation off into the unknown. I spoke deliberately quickly. 'You might even call it a crisis. You could say we're in uncharted waters. I've even begun to think that perhaps I don't really know my colleagues at all, and that's not a good thing going forwards. Of course, you don't have to tell me anything you can't or don't want to. But it might be a good idea if I know where we stand with each of the employees, so I can avoid the worst of the potential pitfalls. If we start with Mirka, for instance, I get the impression that recently she's been more worried than usual. Have you noticed that? Any idea why that might be?'

Everything I had said was true, and could be read in several ways. Still, I hoped that Erkki would understand my concern in only one way: that in order to start work as his replacement, I needed information. I didn't plan to mention that the main reason I needed this information was because I was investigating two murders for which I was the prime suspect.

Erkki had picked up his knife and fork again and seemed like he still wanted to change the subject. Then his blue eyes looked at me, and simultaneously stared somewhere into the distance, as though he had given up and agreed to a conversation he found a little unpleasant.

'Mirka came up through the profession,' he said. 'We first met at the Sauna and Bathing Fair in Jyväskylä. She was presenting hot tubs. I remember noting how dedicated she seemed, as though her whole life revolved around that hot tub. A thing like that can really make an impression on you. My initial thought was that she would make an excellent sales rep, but then I noticed the care and responsibility that she demonstrated towards our stoves. As you've noticed, she has become an excellent stockroom and logistics manager. At least, until last year...'

I waited, ready, should Erkki try to veer off in another direction, to guide him back to the matter at hand.

'...when I began to notice that stoves were going missing. First one, then a second, and eventually a third. I can still tell at a glance exactly how many stoves there are on any given shelf or packed into any delivery van. In total in the last eighteen months, three stoves have gone missing.'

I didn't know what I'd been expecting to hear, but this certainly wasn't it. While it surprised me, the information also explained a lot. At the very least, it explained why Mirka had been so reluctant to conduct an inventory with me or to come up with a special offer. Still, this new information left many things unexplained.

'I don't understand,' I said honestly. 'Three stoves over a period of eighteen months obviously won't put us out of business – it's a small matter – but isn't it still theft? And wouldn't this be grounds to fire her, or at least give her a stern warning?'

'Mirka hasn't stolen the stoves,' said Erkki.

I stared at him. He had the appearance of a man on holiday, enjoying a fillet of pike for lunch.

'How do you know?' I asked.

'I asked her,' he replied. 'She doesn't know where the stoves have gone, and it troubles her greatly. As you've noticed. she's never been so wracked with worry.'

My lunch was still almost untouched. The edge of the plate felt as hot as a cooker top. I decided to commit the information about Mirka and the three missing stoves to memory and move on.

'What about the others?' I asked. 'Jarkko...'

'He's a sharp one,' said Erkki. 'Always keeping an eye on me and takes meticulous care of his own work. If I so much as hold out my hand, a pen or a towel – or whatever else I need – appears almost immediately.'

'Have you noticed any—'

'Changes in him?' he interrupted. 'None whatsoever. Except that the miniature models he sells have been getting bigger and bigger. I bought one of his aircraft carriers. Did you?'

I told him that I'd politely declined the offer, and I was about to ask a follow-up question when Erkki continued.

'Then there's Susanna,' he said, gathering the remains of his mashed potato on his fork and seeming to hurry not only with that but with his words too. 'No change there either. She reports everything down to the last cent, as you know. I had to have a little word with her about you. You see, you were paid a little too much in travel expenses, and this seemed to concern Susanna most terribly. It was something to do with the kilometres you filed. I told her, when you drive a lot, one kilometre here or there doesn't really matter. She replied that a kilometre is one forty-two-thousandth of the circumference of the earth, so using this logic, does that mean our employees can joyride around the world at Steam Devil's expense? I told her this isn't a joyride. You're not joyriding around. Not yet, anyway.'

I wasn't entirely sure what Erkki meant by these last two

sentences, but neither did I intend to get bogged down. We'd have time to talk about me later, I thought; right now, the most important thing was to continue along the path I'd chosen.

'Besides, I wasn't exactly trying to circumnavigate the earth,' I said. 'I was simply—'

'Of course,' Erkki nodded, and I didn't know whether he agreed with me or not. 'And that brings us to Kaarlo ... Well, quite... this is rather more difficult...'

I didn't tell Erkki this was the bit I'd been waiting for, that I'd hoped we would eventually get to Kaarlo – that it was him I was most interested in. Because Kaarlo *had* changed. He'd shouted at me from the doorway, he'd been flirting with Mirka out on the jetty and while the flag was at half-mast. Both were completely new facets of his personality. But perhaps most noteworthy of all was the fact that I still didn't really know why he had been hired in the first place, and in particular I didn't know why he hadn't retired yet, though he'd been eligible for his pension for almost two decades.

'I owed him one,' Erkki said eventually. 'Not financially, you understand, but in another way. I owed him a favour ... a considerable one. And the favour Kaarlo requested was a little surprising. He wanted me to hire him at Steam Devil. I didn't know that ... well ... He's turned out to be much more ambitious than I'd expected.'

I waited for Erkki to continue, but he had turned to face the lake and was, it seemed, trying to steer his thoughts in that direction too. I wanted to return to Kaarlo.

'More ambitious in what respect?' I asked.

Erkki's head turned back slowly. His eyes were so lake-blue that for a fleeting moment I wondered whether something extraordinary had happened between him and the waters of Lake Puhtijärvi.

'Kaarlo...' Erkki began '...wants to run the company. In fact, he's wanted to run the company from the moment he joined it. And when I say he *wants* to run the company, what I mean is that to his mind the matter has already been decided and, well, this has caused a little – how should I put it? – friction between us.'

⸙

I ate what was left of my pike. It was tasty, generously salted and with surprisingly few bones. When I thanked Erkki for the meal – and particularly for the lack of bones – he nodded, sighed and eventually smiled (upper left, twenty-one, and upper-right, eleven: a strip of cherry tomato) in a way that reminded me of the old Erkki. Back then, everything had revolved around stoves and how to sell them. Despite my best attempts, I hadn't been able to get Erkki to return to our conversation about my colleagues, and eventually I gave up. He had clearly told me everything he was going to tell me. In fact, I wasn't sure he knew any more than he'd divulged. Of course, he hadn't disclosed the precise reason why he owed Kaarlo a favour, and it seemed like something he was going to keep firmly under wraps. Besides, I felt I'd already heard the most important thing I needed to know about Kaarlo.

I took Erkki up on his offer of coffee, though drinking something hot took a lot of effort on the sweltering and still shade-free patio. As Erkki walked off to fetch the blueberry pie he'd just made – 'I got a little carried away' – I caught a glimpse of him from behind. The Stove King walked off in one direction, stopped, seemed to hesitate, changed course, then, still watching his step, disappeared inside his four-hundred-square-metre villa as if into the jaws of a whale, leaving an impression that was less majestic and more of someone a little lost and disoriented.

24

Age is just a number.

Few proverbs lead us more astray than this one. Age is something very concrete indeed, as anyone who has done any kind of sport or who has danced in their youth knows only too well. Our legs lose their power, and no matter how much we try, it's difficult to adapt to new forms of music. Time marches onwards, whizzes past us from left and right, it doesn't care how many hoodies we own or how we try to be friends with our kids instead of an authority figure, our bald patches gleaming, leggings chafing. The more we try to hide the year of our birth, the more the young reward us with pity.

Age is not just a number.

Age is about facts building up, and the higher the number, the greater the number of facts.

Naturally, I was thinking about myself and my own situation. Not that I tried to follow recent trends in music or attempted to ingratiate myself with the youth of Puhtijärvi, but I too had tried first to ignore the passage of time, then to stop it altogether. It seemed I hadn't accepted facts after all, at least not completely.

At some point, and for quite some time, Erkki had been an *older* man, who, because of his age, I'd assumed, without giving it much thought at all, would always remain a constant distance ahead of me. Now that distance seemed to have shortened dramatically. What had once been far away on the horizon was now at arm's length. Erkki was only twenty years older than me.

Twenty years.

Suddenly, I found it hard to imagine a shorter span of time. Of course I understood that a second was shorter than a minute in factual terms, and that the last week had felt very long indeed, and still did. But when I looked a little further back into the past, twenty years felt like nothing but the flap of a sparrow's wings.

Marriage, selling sauna stoves, heating up the sauna, the greenery of spring, the darkness of winter. A few sprats, plenty of solitude.

But even this wasn't the crux of the matter.

It wasn't looking backwards that was causing me such anguish, rather it was turning in the opposite direction.

What if I too had twenty years left? Or would it be more honest and direct to say: what if I *only* had twenty years left?

I pulled into the car park outside Steam Devil and was reminded that my restless thoughts and the resulting slight deviation from the task at hand had started with Erkki's doddery steps, with the way he'd changed direction, which was something very different from simply changing one's mind; this was something much, much more significant.

The symptoms had been right in front of me over the last eighteen months. I'd regularly wondered at or simply noticed Erkki's change of attitude, not only towards his own company but to everything else too. Moreover, I'd noticed a change in the way he talked, his general hesitancy, and the difficulty he had making decisions, all of which had been more marked of late. And now, in recent weeks, there was his vague and rather phlegmatic response to the problems that had befallen Steam Devil, problems that I thought were of the highest order. Two members of the board of directors had been murdered, but Erkki thought it was most important to talk about almost anything else. Then there were the bits of food stuck between his teeth. In fact, maybe it was this that had helped me join the dots. The Erkki I thought I knew would never have smiled like a little boy when he was praised for how well he'd filleted a pike while the company's staff were being violently cut down one after the other. And especially not with a sliver of tomato skin between his teeth. I wasn't a doctor, but I thought the diagnosis was pretty clear.

Erkki had dementia.

When I finally got to my office and switched on the computer, I didn't even look towards the windows. Once the computer had booted up, I opened the company calendar and the bookkeeping programs. My last look through this data had taught me not to leap to conclusions quite so quickly. Now I knew what such rash decisions can lead to: witnessing death by ladle in an abandoned sauna.

During the following half an hour, I went through all my colleagues' diary appointments and all their expenses claims for the last two months. I tried to be meticulous, taking everything Erkki had told me into consideration, and going through my colleagues in the same order as I had with Erkki.

Mirka seemed to have accrued a very moderate amount of expenses. Furthermore, she didn't seem to want to bother the rest of us by putting any external appointments in the shared calendar. When she did meet our business partners, it appeared that she only ever met them here at the office. From the evidence of the calendar it looked as though Mirka either didn't like leaving the village or that everybody she did meet with face to face came to her. I genuinely couldn't say whether either scenario was the truth.

Jarkko's activities, which I'd assumed would be easier to track, proved considerably more complicated than I'd thought. He was top of the list when it came to booking the conference room. This was because he added himself to every one of Erkki's meetings, though he only took part in a handful of them. (A quick examination of the calendar revealed that Erkki himself hadn't called any meetings this year.) To complicate things further, Jarkko also made bookings for other people, and though he was nowhere near the meetings in question, it still looked like he was an active participant. Which meant that on certain days he seemed to have been in two places at once, taking care of two very different matters. Ultimately, though, it was easy to make sense of Jarkko's comings and goings: everything he did was strictly linked to his job as Erkki's assistant and as the company's general manager. The same applied to his expenses: without exception, they were all related to his work; everything was itemised, from paperclips to mending the sofa in the foyer.

Susanna treated her calendar entries and expenses claims with the same painstaking care and accuracy as she did everything else. None of her meetings lasted half an hour or an hour; they lasted thirty-five minutes or an hour and ten minutes. In the last two months, she had claimed zero euros in expenses. When it came to Susanna, everything was exceptionally straightforward. There was just one but: Susanna was the person who oversaw the entire system. If she wanted to, she would have had ample opportunity to change the information in it in any way she wanted; nobody else had clearance to do so. I didn't know what to make of this. I pondered this for a while, but I felt no more enlightened.

And then...

Kaarlo really seemed to have been up to, and was still up to, all kinds of things. Having said that, there was no clear evidence to suggest that he'd been involved in the matter with the handle on the fire chamber or that he'd visited other villages, where our competitors manufactured their stoves. According to the entries in the calendar and his expenses claims, he stuck his spoon into as many broths as possible; and almost without exception, each for a very short time. It wasn't against the law, but naturally it begged the question as to what his real role was in this company that he had been so keen to work for. And there was an even greater question – about his desire to become the new CEO of

Steam Devil. There was no disputing that he was in good shape, astonishingly so, but this didn't explain why someone, at the ripe old age of eighty-two, was so eager to run a sauna-stove factory. The more I thought about it, the more certain I became that if I knew the answer to that question, I'd know a lot more besides.

And with that, my mind was made up. I would start with Kaarlo, but not in the way I'd started with Porkka. This time I would proceed with greater care; I would check and double-check everything several times. And I would contact Janne before the situation became too life-threatening.

If it became life-threatening.

As paradoxical as it sounded, I'd reached the conclusion that I was safe for the time being. They needed me. The dead did not commit murder, so for as long as there was a chance I would be framed as the guilty party, there was simply no good reason to bump me off. Besides, my assumed guilt allowed the killer to keep on killing – if that was their plan. I suspected it was. Whoever killed two people at the same stove company would hardly think twice about killing a third.

At this point, however, I was faced with another, even larger question. If this was about the race to succeed Erkki, then killing Ilmo made sense. But killing Porkka didn't. On the other hand, if we imagined that Porkka's fate was tied to the fire-chamber handle and some potential industrial espionage, that wouldn't explain why Ilmo had to be got rid of. The two murders seemed to cancel each other out, at least in terms of their motives.

I got out of my chair, looked outside. The spruces seemed about to march towards the lake; the lake looked like at any moment it was about to pull a plug at the bottom and drain itself into the depths of the earth.

I was already on the way to Kaarlo's office when my phone rang.

25

Kiimalainen's face seemed to belong to a man who had already caught the scent of victory. Of course, this was just my interpretation, and an instant one at that, but it was a conclusion that was hard to avoid.

Kiimalainen was sitting opposite me, leaning his elbows on the desk and keeping his eyes fixed on me, the way people do when they're on a power trip. His expression was deeply disdainful but also relaxed, because he knew he would win. Janne was also present; he was the one who'd called me and asked me to come to the police station. On the desk was a large, light-brown jiffy bag, bulging in the middle.

'Weather's been nice,' said Kiimalainen.

I was sure nobody present thought for a moment that we had gathered in this cramped, unpleasant room to discuss the weather.

'August,' I said. 'It's been exceptionally warm and beautiful.'

'Exceptionally,' Kiimalainen repeated. 'Interesting choice of word. I couldn't agree more; this August has been very ... exceptional.'

Kiimalainen had managed to steer the conversation in the direction he wanted. It didn't really matter which word I'd used, Kiimalainen would have latched on to it in exactly the same way and eventually got to his main topic of conversation. He was enjoying this moment; I could see it.

'I mean,' he began, 'Puhtijärvi isn't exactly Midsomer – a picturesque little hamlet with neat hedgerows, where, even in a normal week, at least six people are bludgeoned to death. In

Puhtijärvi, such activity is, as you've said yourself, exceptional.'

I said nothing. I concluded there was no need.

'As you can imagine,' he continued. 'This has put a great deal of pressure on me. The locals want me to arrest someone, and fast. Yesterday in the shop, for instance, the whole queue behind me at the checkout was shouting, "You'd better catch him, Kiimalainen, and make it quick." Do you know what I said?'

'I don't,' I replied, honestly.

'I told them that when I arrest someone, I'll be arresting the killer.'

Kiimalainen pulled the envelope towards him across the table and tapped it knowingly a few times. 'And right here,' he said, 'is just that. The killer.'

He slid his forefinger under the flap and, from what I could see, began trying to tear the envelope open, using his forefinger like a somewhat chunky paper knife. His first attempt failed, then his second, his third and fourth too. The jiffy bag seemed unwilling to be torn open, presumably due to the plastic bubble wrap inside. Kiimalainen continued to poke his forefinger into the envelope with increasing agitation, his face reddening all the while. He huffed and puffed, and the jiffy bag rustled. There might only have been three of us in the room, but it seemed to be filled with noise and movement.

I glanced at Janne. His expression hadn't flinched.

I'm not sure how long we waited in the end, the two of us, or how long Kiimalainen was fiddling with his jiffy bag.

Finally it gave way just enough for Kiimalainen to slip his hand inside (it still refused to tear fully). He looked up at me again now, looked me right in the eyes. He slowly removed his hand from the envelope, took out a small item in a plastic evidence bag and placed it on the table.

I recognised it.

It was one of my sauna ladles. In fact, it was only half of my ladle. The ladle bowl had been removed, the handle shortened and the end filed to a sharp point.

The handle still bore dark, in parts blackened, stains: Porkka's blood. But there wasn't enough blood to cover the name engraved on the handle: my name.

'I suppose this was stolen from your sauna too,' said Kiimalainen.

I looked from the handle to Kiimalainen. There were small beads of sweat on his temples and cheeks, presumably from his recent struggle with the envelope. As I examined the sauna ladle more closely, I realised something crucial: I couldn't officially know what the handle had been used for. Officially, I was seeing it for the first time. In many ways, all this was true. At the time of the murder in Aurinkoniemi, I hadn't been aware that I'd been looking at my *own* sauna ladle and didn't know what it had been turned into: a dagger. So I was telling the truth when I said:

'I don't understand.'

'I think you understand only too well,' said Kiimalainen. 'You know perfectly well how your sauna ladle ended up in Mr Porkka's forehead.'

'I certainly didn't put it there,' I said. 'And I haven't used that ladle for a long time. That's why I didn't notice it had been stolen. It was probably taken from my sauna at the same time as the bumlets.'

Again, Kiimalainen leant his elbows on the table. He had clearly put the episode with the envelope behind him now and had regained his sense of power, his self-assuredness.

'Of course,' he said. 'And what else was taken? The benches, maybe? The stove? The whole sauna?'

He seemed visibly pleased with his own wit – and might have been only too happy to continue this line of questioning, if he'd been able to think of anything else that might have been stolen from my sauna. I wasn't going to help him. I needed to change the course of this conversation.

'I am not a murderer,' I said. 'But I've got some thoughts about who might be.'

First I looked at Kiimalainen, then glanced at Janne, and their faces told me two things: Janne had no intention of taking part in this conversation; and he hadn't told Kiimalainen about my theories. I doubted Kiimalainen would have listened to them anyway. He smiled, but it wasn't a friendly smile.

'Of course you do,' he said. 'It's good to have thoughts. I've got plenty of them, and sometimes a really big one comes along...'

While Kiimalainen continued his monologue about what kinds of thoughts he'd had that morning – one had come hurtling out of nowhere, another racing in the other direction – I turned my attention back to the ladle's handle and tried to avoid a full-blown panic attack. When I'd arrived here, I'd already assumed the situation had become even more unfortunate for me – they wouldn't have asked me here otherwise – but I hadn't imagined anything like this. I had to work hard to stay calm, to remain as natural as possible, though all the while an unpleasant chill had begun to spread through me. I was grateful that nobody else could hear the whirring in my ears.

'...a confession...' I heard Kiimalainen say.

'Excuse me?' I asked.

'If your little thoughts,' he continued, 'are that you've decided to confess, then this is the best time to do it.'

'I cannot confess to—'

'The results of the lab tests will come back in a few days,' he said, as though he hadn't heard me, which was entirely possible. 'And then a confession will be pointless; we'll be able to move forwards without your help. That said, today would be a good day to hear a Korpinen finally regret what they've done.'

At first, Kiimalainen's final sentence passed me by, then it was as though I heard it for a second time. I sighed.

'I can hardly believe I'm saying this out loud,' I said, 'but isn't today the anniversary of the felling of the Great Elk?'

'I told your father long ago,' he nodded, 'that there's no statute of limitations on felling another man's elk.'

'Once again,' I said. 'There was no crime, and an elk does not—'

'Where are the antlers?'

'What?'

Kiimalainen wasn't smiling. Now he looked every bit as agitated as the last time he'd brought up the subject of the elk. His cheeks were again flecked with red, just as they had been while he was wrestling with the jiffy bag.

'The Great Elk's antlers,' he repeated. 'Where are they now?'

I glanced at Janne, who seemed to be detached, observing the conversation from a distance.

'What have the antlers got to do with anything?' I said. I knew I should have kept my mouth shut, but I'd started to become agitated myself. 'Why ask a thing like that?'

Kiimalainen hesitated, but his hesitation was gone in an instant. 'This is a police matter.'

I looked at him. 'Are the antlers suspected of murder too?' I asked.

Kiimalainen's eyes had taken on a powerful gleam; they were like two small, moist coins. 'Do you find this funny?'

'What, an old set of antlers?'

Kiimalainen leant forwards. It seemed as though, were there not a table between us, he would have kept leaning, until he touched my face.

'No, murder,' he said, his voice hoarse. 'I'm going to arrest you on suspicion of murder. Two murders, in fact. You can joke about it for a while longer, but your time will be up soon enough. You Korpinens might think you always get the last laugh, but I'm going to make sure you—'

'So, to summarise this interview,' Janne interjected, as calmly as if he were concluding a peaceful, constructive conversation. 'Obviously, we'd like you to stay in town and to keep your phone with you so that we can contact you if anything comes up.'

I didn't know whether I was reading too much into the cadence of Janne's voice, but I was sure he was particularly keen that I keep my phone with me at all times. I hadn't had my phone with me at Aurinkoniemi, and now I felt as though I'd been caught out about that – as if there was a suggestion that I'd left it at home deliberately. I made sure not to show this outwardly.

'I'm not going anywhere,' I said.

'Except prison,' added Kiimalainen.

26

The shadow of the birch tree played on the yellow wall of the house, gently running backwards and forwards, unwilling to stay put. I took a deep breath; perhaps the birch and its shadow could afford such joyful, unruly behaviour. I certainly could not.

I'd driven straight home from the police station, intending to gather my thoughts in peace and quiet. I'd been convinced that Santeri was away, somewhere in Finland or in Europe, potentially on semi-illegal business. So I was surprised to find his car right in front of me as I pulled into the drive. Upon seeing it, I'd been ready to jump out of my moving Volvo, dive into the house and demand some answers from him.

But I'd managed to restrain myself. So-called direct action didn't always achieve as good results as a more considered approach.

And so, only now, almost ten minutes later, did I finally take my other hand off the steering wheel. My palm felt almost numb, my fingers ached, my wrist seemed to have stiffened into position. I concluded that thinking about Santeri didn't just hurt my head; it hurt other parts of my body too. I shook and clenched my hand a moment longer, watching the dancing shadow on the wall all the while. It didn't seem to tire at all. Eventually, I left the shadow to dance to its heart's content and went indoors.

Inside, everything was familiar.

Niki Lauda was in the lead, with Andrea de Cesaris on his tail. Rene Arnoux was determined to keep Keijo Rosberg behind him – very unsportsmanlike, something I knew riled Santeri almost four decades after the fact. The sound world was such that if a death-metal band had been playing in the next room, worshipping Satan at the top of their lungs, I wouldn't have known anything about it. Santeri was half lying in his chair. He hadn't noticed my arrival and seemed consumed by the fuzzy images of the grand prix on the screen – not in the real world at all.

(Was I looking at a murderer? A man who first burned someone to death in their own sauna and then sharpened the end of a ladle handle and thrust it between someone's eyes? They say anything is possible, but was it really? I tried to dismiss these ideas and thought instead that the most important thing was to follow my plan: start at the beginning – calmly sensing my way forwards.)

I followed events in the room, or rather, the lack of events, first from behind Santeri, but after another two laps I stood beside him. I had to wait another half lap until he noticed me.

Seeing me prompted two simultaneous reactions: he flinched, perhaps even with fright, then, quick as a flash, he looked around, as though he was expecting to see other people arrive too. I didn't know who else he expected to see apart from me. I'd never brought anybody into his shrine – for various reasons. After shaking his head, he stared at me, then seemed to become aware of the roar in the room and the screaming commentary. The remote control looked like a bionic extension of his hand as he pointed it at the screen and Riccardo Patrese froze on the circuit.

Santeri all but crawled out of his armchair and gave his Ferrari shirt a tug to straighten it out. And as he pulled himself to his feet, a little cloud of scent seemed to waft around him. The scent didn't belong in this room, didn't belong on Santeri, but I thought I recognised it from somewhere. There was something light about it, a hint of fabric-softener freshness but with something more refined too. I'd smelt this somewhere before, but I couldn't think where. I didn't want to spend time dwelling on it now though; I didn't want to lose the element of surprise.

'How were things in Stockholm?' I asked. 'Everything went well?'

Santeri gulped, I could see his Adam's apple bobbing upwards, then down again. 'It was okay,' he said.

'What was the weather like?'

'What, in Stockholm?'

'Yes,' I said. 'Where you were.'

Santeri quickly glanced out of the window then turned and looked at me again. 'Same as here, really,' he said.

'Pick anything up?'

'What?'

'Collectibles,' I said. 'Which you went there to buy.'

For a moment, Santeri looked like a man who had forgotten one thing only to remember another. He took a few steps towards Häkkinen's tyre and stood next to it, trying to muster that boyish self-confidence. I didn't usually believe in the supernatural, but now I was almost sure that I was witnessing something like it. It seemed as though the tyre was giving off some kind of mystical power, transferring it into the man standing next to it. Santeri ran his fingers through his surfer's hair, letting it fall freely to the sides. I used to find this gesture attractive.

'The company's in a really good place,' he said, sounding like he'd just read or heard this phrase somewhere. 'I've been thinking – we need to either expand our operations and make them more general or become even more specialised. In business, you can't stand still. The market doesn't like the status quo. Apple's a good example of that.'

I was convinced Santeri had no idea what he was talking about. But, in a way, I was impressed. He'd clearly internalised ...

something. I couldn't say what it was. I was about to ask what this might mean in practice when he began talking again.

'So I've started scouting around for potential new partners,' he said. 'I've already had a few productive conversations. The timetable is still quite open-ended, but I think it's possible that either this quarter or next there'll be some surprise news about profits. These are the kind of strategic decisions a successful business has to make. You've got to have a vision, of course.'

Now I wasn't just impressed; I was beginning to suspect this might be a phenomenon I'd once seen in a late-night movie where people retain their exterior form, but their souls are abducted and changed beyond recognition.

'Sounds interesting,' I said, and I meant it.

'Yes,' said Santeri, raising a hand to stroke Häkkinen's tyre. 'This might all sound a bit surprising, but like I said, I've been thinking about it a lot. I'm the founder and owner of my company. So's Richard Branson. And anyway...'

He looked like he'd been practising for this very moment, this very speech, for some time. He ran his fingers over the surface of the tyre as if it were the finest silk.

'I'm not just about worn-out old clutches, jumpsuits and helmets,' he said. 'I'm much more than that.'

Where had I heard the very same thing recently? From Erkki's mouth. He wasn't just about sauna stoves. I didn't know what was going on. At first I thought this might be a men's problem – they were getting old and beginning to think about life and its meaning.

'And I suppose I've come to realise,' Santeri continued, still sounding like he was repeating something he'd heard elsewhere but also as though he was finally getting to the point, 'at the end of the day, I'm more of a ... creator.'

I looked him in the eyes, trying to see as clearly as possible what was going on in them. 'So,' I asked, 'you're God?'

'No,' he said with a shake of the head. 'Not *the* Creator. *A* creator. I'm a creative type, an innovator.'

On the one hand, I was relieved that Santeri hadn't completely lost his mind and imagined he had dominion over the universe, but on the other I'd slipped quite far from what I'd come into this room to do. I was investigating two murders, and no matter what Santeri thought of himself or how many business self-help guides he was able to quote, he was still part of my investigation.

'Right,' I said eventually. 'By the way, have you noticed anyone visiting our sauna or the yard in the last few days or weeks?'

Santeri took his hand from the tyre. He shook his head. 'The sauna has always been your domain,' he said. 'I don't have saunas. It dries my hair out, as you know. The bounce and shine disappear.'

'I know,' I said. 'But I meant have you noticed anyone *else* around there—?'

'Have you been talking to that Janne Piirto?' he asked. 'Because he was asking the same stuff about the sauna when he visited.'

The way Santeri said Janne's name was all too familiar. Santeri didn't like Janne, I knew that, and he didn't like talking about Janne. I decided to skip this aspect of the conversation for now.

'And what did you tell him?' I asked.

'That I hadn't seen anyone around there,' he replied. 'But I might have seen some*thing* – or thought I saw something.'

'Why didn't you tell me about this?' I asked, trying to keep my voice calm. 'If someone has been in or around our sauna—'

'It was probably nothing,' he sighed. 'And it was in the middle of the legendary Hockenheim race from eighty-two. Tambay had just dropped out, there was oil on the track, they were all driving in a long convoy and—'

'The sauna,' I said as gently as I could. 'Let's go back to the sauna. What exactly did you see?'

'Well,' Santeri nodded. 'I went into the kitchen for a cold Red Bull, and I looked out of the window, and to me it looked as though, next to the sauna, sort of on the veranda and walking by the sauna, there was an elk.'

'An elk?'

'Yes,' said Santeri. 'While you were having a soak or out swimming, but...'

I waited patiently, trying to keep my cool.

'...then I got my Red Bull,' he said. 'And suddenly Watson was right behind Prost, and I was in a bit of a hurry to get back to trackside. Then Watson made a mistake in the chicane and Prost got away from him, and I thought, it was a pretty odd-looking elk. It was moving differently from how elks usually move. I started wondering whether I'd imagined the whole thing and what this was really about. So I went back into the kitchen and looked out towards the sauna, but there was nothing there. No elks, and nothing else either. And then I thought you would have noticed if there'd been anything out there, and so what if it was an elk? The forest's full of them. And after that I forgot all about it.'

Again, he ran his fingers through his hair, blew the air from his cheeks. The story seemed to have taken its toll on him. I didn't tell him what I thought about his stalling tactics or the fact that he hadn't told me any of this before, because I knew that even the slightest criticism would be met with the silent treatment. I'd got used to Santeri's thin skin over the years – perhaps too used to it. If I hadn't been talking to him as part of my murder investigation, I might not have treated him with such kid gloves. But the problem wasn't with him. It wasn't him I was actually questioning; it was me, my own choices.

'Did you talk about anything else?' I asked. 'You and Janne?'

Santeri looked pained. 'Not really,' he said. 'He went on about the sauna, just like you do, and he asked about you too. Nothing out of the ordinary – whether you ever talk about Steam Devil's business at home. I said you tell me bits and pieces, like you do. And he asked whether you've been behaving out of the ordinary lately, and I said not at all, you're exactly the same as you've always been, haven't changed a bit.'

Santeri might not have been aware of it himself, but his last sentence might well have been the first honest thing he'd said in this entire conversation. It sounded like he'd been holding this thought inside for a long time, and it had finally burst out into the open. He looked at me, and I realised his expression was supposed to be grave and serious.

'I don't like Janne Piirto,' he said. I could hear the contempt in his voice. 'And I wouldn't tell him even if I was the murderer.'

27

At six in the morning, the lake looked like a black mirror on the earth's surface. All I could hear was my own breathing and the flapping of the wings of the occasional bird as I climbed down the ladder at the end of the jetty and pushed myself off and into a long, gentle stroke.

Swimming felt necessary after a night of sleeping in fits and starts. I didn't feel tired though – it seemed that being the prime suspect in a murder investigation meant I needed far less sleep. During the night, I'd reached so many decisions and conclusions and drawn up so many different strategies that it was only sensible to slow down a bit and try to put them all in some kind of logical order.

I hadn't spent any more time thinking about Santeri than absolutely necessary. Our conversation had ended in the usual way, with him informing me he had to take part in an inter-national online conference on the subject of Michael Schumacher's overtaking techniques in the 1994 Formula One season. It didn't matter; I'd heard everything I needed to. Santeri had spent the night in his shrine, while I was in the bedroom with the door locked. In the light of the morning, this felt like something of an overreaction.

Erkki's dementia was anything but good news. It was very sad news for Erkki, and for Steam Devil it could prove catastrophic. My colleagues were still a mystery to me; it seemed I hadn't managed to dig up anything important, let alone decisive. Kiimalainen's obsession with the elk was beginning to feel pathological, but it explained a lot. As did his choice of words when he got angry: *For a while.*

Of course, I didn't know what kind of timetable he had in mind, but I doubted he would wait very long before arresting me. Surely only a matter of days. And the more I thought about it, the more I was inclined to think that Kiimalainen meant two days, three at most. So, that's how long my 'while' was.

I returned to the shore, climbed up the ladder and back onto the jetty. The air felt warm and soft against my skin. I turned to look at the rising sun, took a deep breath and set off.

Janne lived in a house I knew very well but had never actually visited. The reason it was so familiar was because we used to see it on our rowing trips thirty years ago; we'd sometimes looked at it from afar and dreamt that one day we would live there. Janne eventually fulfilled that dream, and I still didn't know what to think about that. I still remembered the moment when I heard he had bought the house, and I wasn't proud of what I thought and felt.

The house wasn't big or remotely fancy or luxurious, but in one respect it was truly exceptional. It had been built long before today's building regulations had come into effect, which explained the second floor propped up on columns and reaching out into the lake. With its large, wide windows it looked like something between the bridge of a ship and a dark-brown, wood-panelled air-traffic control centre.

Janne had told me he now lived alone, so it was only natural that there was just one car in the garage to the right of the house, though there was enough space for two. I parked my own car in the garage next to Janne's, switched off the engine and stepped out. This part of the lake had always felt quieter than where I lived, though there was really no significant difference between the two areas. Perhaps it was something to do with the surrounding peninsulas, the thickness of the forest and the height of the trees, the way the wind passed through the area and how sound carried across the water. The drive had only taken twenty minutes, but it felt as though I'd travelled thousands upon thousands of kilometres only to end up exactly where I'd started.

Which, in many ways, was true.

I was concluding the journey that had begun the moment our fishing boat had left shore thirty years ago.

I walked across the gravelled driveway, took the steps up to the porch, rang the doorbell – and Janne answered before the shrill peal of the bell had stopped.

'I heard a car,' he said.

I told him it was mine and gestured towards the garage, then started apologising for coming so early, but Janne replied that it didn't matter, he'd gone for his morning swim in the lake before six. I told him I'd done the same, and we agreed that the water was cool and refreshing. After this, we stood in silence for a moment, Janne in the doorway and me in the porch, then he asked if I'd like to see something.

That something was the landscape, the view from the windows. It was the view that we'd talked about and that we'd tried to imagine in the rowing boat. The sun was rising in the east, to the right of the house, turning the lake golden in front of us and making the little peninsulas look like soft, dark-green fingers holding a pot of gold. Sturdy spruce trees grew on both sides of the house, their gnarled branches stretching out towards it but not quite reaching, framing the landscape like a Renaissance painting. I said that sometimes it's nice to notice you were right all along. Janne smiled, said nothing.

Inside, the house was just as cosy as it looked from the outside, with lots of exposed beams. The living-cum-dining room was compact, and I noted how new many things looked – the sofas, the dining table, the light fixtures. Then I realised why, and Janne seemed to read my thoughts.

'I had to buy quite a lot of new furniture,' he said. 'Ikea must make a lot of money out of divorces. Of course, most of their customers are young couples, people starting a family, and nobody wants to tell them, "Decide now which one of you is going to be back here in a few years' time, alone." But I wasn't the only person there by himself. Many of the sofas I tried out had a man of about my age sitting alone at the other end, and we didn't need to ask each other why the other was there. We both knew. I don't know if I've felt more alone than when I had to choose new sheets with all those other lonely souls. But...' he turned a little, looked at me '...you didn't come here to hear about my interior-design skills. You want to talk about something else.'

'Well,' I began. 'I came to talk about ... what happened back then.'

Janne brought me a cup of coffee and topped up his own. It seemed we both still took our coffee black. Beyond the windows, the lake glowed golden, the spruces leaning in towards it. I caught the smell of coffee and wood. Somehow, I felt the earth disappear from under my feet, and it wasn't because the living room was built over the lake. Wherever I was at this moment, I would be stepping into thin air. And I knew that, despite my emotions, I had to move on. To move on in order to move on.

'It was the beginning of October,' I said. 'You'd just started working as a policeman in the neighbouring town, and you were doing the shifts the older officers were only too happy to leave to the new recruits. Which meant you were away from Puhtijärvi, sometimes for a couple of days at a time. That summer I'd started working at Leinonen's Nets & Lures. The work was interesting, as I told you many times. But then one Monday, a man came into the store. He didn't look much like a fisherman. Leinonen took him into the back room, but I could hear them talking. Turned out that Leinonen owed this man money – a lot of money. And, needless to say, Leinonen didn't have any. Nets & Lures was only just keeping afloat; I knew it even back then. As their conversation went on, I learnt that it was Leinonen's son who had run up the debts. He'd been living a jet-set lifestyle in Helsinki, and as far as I understood he didn't pay for all of it himself. The man left, said he'd be back the following day. I didn't tell Leinonen I'd overheard their conversation. The next day, I was at work again. And the man kept his promise; he came back just before closing. Of course, Leinonen had no more money than he'd had the day before. We'd sold a total of three lures that day, and that wouldn't pay for anyone's cocaine habit. The man threatened Leinonen in the back room, then came out into the store, looked around and said he'd give Leinonen three hours to get the money together, and in the meantime he'd be going fishing with "this woman".'

I pulled my coffee cup towards me but didn't pick it up. I didn't dare. Janne said nothing; he sipped his coffee.

'That woman was me,' I said. 'And so, we went fishing. Of course, the man was useless. I had to get everything ready for him: the rod, the line, the lures, everything. In normal circumstances, it would have been a good evening for fishing. It was calm, the fish were hungry and on the move, the moon was bright. But the man couldn't do anything ... anything at all. I tried to tell him what he needed to do, and he started to get annoyed. So I suggested we head back to the shore. He was quiet for a moment, and at first I thought it was because he agreed. Then he said he wasn't going to take lessons from a little bitch like me, that, on the contrary, he was going to teach me a thing or two. He pulled down his trousers and came towards me. From this point, everything happened very quickly – quicker than anything had ever happened before. The boat started wobbling.

I reached out a hand, fumbled for Leinonen's box of lures and snatched the first one that I managed to reach. It was one of those giant lures, made of steel, sharp as a filleting knife, made for ten-kilo pikes, the kind that Leinonen pulled from Lake Puhtijärvi every autumn. The man grabbed hold of me, pushed me down into the bottom of the boat and ... I lashed out. With the lure. I didn't see where I hit him. My eyes were closed...'

As I looked up at Janne, then out at the lake, I knew that my eyes were open. And yet it felt like I was back in that boat all over again.

'The man let go of me,' I continued. 'He stood up. The boat lurched from side to side, more forcefully than before. I was lying at the bottom of the boat, but I still had to hold on to avoid being thrown overboard. I opened my eyes, saw the man for another second or two. The lure was sticking out of his right eye, and it looked like he was trying to pull it out, but there are sharp little teeth all along it, so ... Then he fell backwards. Into the lake. I must have been in shock. I just lay there in the boat – for how long, I don't know. Everything was silent when I finally sat up and looked around. I don't think I've ever seen the lake that still. The moon was so close that it looked like it was touching the surface of the water. I started the motor and drove back to the shore. Leinonen was waiting for me. I didn't need to explain anything to him. We never spoke about what had happened, ever. And a few years later he took the secret with him to his grave.'

I paused briefly, glanced at the lake. The coffee seemed to have cooled, a small oily blotch was slowly moving in a circle on the surface.

'And the lake,' I said eventually, 'took that man, that complete stranger.'

Janne turned his own coffee cup on the tabletop, then looked up at me.

'One-Eyed Salmela,' he said.

28

It was a mirage, of course, purely in my imagination, but it felt as though we were flying, as though the whole house was suddenly gliding across the golden lake. But we weren't flying; Janne was still sitting in front of me and didn't look like he was thinking about take-off or landing. He looked calm and certain. He looked like himself. I wasn't calm or certain in the least, though, and I noticed I'd gripped the edge of the tabletop with my left hand. This felt somehow bizarre, but nonetheless necessary.

'One-Eyed Salmela,' repeated Janne. 'That's what we used to call that stranger. I mean, that's the name he was given back then. Before that he was just Salmela: a professional criminal and a wanted man. A police unit found him soaking wet and wandering aimlessly around Verkaistenlahti, about thirty kilometres from Puhtijärvi. He didn't know how he'd ended up there, and nobody else seemed to know either. He had no short-term memory at all, which was hardly surprising: a long, steel pike lure was jutting out of his left eye socket. It's a wonder he was still alive. He was transported to hospital and from there to prison, where he got his nickname and where he eventually died. Of natural causes. I wasn't at Verkaistenlahti myself, but I heard about the case. The reason it was never talked about publicly and why nobody knew much about it was because of his criminal history.'

Janne looked out at the lake, then turned to me.

'So, you did not kill Salmela that evening thirty years ago,' he said. 'You can forget that thought.'

'I don't know ... what to think.'

I didn't know what I felt either. Some form of relief, I guess. Joy, even. Yet at the same time ... everything felt somehow unreal. All of a sudden, thirty years felt both like the age of the universe and like some malevolent sleight of hand.

'I didn't kill Salmela,' I said. 'But I did kill ... us.'

Janne was quiet for a moment.

'I've said before, if things had turned out differently, maybe we wouldn't be here right now. I can't say I don't understand why you broke off our engagement. In your shoes, I might have done the same. Life isn't easy.'

I took a deep breath. The lake glinted, golden.

'No,' I said. 'It isn't. It's also completely different from what I once thought it was.'

Janne said nothing. He was clearly giving me some space. It seemed to work. After some time had passed, I released my grip on the edge of the table and noticed that I didn't fall into the lake or anywhere else.

Janne must have been watching me because he asked: 'What do you want to do next?'

I looked at him, then down at my oily coffee. 'I haven't had breakfast,' I said. 'Maybe I should eat something.'

'I meant in general,' he said. 'But breakfast is a good start.'

'Right,' I said. 'I don't know. I mean, I do know. I know a lot. I know very well what I want. But there are some things that feel like they can't be undone.'

'More bodies in Lake Puhtijärvi?'

'What?' I snapped. 'No. I've said a thousand times—'

'It was a joke,' said Janne. 'A bad one.'

I looked at him. I'd already told him the truth about the past, so why shouldn't I tell the truth about the here and now?

'I mean you,' I said.

Janne might have smiled a little. 'To be honest,' he began, 'I was hoping you'd say that. When I pulled you over on the ridge, I had the feeling there was still something between us, something unfinished.'

I was reminded of the things I'd been thinking lately, my sense that something was happening, that a potent, unknown power was waiting for me under the surface. Until now, I'd thought it was to do with the secret I'd been keeping all these years. There was no secret any longer, but I still felt the presence of that underwater power, the sense that something was about to happen.

'I'm not exactly a lottery win, you know,' I said. 'I'm married, your boss suspects me of two murders, and I've already broken off our engagement once before.'

'I don't know if I'm much of a catch myself,' said Janne. 'I'm divorced, I go to bed at nine in the evening and I pick the green jellybeans out of the bag.'

We stood up at the same time. We walked around the table, met at the spot where the sun, reflecting off something, cast a bright, gleaming strip across the floorboards. I could feel its warmth in my feet. And I realised that what was happening now wasn't what I had come here for; but it was what had been waiting for me under the surface all these years. I took another short step and switched the warmth of the sun for another warmth.

Janne's arms, his body, his face.

Then his lips, their form and feel.

I knew where I was.

29

The sauna whisks in the reception area looked like dry, withered bunches of branches. Which, of course, they were. I didn't know why the shrivelled leaves, yellowing around the edges, caught my attention right now. For a second or two, I tried to remember who Erkki had put in charge of looking after the whisks, and replacing them, but then it felt rather pointless. This wasn't a pressing matter. I had matters that *were* pressing, and wondering about old sauna whisks didn't help me.

I stood in the foyer a moment longer, listening to the sounds of the building, and concluded that everybody was at work.

I walked to my office, switched on my computer and quickly answered a few emails. Promoting our sauna stoves still felt important. To some degree this provided a sense of security – stoves represented stability, permanence – but at the same time I felt very strongly, perhaps more strongly than ever now, that Steam Devil's business was my business too. The idea had come into focus as I'd been driving here from Janne's place. The past no longer weighed me down, no longer zapped my strength, even subconsciously.

The swiftness of this change was bewildering; it had all happened so suddenly. I was still able to recall those unpleasant memories, but they no longer held me in a vice-like grip. I could still see those images, accept their existence, their reality, but now I could quickly push them from my mind. What's more, they no longer left me with that cold sense of regret or brought out the desire to flee. They were simply ... a part of my life. Which was probably the most merciful thing one could say about anything.

Once I'd sent a few emails, I stood up, adjusted my jumper and went through my plan one more time. This took about half a second, because the plan was a simple one: I would speak to each of my colleagues once again, but this time in light of the new information I had learnt.

I passed Mirka's room – I had already had a one-on-one conversation with her very recently, and this meant she was currently last on my list – and found Kaarlo out on the patio.

As usual, Kaarlo noticed my arrival at once. He seemed to have a heightened sense of alertness; he was always the first to turn his head, to get out of his chair, to rush towards the door. I walked over to the table where he was sitting, apparently reading a newspaper and a book at the same time: the *Wall Street Journal* and Sun Tzu's *The Art of War*. I thought his choices a bit fake and transparent; I suspected he was keeping them in view simply to make an impression. On whom, I couldn't say, because he was on the patio by himself. I also remembered hearing that Kaarlo didn't speak any English, which would make reading complicated articles about the intricacies of economics challenging, to say the least.

'Has Kahavuori bought those stoves yet?' he asked, before I could say hello.

'Not yet,' I said and remained standing by the railing so that, in order to look at me, Kaarlo had to gaze almost directly into the sun. 'But we're close to signing the deal. Just a few more details to iron out first.'

'A firm grip on the wrist,' he said. 'A quick twist, and, *bingo*, the hand's ready to sign.'

'Right,' I admitted and stared at the Lee Van Cleef of the sauna-stove world. 'Actually, there's something I wanted to ask your opinion about. Our new stoves have the—'

'I've looked into the matter of the handles,' he interrupted. 'It's not industrial espionage. There are no rats on this ship.'

Kaarlo's eyes were like daggers; they seemed to cut into me, even at a distance.

'How did you—?'

'I challenged Porkka to a competition,' he said. 'We went into the sauna, I locked the door, sat right next to him on the bench and started off by throwing a pail of water on the stove at a hundred and thirty degrees. Before long he was begging for mercy. I told him he would have mercy as soon as he told me what he was doing at our competitor's factory. And he told me. He'd flown off the handle, so to speak. He was obsessed, thought everybody was copying his inventions. That wasn't the case; it was a coincidence.'

'Are you sure...?'

'I threw another pail of water on the stove, just to make sure,' he nodded.

Very well, I thought, but we still haven't talked about *you*, and that's what I'm most interested in. I didn't know how to approach the subject, though, and decided to take a short detour first.

'Have you noticed anything different about—?'

'Erkki?'

I tried not to show how taken aback I was at Kaarlo's quick answer. He'd finished my sentence without hesitation, and I couldn't help wondering whether this was another grilling, another pail of water over a metaphorical stove. I tried to shake off the thought, but it was no use.

'Right,' I said. 'Or anyone else...'

'Gone soft.'

'Sorry?'

'He's gone soft,' said Kaarlo.

I hadn't been expecting this either – that we would have reached the heart of the matter so soon.

'Do you mean, compared to when you first met him?' I asked.

'Those were good times,' said Kaarlo. 'We were sharp. Sharp as a blade. I taught him how to dance.'

'Really?'

'Erkki didn't have a clue how to dance,' said Kaarlo. 'And back then you had to know how to mambo if you wanted to meet any ladies. I taught him that dancing is like a battle. I danced with him, showed him how to lead, how to treat your partner like a rose. Then I let him lead. He was a good pupil, and that's how he met the mother of his children. He's been dancing ever since, as I'm sure you know.'

The sun was behind me, but I still felt as though I was the focus of a bright, very unpleasant light. On the plus side, now I knew the nature of the debt that Erkki had mentioned.

'The rumours you've heard aren't true,' I said eventually. 'Erkki and I aren't ... doing the mambo ... or anything else of that nature. But right now, I'm—'

'I don't like saying this,' Kaarlo interrupted again, probably without even noticing. 'and I'm not trying to walk all over your ambitions, but because of Erkki, because he's going soft, I think it's best if I take the reins from here. So the place doesn't turn into something between a flower shop and a bag of cotton wool. It needs to be damn clear that we make the hottest stoves around – pure steel that'll tear the skin off even the toughest back.'

Was Kaarlo the murderer? Would the culprit really talk like...?

'For a moment there, I thought you might be our killer,' he said, once again as if he was reading my mind. 'But now I don't. Not after Porkka. This killer has skills that you don't have.'

Kaarlo's last sentence confused me for a moment. In a strange way, I'd taken offence: Lee Van Cleef was questioning my killing skills, he didn't think I had it in me. The absurd thought quickly disappeared.

'What kind of skills are those?' I asked.

'You've been working on the Kahavuori order for months without results,' he said. 'In just a few weeks, this killer has sent two critical members of our team to the morgue. I'm sure you can see the difference in terms of initiative, determination and the drive to see projects through.'

I admitted that one could see it like this. Then I asked him what other skills or qualities – positive or negative – he thought a murderer should have. Kaarlo looked pensive, his dagger-sharp eyes glanced at the lake, then bored their way into me again.

'The killer wants to save money,' he said.

'Sorry?' I said for the second time this conversation.

'Ilmo's salary was about to become the second largest in the company, after Erkki's,' Kaarlo explained. 'And Porkka was due for an unprecedented bonus after securing those patents. Now none of that is going to happen. Both men took the ultimate pay cut, at exactly the right moment.'

I stared back at him and recalled the suspicions I'd had about his guilt a moment earlier. I wasn't sure whether those suspicions had diminished or not.

'You and Mirka seem to be very close,' I said, leaving as much innuendo as possible floating in the air.

But my insinuations didn't appear to have the least impact. Kaarlo's expression remained unchanged. His hands neither flinched nor trembled.

'We wanted to wait,' he said, his voice like sonic concrete, 'until we were both certain. Now we are, and we'll be telling everyone soon. We're starting a family, and we're expecting a baby around Christmas. I'm excited to bring little Arnold into the world.'

I went into the staffroom to get a diet cola and managed to force myself into a chair. Sitting down felt like a waste of time, but rushing felt potentially dangerous. Not that I thought the killer was going to strike again – at the Steam Devil offices and in broad daylight. But the conversation I'd had with Kaarlo was yet another example of how quickly things can change and how quickly I needed to change my understanding of the situation. In one fell swoop, I thought, Kaarlo and Mirka had both become both more and less suspect, and I couldn't decide which. My mind conjured up images of infamous serial-killer couples who had found each other in the most depraved ways. Then I quickly had to admit I wasn't an expert on these kinds of relationships. Kahavuori might have had some historical knowledge of the subject, but I didn't plan to take my theories to him, of all people.

All the while I was trying not to think about what had happened on my visit to Janne's house, but that was nearly impossible. Being released from the weight of the past felt both breath-taking – in a pleasant way – and completely incomprehensible. The same could be said for the second surprise of that morning.

Afterwards, we were both a little bewildered. We agreed that, though what we had done was something we had thought about and secretly wished for, it was also, at least when it came to the timing, inappropriate to say the least.

Maybe it's best if for the time being we don't...
No, of course not, as long as you're still investigating and I'm...
After all, I am a police officer...
And I ... sell sauna stoves...
But it might be a good idea to talk...
Yes, it would be nice to meet up...
If it's possible, of course...
Of course, we'll fit it around your...
I love you...

I've always loved you...
But maybe it's for the best if we...
Right, yes, the timing couldn't be worse...

And so on until Janne's phone rang and he had to go. We did take the opportunity for one last kiss, nice and thorough, and very long indeed, because we both knew that we were being forced to go our separate ways and wouldn't be able to continue these activities for a while.

In my car, I had still been able to taste Janne in my mouth, feel his bare skin against my bare skin, and I'd tried to avoid the thought of how much I wanted to taste and feel him again, as soon as possible, as often as possible. I wasn't very good at avoiding that thought, though. The truth, as awkward as it felt, was that I was combining middle age and teen age in the most convoluted way.

I finished my Coke.

⸙

Jarkko was sitting behind his desk the way he usually did, tapping away at the keyboard in front of him. Although he looked absorbed in what he was doing, I knew that he was constantly on the look-out for anything going on in the corridor, at the end of which was Erkki's office. I wasn't at all surprised, therefore, when, without looking up from his computer, he said that Erkki was out and that I should run any potential meetings by him.

I thought it best not to tell him outright that I hadn't come here to meet Erkki or even to talk about him. I was acquainted with Jarkko only superficially, but I knew that he was happier to speak as Erkki's representative (which he was not) than as himself. Which meant I would have to proceed via Erkki anyway, one way or another.

'Is there a full day free in the diary?' I asked. 'Preferably as soon as possible, perhaps even tomorrow?'

Jarkko's fingers stopped in mid-air, his head turned. His expression was both deadly serious and perhaps a little frustrated.

'There's a special protocol for booking an entire day, and it needs to be done well in advance,' he said. 'As you know. And we need to have a detailed outline of what the booking is for. And this information should be submitted in advance, in writing—'

'How about we just sort it all out here and now?'

Judging by Jarkko's expression, you'd think I'd just suggested a coup or an immediate cranial operation.

'Nobody can possibly—'

'But you coordinate Erkki's schedule,' I said. 'You can move anything, anytime you like. You can *make* time.'

Jarkko didn't answer right away. He pushed himself back from the desk a little, perhaps to get a better view of the adversary he had suddenly encountered.

'There would be chaos around here,' he said, 'if there wasn't somebody to make sure people didn't just move things willy-nilly or come up with all kinds of "fudges".'

I understood the air quotes. Jarkko even enunciated the word inside them as though it was the most unrealistic thing he'd ever heard.

'Are you afraid of chaos?' I asked. 'Or is Erkki afraid of it?'

'What do you mean?'

'Which of you two actually makes the decisions around here?'

'Erkki,' he said. 'He's the Stove King. And the king makes the decisions. Always.'

I hadn't quite got where I wanted yet, but I could see that Jarkko was a little irritated. This was highly unusual. He often suggested and demanded things that nobody else seemed to agree with, but genuine irritation was very rare for him.

'What if the king disappears?' I hazarded. 'Abdicates, relinquishes his crown?'

By now I knew Jarkko was very agitated, but he was doing a good job of hiding it. 'We all know you're the favourite to succeed him,' he began. 'But you're also a murderer. Or so everybody says.' Jarkko looked as though he truly believed what he'd just said.

'Who's everybody?' I asked.

'What?'

'Everybody?' I asked again. 'Does Erkki say it?'

It looked as though he didn't even have to prepare an answer. 'That's what the police think,' he said, and now he sounded as though he was simply stating the obvious. 'And, quite clearly, they know best.'

Jarkko's eyes told me everything I needed to know. He was convinced of my guilt. I decided it was pointless trying to continue in the same vein and that I'd be better served moving the spotlight onto him.

'What would you do differently then?'

Jarkko didn't seem to understand my question, he was too flustered. 'In what sense?' he asked.

'You're in the race to succeed Erkki too,' I said. 'So you must have some ideas about the future of Steam Devil. I've heard other people's ideas, but I don't think I've heard yours. What would you do differently? What would change?'

For a moment longer, Jarkko appeared confused. Then it seemed that he finally understood the question. He now looked considerably more sure of himself, in every sense.

'Nothing,' he said. 'Obviously. Steam Devil would continue exactly as it has until now.'

We gazed at each other.

'Do you still want to reserve a slot?' he asked eventually. 'Let me warn you in advance, Erkki's diary is full, so I can't make any promises.'

I didn't tell him that Erkki was quite happy to arrange meetings with me privately, and on his own patio no less – and I certainly didn't mention my other recent observations about Erkki's health. I wanted to continue the conversation with Jarkko, and to do that I had to submit to his scheduling gymnastics. Eventually, after some tortured manoeuvres, we managed to arrange a fifteen-minute meeting the following week. It was interesting that Jarkko really did seem to believe he had complete control of the company diary, and as far as I could tell he wasn't remotely aware that I'd met Erkki only the previous day. I was about to ask my next question, but Jarkko got there before me.

'If it's all the same,' he said, 'I've got work to be getting on with.'

I glanced towards Erkki's office. The door was closed; I didn't know whether he was in there or not.

'Do you remember who's responsible for the whisks in the foyer?' I asked. 'It's important to Erkki. In the summer he wants the foyer to smell of fresh birch leaves, fresh whisks. It makes people think of the sauna.'

Jarkko's mouth opened, closed, then opened again. 'What about the whisks?' he asked.

I assumed I'd struck gold.

'They're all withered,' I said. 'And they don't smell of anything. It sort of defeats the point.'

I could see I'd touched a nerve. The sauna whisks must be Jarkko's responsibility; I could see it in his eyes, which were desperately searching the screen for something to fix upon. After an extensive search, he found something.

'A very good point,' he said. 'I'll make a note of it—'

'Should I quickly mention it to Erkki too...?'

'No!' said Jarkko, almost shrieking. Then straight away continued in a markedly calmer tone: 'The whisks will be changed today. Porkka was a legend when it came to making them, but he won't be ... making any whisks ... for us ... any longer.'

Jarkko spent another moment or so tapping his keyboard, then watched as I stood up from my chair. I didn't know whether he was a murderer, but I knew a lot more than I did when I'd stepped into the room. I thanked Jarkko for arranging a meeting with Erkki, then turned to leave. Before I did I carried out one last little experiment. First I walked away from Jarkko and his glass-walled office, then changed direction and started making my way towards Erkki's office. I glanced over my shoulder.

Jarkko had stood up; it looked as though he was about to charge towards me and stop me.

I turned and walked away.

30

I was in my office for only a few seconds. That's why I was so surprised not to find Susanna sitting at her desk. I'd heard her voice a moment earlier, on my way from Jarkko's office, and when I looked at her desk now, everything seemed to suggest she should be there. The bookkeeping programme was still open on her screen; beside the keyboard was an almost full mug of coffee with oat milk – I thought I could feel the warmth emanating from the mug as I stood in the doorway. And everything was neat and tidy, pleasant and impeccable in a very Susanna way.

I thought I'd come back a moment later, but then I stopped.

At first, I couldn't understand why I'd frozen. The feeling was overwhelming; I felt it in every muscle in my body. Then I made a concerted effort to calm myself down and make sure I hadn't been imagining it. I took two steps forwards, stopped in the middle of the room and took a deep breath. The cleanliness, the lightness, the freshness. A faint, classy hint of darker tones and something exotic maybe.

The same sophisticated fragrance I'd smelt in Santeri's shrine.

The very same one. No doubt about it.

I recalled Santeri's strange talk about entrepreneurship, about expanding the business; I remembered my bewilderment.

I turned, started walking. However, I didn't head towards my own office but walked through the foyer towards the main door and stared out through one of the narrow, wall-height windows.

And saw Susanna's small red Audi swerving through the car park.

The angle of the turn felt strange; it didn't seem to have

anything to do with coming in or out of a parking space, and Susanna's speed felt odd too. I didn't think I'd ever seen anybody driving through the car park in such an erratic way and at such speed, and this included the times when Porkka had flown into a rage about something or other and sped away from the forecourt.

Susanna's reckless trajectory took her rather close to the office building, so I could see her hunched over the steering wheel. Her stance looked tense and panicked, not at all stylish or relaxed.

Something had happened. Or something was about to happen.

Susanna was behaving in a way I'd never seen her behave before: suddenly, abruptly, *carelessly*.

And with that, I made a decision.

I ran to my office, grabbed my handbag and pulled out the car keys while hurrying back towards the front door. I opened it and was momentarily blinded by the brightness – the sun shining from a clear sky, again, for the umpteenth day in a row – took the three steps down to the tarmac and strode towards my car. I could see Susanna's Audi heading towards the village. I pressed the button on my key fob, then saw and heard the back lights flashing, the central locking opening. At that same moment, something about the brightness and the stagnant outdoor air forced me to slow my steps and...

I heard a sound, the kind of sound that in another context, at another moment, I might have associated with a ship running aground or a train slamming on its emergency brakes. I saw movement out of the corner of my eye before I realised what was happening. Instinctively I took a step to the side, then another, a third and a fourth, and that was all I had time for.

The Stove came tumbling down, its stones crashing to the ground just left of my head; the metal wrenched, twisted and screeched right in front of me. I felt a powerful gust of air against my face, throughout my body. The noise was dizzying, and the final *crash* was extended, like a car rolling down a mountainside.

And with that, the Stove was on the ground, and I was standing half a metre from its side.

My ears were ringing.

If I'd reached out my hand, I would have been able to touch the wreckage. I didn't have to wonder what would have happened if I hadn't managed to move in time. The whole incident had probably lasted no more than a second or a second and a half. I was still alone in the car park. If I hadn't slowed my steps, if I hadn't taken those steps to the side ... I would be underneath the Stove without any witnesses, without anyone to help me, to save me.

I forced my legs into motion, taking a few steps by sheer willpower. I walked around the defunct Stove and thought that, in a horizontal position, it was even larger and heavier than it appeared when it was still standing. I reached my car, got in and tried for a moment to recall how to start it up. Then I remembered, pressed my foot on the accelerator, first gently, then more purposefully.

Just before turning into the main road, I glanced in the rear-view mirror.

The giant Stove was lying on the ground in pieces. The office door opened, people spilled outside like peas from a bag: Kaarlo, Jarkko, Mirka. They all stopped as soon as they stepped into the forecourt, and in a way I understood why. I didn't know what had happened either.

I caught sight of Susanna's red Audi just before reaching the village. She had slowed somewhat, while I had been getting faster. But now I slowed down too, keeping the distance between us as wide as possible.

The very fact that Susanna had careered out of the car park but was now driving calmly suggested that her initial panic had something to do with events in the Steam Devil car park. Perhaps the way the Stove toppled over was significant. I was the only person who had recently parked in the area of the car park where the Stove had just come crashing down. Of course, this might have been pure coincidence, an accident perhaps. But when I thought of the way Susanna had suddenly left an assignment unfinished, about the full mug of coffee with its carefully chosen oat milk left on her desk, and about the fact that she might have seen or heard what I was doing and could very well have concluded that I would be coming to talk to her next, perhaps there were other explanations. And whether the toppling of the Stove was deliberate or not, Susanna's behaviour was interesting.

Where was she going in such a hurry, and why now?

The red Audi glided through the village, then picked up speed again.

I was more than familiar with these roads. I knew every turn, every bend. Each junction suggested many possible destinations, and I was constantly trying to predict which was the most likely at any given point. We were driving towards the police station, then we passed it. I couldn't see Janne's car in the yard, or any other cars for that matter.

Five minutes later, we arrived at an intersection that I'd been nervously anticipating for some time. The nerves were to do with my fuel situation. If we turned onto the highway towards Tampere, that would entail a much longer drive, one I wasn't prepared for. That morning, I'd noticed the red light flashing on the fuel gauge, but I'd dismissed it. I hadn't imagined I'd find myself tailing my husband's mistress quite this soon or that, in doing so, my average speed would be faster than usual.

The Audi took a right, which was a relief. Nobody drove along this winding and in places potholed road to Kivijoki for long if they could avoid it. I let the Audi pull ahead a little, and at times lost sight of it altogether. But the car's red paint was bright and glowing amid the green of the forest and the fields, so I caught sight of it again every time we reached a straighter section of road.

Eventually, the Audi slowed down, and I followed suit, though rather more abruptly. It disappeared from view, and I continued cautiously. I knew where we were: the lakeshore was to my right, and there were houses dotted here and there along both sides of the road. I picked up my speed a little so that I was just over the limit. I drove for about half a minute, maybe a full minute, and I almost passed the house I was looking for without even noticing it.

The Audi was standing outside a light-brown brick building at the end of a long driveway, and parked next to the Audi was Santeri's BMW. Santeri's car was even easier to identify, not least because of its light-blue paintwork. I knew the car well; after all, I'd bought it, and paid for every MOT too. I slowed down, checked the house's number on the letterbox and continued on my way.

After driving some distance, I flicked on the indicator, turned onto one of the lanes through the woods, which looked like it would be completely overgrown within the next fifty metres, stopped the car and switched off the engine. I took out my phone, opened up a browser and typed in the address I'd just seen – Kivijoentie 224 – then filtered the search results to show only the last month. And I found what I was looking for. The house was for sale. I looked at the pictures and realised that I might be looking at Susanna and Santeri's future home. Or was I? There was only one way to find out. The listing gave the estate agent's number. I keyed it into my phone.

'Leila Tyni,' a chirpy voice answered.

'Hi,' I said, aiming for a similar level of chirpiness. 'I just came across one of your listings, the beautiful old, detached house – Kivijoentie 224...'

'Well, there's a coincidence,' said Leila Tyni, now seemingly even more thrilled. 'I'm showing some people around that one right now. I'm standing in the garden as we speak, and I'll be here until four o'clock, if you'd—'

'Marvellous,' I said. 'The house is just charming. I was afraid it might have gone already.'

'We've just had the first offer,' Leila Tyni explained, and her voice could barely conceal her excitement. 'This was the buyers' second visit, but of course there's still time to make an offer and get into the bidding...'

'That's smashing,' I said, again trying to match her excitement. 'May I ask a quick question first?'

'By all means,' the agent assured me.

'This is a little – how should I put it? – confidential,' I began. I noticed my speech was quickening. 'I've lost out in bidding wars like this before, and before I make an offer I'd like to know who I'm up against, how high they're willing to go, though I'm prepared to go all the way. I realise an estate agent can't give out personal information or anything like that but—'

'I can tell you bits and pieces,' she said encouragingly.

'Well, if it's possible...'

'Anything is possible,' said Leila Tyni, and she sounded like she meant it.

'I don't want to...' I began, trying my best to sound both enthusiastic and hesitant. 'I mean, if I make a higher bid, and it'll be a high one, I don't want to think I'm taking the house away from a young family with children trying to get their foot on the property ladder...'

'There's no need to worry about that,' said Leila Tyni. 'This isn't a family. It's a middle-aged couple – a very stylish and well-heeled couple – so I think a nice high offer is the best way to proceed.'

I wondered whether this might be the right moment to warn Leila Tyni that while she might be dealing with a very high-earning accountant, the same could not be said of the stolen-goods merchant who was with her. I dismissed the thought.

'That's so good to hear,' I said. 'So, when will I need to make my offer in order to be level pegging with this stylish couple?'

'By tomorrow evening.'

I thanked Leila Tyni for the lovely conversation and ended the call, although I could still hear her asking for my name and when she could expect to hear from me again as I hung up. I concluded that if she were to call me again, I would tell her the truth: that I'd decided I was happy in my current house, and perhaps I'd mention that it now felt quieter and more spacious than ever before.

As I reversed my car out of the lane and back to the main road, my mind was awash with flickering images, short fragments that were, of course, the work of my imagination but that I suspected were quite accurate. I could almost hear Santeri's voice telling Susanna that he wanted to surprise her and was about to make an offer on the house they had viewed, and how he had bravely grabbed the bull by the horns and how he – because he was a successful entrepreneur these days, Puhtijärvi's very own Richard Branson, no less – had moved quickly, with great determination. And I imagined Susanna panicking, leaping up from her desk and dashing out to calm him down, to bring some sense to proceedings.

But were Susanna and Santeri murderers? Another star-crossed couple to torment the village?

I didn't know.

But I couldn't imagine either of them carrying out all that bloodshed. And the flickering images seemed to be disappearing now.

I managed to turn my Volvo and drove back the way I'd come. I no longer needed to see the stylish, well-heeled couple standing outside their home-to-be. I already knew everything I needed to know.

I stared at the empty road ahead of me and concluded that middle age did strange things to us all.

31

Kiimalainen's slow, pensive steps were those of a man trying to give the impression he was someone who analysed and examined things very thoroughly indeed. He had paced around the Stove twice already, and in all that time he hadn't said a word. I didn't think the reason that this work of art had collapsed would reveal itself to him on a third inspection either, and I didn't think it was likely that Kiimalainen was really carrying out a profound, wide-ranging analysis of the mass of metal parts lying on the ground.

This was about something else, and I believed I knew what.

I knew that news of the toppling of the Stove would soon reach the police, and that would pique their interest. And if someone from around Steam Devil or the immediate surroundings said they had seen the prime suspect in a double murder investigation speeding out of the car park only moments after the event, that would pique their interest even more. Therefore, it was more natural – not to mention safer – to turn up of my own volition and tell them the truth. And that's what I'd done, as concisely as possible – *The Stove toppled over, I don't know why* – about ten minutes ago, a moment before Kiimalainen had started prowling around the wreckage.

I glanced over my shoulder and saw Kaarlo and Mirka standing in front of the office building, about twenty metres away. Jarkko seemed to have returned indoors. Kiimalainen had ordered them all to keep a distance and invited me to stand by the Stove and watch his steps. He stopped, stared a moment longer at the broken pieces of the Stove, then turned towards me, crunching the car-park gravel under his shoes as he did so.

'It's toppled over,' he said and squinted, either at the afternoon brightness or for some other reason. 'Just like that.'

I'd already told myself that I was no Sherlock Holmes. Now I felt that Kiimalainen was no Watson either. Standing around here was a waste of time, and I was in a hurry to get elsewhere, but I didn't want to let Kiimalainen know either of these things. I agreed with him, the Stove really had toppled over – just like that – and I reiterated that it had been both shocking and earth-shattering.

'I mean ... just like that,' he said coldly. 'How did you manage to dodge it, I wonder?'

I told him once again that I'd acted instinctively. Kiimalainen looked like I'd just said something most unpleasant.

'Your accountant, Susanna Luoto, left the car park only moments earlier, isn't that right?'

'Yes,' I admitted, 'but—'

'Was it intended to fall on her?'

'Excuse me?'

'Was the intention,' he asked, squinting so much now that I couldn't see his eyes at all, 'to pull the Stove over a moment earlier? And when it didn't fall, you panicked, you had to follow her and finish the job some other way?'

I knew where he was going with this. He thought that I, who he imagined went around killing people the length and breadth of Puhtijärvi, was so enraged that my latest attempted murder had failed that I'd set off after Susanna to kill her somewhere else. I wanted to tell him in no uncertain terms what I thought of him and his theories, and the real reason I'd bolted out of the car park, but, yet again, I couldn't do either of these things. If I'd told him the truth about my sudden departure, I would be forced to tell him about Susanna and Santeri and the state of my marriage. I didn't want to give Kiimalainen the satisfaction.

'I did not make the Stove topple over,' I said. After all, it was true.

'You did not make the Stove topple over,' he nodded. 'You didn't sauna with Ilmo Räty, you didn't strike Porkka using a ladle with your own name on it. Quite a lot happens round here without you doing anything.'

We looked at each other. At least, I thought we were looking at each other. I couldn't be certain what Kiimalainen was doing underneath his furrowed eyebrows.

'You used to sell glue, isn't that right?' he asked eventually.

The question took me by surprise, but I managed not to show it. Which was particularly tricky, as it appeared to tell me something crucial – I just didn't know what. Yes, there was a time when I'd sold glue, I'd sold hundreds if not thousands of different building materials before moving to Steam Devil.

'I worked for a company that sold building materials,' I said. 'As you well know. You often visited it yourself. Uitto & Sons. I sold all kinds of building materials, even glue. Why do you ask?'

Kiimalainen didn't answer right away.

'So, you know your glues?' he asked, now sounding very happy with himself.

'I certainly used to,' I admitted, stressing the past tense.

'Glue is glue,' he said. 'You know what holds on what kind of surface, and what doesn't.'

I said nothing. Just then, my phone rang in my bag. I let it ring, didn't look to see who was trying to get hold of me.

'May I leave?' I asked as the phone doggedly continued ringing. 'Nowadays I sell sauna stoves, and I really have to—'

'It's a busy life,' said Kiimalainen with a wave of his hand. 'By all means. Be my guest.'

I thanked him and was turning to leave when I heard his voice behind me.

'We'll be meeting again soon,' he said. 'Very soon.'

I didn't stop.

On the way to my car – still walking with exaggeratedly calm but determined steps – I looked at my phone, which was still ringing.

〜

I didn't see Erkki on the patio, but he'd instructed me to meet him there so that's where I headed. The lake was shining in the dark blue of early evening. A bird flapped itself into flight in the water by the shore. The garden looked the same as last time: large, empty and well looked after.

On the phone, Erkki had said he'd heard about the toppling of the Stove, but he hadn't sounded as though the matter was foremost in his mind. He wanted to tell me something, he said, something personal and urgent, so I should head to his villa at once. I'd wanted to say that I was exhausted, so tired that my whole body ached and my temples were throbbing. I recalled that in one day I'd managed to make love to my former fiancé, who just happened to be an officer investigating the murders for which I was suspected, that I'd heard some shocking news about my past that had released me from my decades-long anguish, that I had made progress with my own investigation, had almost ended up crushed by a fifteen-metre-tall ornamental stove, and had found out that my husband and the accountant at our sauna-stove business were having an affair. At this point I was ready to warm up my own sauna, sit on the benches and think about what to do next.

But when I'd considered my own situation – and Erkki's – I could see I needed even more evidence to prove my innocence, and Erkki needed ... help.

My feet tapped on the paving stones, then the wooden steps and then the patio. The table wasn't laid and there was no smell of food. Apparently, this visit would be different from the last one. The French windows were open and I could hear music coming from inside. The song had started playing just as I'd arrived on the patio. I recognised it from the first few bars. And by the time the singer began, I was sure of what I was hearing.

Dean Martin.

That's Amore.

I looked over my shoulder. The garden, the lake, the leafy green birches, further off a row of dark spruces.

I carefully opened the French windows a little more, one centimetre at a time. Just then – I was sure of it – the volume of the music increased.

When the moon hits your eye like a big pizza pie...

Dean Martin was singing as close to me as the sadly departed crooner could possibly have sung. I could make out the resonance of his voice, almost feel his lips against my ears. Erkki was never lavish or wasteful, but he had certainly spent a lot of time, effort and money on his sound system.

When the stars make you drool just like a pasta e fasul...

I couldn't shout or call for Erkki; the music was too loud. It took a moment for my eyes to adjust to the dim in the living room, which seemed like it was deliberate. The curtains had been drawn across the windows, and in the furthest corner, on a small round table that looked more like a plinth, was the only light source in the room, and it was faint and yellow. Then, on the coffee table in the middle of the room, I made out something that didn't seem to be a permanent part of the furnishings.

When you dance down the street with a cloud at your feet...

It was a bottle of champagne in a bucket of ice, two glasses and something else. I didn't spend long looking at the steel bucket and the gleaming, steamed-up bottle, because I wanted to find Erkki or the volume button. Either would do, I thought.

When you walk in a dream but you know you're not dreaming, Signore...

A face appeared around the wall beside me, looking as surprised as mine must have at this moment. Then the surprise changed to a different expression, which was far harder to interpret. I didn't have time to do anything.

That's amore.

Dean Martin carried on singing about old Naples as Erkki grabbed me and spun me around, and with that we were dancing, but in a bizarre way, because as far as I was concerned I wasn't involved in the act at all. We spun around, turned, spun again, twirled in and out of each other. I felt Erkki's cheek against my temple, then it disappeared as I started flying through the air, first one way then another, and the room seemed to dim as the brightness of specific items – the champagne bottle, the ice bucket, the glasses – increased, and I wondered if this was what people meant when they said they were seeing stars.

I tried to extricate myself, but it felt like trying to jump off a moving train. I attempted to say something, but Dean Martin's voice smothered my own. Then Erkki leant or curved backwards, I saw his face and eyes, and realised I really was on a moving train. A train that had set off decades ago.

Erkki was leading this dance, that much I understood, and he was doing so in a way that was quite irresistible. Both literally and figuratively.

My thoughts came in fits. I managed to make an escape plan and decided to set it in motion once the song came to an end. We spun, skipped, spun again. I could hear Dean reaching the end of the story, and I felt Erkki ramping up the intensity. We were about to reach some kind of climax. I tried to keep my eyes firmly fixed on the French windows and patio. Erkki swung us around one last time, and the French windows were now right behind me. One step backwards, and I would be on the patio. And then – the climax.

Which was an even greater surprise than the one I'd been preparing for.

Dean stopped, the orchestra stopped.

And Erkki started.

Kissing me.

Using all my strength, I lunged backwards, but I hadn't taken the doorsill into consideration. I struck it with my heel and lost my balance. My arms flew out instinctively and I grabbed the first thing I could, the front of Erkki's shirt, I fell backwards, pulling him with me. We were on the patio, I was still falling, I fell, still pulling Erkki…

…onto the long wooden bench in the middle of the patio.

The air was knocked out of my lungs, and though I heard that the music had stopped, I couldn't shout out or say anything. Erkki was on top of me, he was between my legs and my legs were high in the air because I was trying to get up and shake him from on top of me all at the same time. But he seemed to understand my writhing in completely the wrong way. He tried to kiss me again, his lips pursed. He groaned, a long wheezing sound came from his throat, and a glazed expression settled on his face.

Then, just as my arms were starting to feel exhausted, there was another change in Erkki's expression, just as abrupt as the previous one. His eyes brightened and focussed on the here and now: the August evening, his patio, the two of us, our panting bodies pressed against each other.

'Anni,' he said. 'What on earth are you doing?'

32

I threw another ladle of water on the stove, placed my feet on the railing and glanced at the thermometer. Exactly ninety degrees. At least there was one thing I still knew how to do right.

The heat and moisture descended over my skin, revitalising my exhausted body. As I watched the window steam up then gradually become clear again, allowing the darkened lake to come into view, I tried to imagine how I would explain all this to the one person I felt I could trust right now.

Because I needed help. I was too tired and too alone.

But would Janne be as understanding as he had been about One-Eyed Salmela? This event – these two events, in fact – were much more recent, and I'd kept certain things to myself that I should have told the police a long time ago. Of course, I had good reasons not to tell them, but the more I thought about it, the harder it was to see Janne, a police officer, nodding along to my accounts of unexplained murders or to the way I'd hidden things that might have helped the investigation. This alone felt like reason enough to keep my distance.

And if I thought about Janne truthfully – acknowledging the facts, that he was the man I'd always loved – things got even more complicated.

For the past was now finally in the past. Each time I thought about it, the revelation felt new and lightened my burden. I simply felt joy. Joy that I had finally returned from that autumnal lake and that upon reaching the shore I had found the one person I'd always hoped I would find.

Janne.

We'd made a new beginning. Which, in light of recent events, felt like stepping out of a long, arduous winter straight into the warmth and ease of summer. I'd been trying to keep my thoughts about Janne – and especially about what had happened today – at a neutral distance, but I knew this buffer was illusory, an ephemeral protection zone. In reality, there was no buffer and no protection. Janne had always been nearby, and now it felt as though I'd let him approach. I felt it mentally and I felt it physically. Did I really want to tear myself away from him yet again, for what would surely be the last time?

Revealing everything I knew came with risks too. My stories might yet turn against me. In fact, this was more than likely. Kiimalainen would never allow my stories to quash his theories. On the contrary. To him, my stories would be a confession, or something similar. This wasn't just probable; it was inevitable.

But ultimately, what were my options?

And, more specifically, which of those options were realistic?

I threw another ladle of water on the stove. The window steamed up, the view disappeared. The answer to my questions was the same as it had been at the beginning of my sauna.

I didn't have any options.

At this point, the idea that I would get to the bottom of two murders before Kiimalainen arrested me for them felt like such wishful thinking that it almost made me physically sick. I'd been trying to solve these murders by myself, and in the process I'd found myself in an abandoned sauna, almost buying a house and pinned to the patio in Erkki's villa. And, if I was honest, I didn't know any more than when I'd started. At least, I didn't know anything that might have helped me. It was time to call it a day.

I went for a swim in the lake, then pulled on my dressing gown. I picked up my phone, sat down on the bench in the porch and took a deep breath. The sun was shedding its last beams, the lake was becoming dim, the opposite shore rising up from the horizon. I might lose this, I thought. I might lose everything, but I didn't know what else to do. I pressed the call button.

Janne didn't answer.

))

Morning came suddenly and unexpectedly. At first I didn't understand what had happened, but then I concluded that I must just have slept very well. This felt strange – for a moment almost alarming. Until I remembered the decision I'd made. I hadn't been able to get in touch with Janne, not even on the second or third attempt, but the fact that I'd made up my mind seemed to have removed a tension inside me, a weight. And so, after locking both the front door and my bedroom door, I'd quickly fallen asleep. And this despite the fact that I'd tried to lie with my eyes wide open, waiting for the phone to ring and for Santeri to pull up outside. But neither of those things happened.

After getting up, I revised my last thought: neither of those things had happened *yet*.

Janne still hadn't called me back and Santeri's car still wasn't in the driveway.

After my morning chores, I didn't think about Santeri at all, not even when I was making some coffee and breakfast in the kitchen. I thought of Janne and decided to call him as soon as I'd eaten. I'd taken my first bite of rye bread when I heard a car approaching. I automatically assumed this was Santeri returning from wherever he'd been – stealing or dealing in stolen goods, or cavorting with our accountant or making offers on houses he would never pay for – but as the car appeared from behind the birches, I saw I'd been mistaken.

Janne got out of the car, then remained standing beside it for a while, holding something dark in his hand.

Everything was happening so quickly. Maybe that's why I didn't jump up from the kitchen table. I checked my phone: no, he hadn't called to say he was coming. He was clearly waiting for me to come out of the house. I looked at him, thought about the decision I had made. Maybe it would be best if we were outside. There was more space, more air. Maybe Janne sensed what I wanted, and that's why he was waiting there. It felt logical, sensible, considerate even. It was all very Janne-like. I stood up, left my full coffee cup on the table alongside the half-eaten rye bread, and stepped outside.

The morning was August at its most glorious: warm and yet still somehow fresh.

Janne saw me right away, we said our good mornings, and I walked towards him.

'I tried to call you,' I said.

'I noticed,' he said.

I stopped, looked at him more closely, and suddenly I couldn't tell whether the wrinkles and furrows in his face had deepened from the previous day or whether this was simply a result of the morning sunlight.

'You noticed?'

Janne didn't answer this question. 'I'll get right to the point,' he said instead. 'If that's okay?'

The way Janne asked this instantly knotted something inside me. But all I could say was that getting straight to the point was fine.

'As I said,' he began, 'I noticed you'd called. But I thought it better to have a conversation like this face to face, plus I had to check a few things first.'

'Right,' I said automatically.

'I received an email yesterday,' Janne continued with a nod. 'An email that, as we see it, is directly linked to the ongoing investigation and, therefore, to you ... and me. I can only blame myself. This sounds like a cliché, but in the circumstances I have to say it. I should have known better.'

What Janne had just said contained several words and phrases that felt like a cold, sharp implement being thrust into my body. *As we see it. I blame myself. I should have known better.*

He flipped open the cover of the iPad he was holding, then spun it round to face me.

Despite the morning brightness, the image on the screen shone as if something were on fire.

Me kissing Erkki. Janne swiped to the next image: me kissing Erkki more intensely. Another swipe: Erkki between my legs; me looking positively elated. Another swipe: Erkki and me lying on top of one another, languid.

Janne flicked the cover back into place. I felt as though I was falling. I felt everything I'd been thinking about, everything I'd decided, crumbling, disappearing before my eyes. I knew right away what these images would mean to Kiimalainen, and I knew that when Janne had said 'we', it wasn't the royal we. He believed exactly the same as Kiimalainen. And because I couldn't tell Kiimalainen everything I knew, I couldn't tell Janne either.

But that wasn't the worst of it. The worst thing was what I saw on Janne's face. Yes, the furrows had deepened since yesterday. Yes, the shadows had darkened. Even this incredibly beautiful morning had suddenly become almost unrecognisable: the birches looked dry, their branches bony, the green of the grass now had a mouldy tinge, the lake looked like a grimy pond.

'This isn't...' I began. 'And that ... isn't...'

'Looks like you had a busy day yesterday,' he said, and I could hear the personal, emotional charge in his voice. 'First the police, then the founding father. And what do I know? Maybe you had time for more. Well, it's none of my business. Not anymore. And...'

I said nothing, didn't interrupt him. It wasn't because I had nothing to say or that I didn't want to interrupt him. I could sense that there was more bad news to come.

'There's been a change in the timetable,' Janne continued. 'The forensics report came back from the lab ahead of schedule. It's your DNA – on the bumlet and the ladle. I can tell you now that we're certain of it. We know who to arrest today. I didn't tell Kiimalainen I was coming out here. I don't want to be here when he shows you these photographs.'

He held a brief pause.

'In fact, I don't really want to be here at all.'

We stood on the spot for a moment. I still couldn't think of a way to tell him what I knew without putting myself in an even trickier position. In fact, I wasn't sure I could speak at all. I wanted to change everything. I wanted everything to be different. The weight and the tension had returned to my body, a cold drill was churning inside me, bringing black mud up to the surface. There was nothing I could say.

'Thirty years,' said Janne. 'That's how wrong I was.'

He turned, got in his car and drove off.

It was a bright morning, in the middle of the night.

33

The coffee was cold, the sandwich toppings room temperature. From this, I concluded that I must have been sitting in the garden chair much longer than I'd thought. The wall clock seemed to be telling me that around an hour had passed since Janne had pulled up in my drive. I didn't have a clear memory of how I'd ended up in the garden chair or what I'd been thinking. Probably nothing. I knew that some time had passed before I'd heard a blackbird singing, further off at first, then closer, and seen the smooth surface of the water shimmering in the wind. Not that these would have changed the course of my thoughts, but at least I'd become aware of where I was.

I poured the cold coffee into the sink, refilled the mug with the coffee that had been standing in the machine and sat down at the kitchen table. I pulled the plate with my sandwich towards me, as though that might make the slices of tepid turkey more appetising. It was an attempt to make the morning feel a little more normal, but it failed. Of course. The morning had been and still was anything but normal. I stood up from the table, left my miserable breakfast behind and walked...

Well, where exactly?

Where did a person go when they walked out on their own life?

Everything would come with me.

It was delusional to think otherwise.

I stood in the middle of the living room and didn't even try to control my thoughts. They crashed through my mind like waves – emotions ranging from self-recrimination and regret to rage and anger, and eventually to confusion and despair. Of course, I knew that right now I was being treated unjustly, but one thought was harder to accept than all the others: I hadn't been a beacon of virtue and innocence myself. Which in turn led to more recriminations and even deeper regret. The spiral was gathering pace.

And for the first time in a long, long while, I had no plan at all, no moorings, no objectives. Perhaps this was what waiting to be arrested was like: when the police are going to come knocking at your door, it's hard to fill your diary.

While I'd been switching between blaming myself and blaming others, I'd started moving, almost involuntarily. And ended up here, maybe to maximise my accusations against myself, maybe to remind myself of quite how many bad decisions I'd made.

Santeri's shrine.

Full of Formula One paraphernalia.

Overalls, gloves, car parts, ribbons, badges, VHS tapes, posters, pictures, helmets – and then my eyes stopped abruptly. It was as if they were glued to the spot, so powerfully that I could feel it physically. Socks.

A tall pile of clean socks.

I looked at it for a moment, then walked around the table of trophy reproductions until I ended up in front of the pile of socks on a shelf.

For some reason, I'd imagined – more subconsciously than consciously – that the story about Mika Häkkinen's socks had all been in Santeri's imagination; that such things couldn't possibly exist and that the whole idea of the socks and sourcing them and picking them up had been another one of Santeri's pie-in-the-sky business ideas. Now, as I looked at the socks, I felt genuine confusion. There must have been a few dozen pairs. Each one of them had something scrawled on them in felt-tip pen; it certainly looked like Mika Häkkinen's signature. I wasn't a Häkkinen expert, but the capital M and capital H told me all I needed to know. I picked up a pair and examined them. They had clearly been washed at some point between the race and ending up in my hand, but in all respects they felt real.

I was about to put the socks back on the pile and was asking myself whether I might have underestimated Santeri in other respects too, whether I'd removed him from my list of suspects a little too easily, when my eyes lit upon something I'd thought I would never see again.

I'd given it to Santeri as a Christmas present some years ago, mostly because I hadn't been able to think what to do with it. Most gifts are like that: items and objects that nobody needs and that manage to disrupt quite a few people's lives before ending up in landfill. I put down the socks, and reached up to the shelf and the box that had been there for years. I gripped the box firmly, and carefully lifted it over the mountain of socks.

A miniature Spitfire, the pride of the Royal Airforce. Of course, it had never been put together; the kit was still in pieces in its original box, and the box was still sealed inside its plastic wrapping.

I remembered very well how I'd come across the Spitfire. And that was just the beginning of a chain of thoughts. With the box in my hands, I walked to Santeri's so-called desk, looked for something sharp, found my kitchen scissors, which I thought I'd lost long ago, cut the plastic and opened the box. On the top was what looked like the instructions. I had no use for them, and put them on the desk. Then I took the plastic pieces of the Spitfire out of the box one at a time and placed them on top of the instructions. Eventually I found what I was looking for. The tube wasn't big, and it wasn't necessarily the right kind, but to a connoisseur this might serve as inspiration and, later on, with a little adaptation, a tool.

But why was I thinking this?

I had Kiimalainen to thank: him and his question about glue, which I'd realised was important, but I just hadn't known why. At the time, I hadn't realised that this was the answer to my own question about why Ilmo Räty had stayed put on the bench of his sauna – or rather, what was keeping him there. Now I knew: he was glued to it. The forensics investigation had turned up a strange adhesive on the wood that didn't belong there; that's why Kiimalainen was so interested in the subject, and that's why he had seen it as yet another piece of evidence pointing to my guilt. Of course, it *was* true that I used to know a thing or two about glues and all their various uses, and back then I might even have been able to mix different glues together to form the kind of adhesive that would hold something tight. But because I hadn't been working with glues for decades, I didn't have the means to spread glue on the benches in Ilmo's sauna.

I returned the plastic parts to their box, placed the instructions on top, and closed it. Santeri hadn't built a miniature model in his life. However, the person from whom I'd bought the Spitfire had built dozens of them, perhaps even hundreds. This person had sold them too, mostly to members of the football club, and had offered me another one only very recently.

I thought of Kahavuori's account of the bicycle tyre marks at the lay-by on the edge of the woods. Of course, the tracks belonged to the same mountain bike with thick tyres that had been parked outside Steam Devil many, many times. I thought of how, as I was standing talking to Kiimalainen after the Stove had collapsed, I'd glanced over my shoulder and only seen Kaarlo and Mirka standing in the doorway. Finally, I thought of the elk Santeri had seen by the sauna, which wasn't an elk at all but a very large man. I was thinking of none other than Erkki's personal secretary and Steam Devil's general manager: Jarkko Mutikallio.

But it was there that my train of thought stopped.

Why?

Jarkko had just told me that he wouldn't want to change anything if he were to become the new CEO of Steam Devil. In fact he'd been at pains to assure me he would change nothing. Moreover, I couldn't remember a single time he'd ever expressed an opinion about Steam Devil's products or business model, let alone its future. The more I thought about it, it was entirely possible that he didn't have any such opinions. Besides, I'd heard him say that he was content with his role in the company, happy even. And for as long as I'd known him, his interests and passions when it came to Steam Devil had been confined to scheduling and organising things, and no matter how much I thought about it, I couldn't accept it as a reason why he would suddenly start murdering people. Why would he want to secure a position that didn't seem to interest him in the slightest?

I returned to the bookshelf, placed the Spitfire back where it had been, looked at it one last time, and I was reminded of something Jarkko had said.

Erkki. He's the Stove King. And the king makes the decisions. Always.

I'd been coming at this from completely the wrong direction.

34

The phone trembled in my hand. It rang for a long time, and I sent a prayer, a sincere wish, to whatever or whoever it was who could slow down dementia or at least punctuate it with moments of lucidity. When Erkki picked up I was almost certain that my prayers had been heard. I got straight to the point.

'I'm calling to ask about the race to succeed you,' I said.

'You're still my favourite,' Erkki began. He sounded almost like himself. 'Though what happened yesterday came as something of a surprise, at least to me ... I can't say it was unpleasant, on the contrary, I'm just used to taking things a little slower ... And I assure you, there's no need for you to shore up your position as my favourite candidate in such an ... intimate fashion.'

I knew that, at some point, I'd have to correct Erkki's misunderstanding of what had happened. I'd been too tired to do it yesterday, and now there was too little time. I had to move on.

'That's nice to hear,' I said. 'But the race is still officially ongoing, and we are all still candidates – Kaarlo, Mirka, Jarkko and me – isn't that right? What I mean is, your successor will be chosen from these four candidates, correct?'

I had deliberately stressed the number of candidates and their names. Erkki didn't answer right away. This was a good sign.

'Or is there some aspect of this race,' I continued, speaking in such a way that Erkki would understand even if he wasn't at his brightest, 'that I don't know about or that I've overlooked?'

'Well...' he said eventually. 'Well...'

'Has anyone dropped out of the race?' I asked.

Long, humming, agonising seconds that felt like hours.

'One person you mentioned was never in the running in the first place,' he said finally. 'Jarkko, that is. He asked me not to talk about it, so that people would think he was in the running just like everybody else. I didn't quite understand why, but it seemed important to him.'

It seemed important because he wants you to continue. For all eternity. You are the Stove King, now and forever. He is prepared to take out everybody, to sweep any potential successors out of the way so that you will continue. So that you must *continue.*

I didn't say any of this out loud.

'Thank you, Erkki. This has really cleared things up,' I said instead.

'I truly hope,' he said, 'that these terrible things will be resolved quickly. I am ready to name you as my successor. And it ought to be done soon.'

I thanked him once more and ended the call. I almost made another call as soon as I'd hung up, but I realised that even if someone answered – which, based on my recent experience, was unlikely – the call probably wouldn't have the rapid, decisive effect I was hoping for. I went into the hallway, snatched up my car keys and hoped I would come up with a better plan on the way.

I'd just reached my car when Santeri appeared from behind the birches and swerved into the drive.

I saw him in the driver's seat. He was wearing a black McLaren cap, and the closer he came (this might have been the slowest he had ever driven into our driveway), the lower the cap seemed to sit. The car came to a stop, Santeri got out, still keeping his cap pulled over his head, the front hiding his eyes. Then he walked around the car until he was standing about four or five metres away from me. Finally, he must have realised what an ostrich-like impression he was giving.

His cap rose.

He looked like a little boy who had just spent his first night at a friend's place. In a way, he was. Santeri *was* a little boy and he *had* been out all night. I felt a whole raft of emotions, but perhaps the strongest among them was sympathy.

'I've made a number of plans and decisions,' he began, and he sounded like he was either imitating somebody or as if he'd been rehearsing what he was about to say many times – or both. 'That's why I didn't come home last night. There's something I need to tell you. It's sad, but it's also fair...'

'You want a divorce,' I said.

Santeri looked bewildered.

'It's fine,' I continued. 'Remember to eat the rest of the turkey slices today before they go off. Was there anything else?'

Santeri looked as though someone had snatched something very important from him.

'I ... the turkey...'

'Does Susanna know you sell stolen goods?'

He stared at me as though I were an invisible tree he had bumped into while running. I didn't think I'd ever seen him looking this befuddled, and that was saying something. His mouth opened and closed, then he said:

'Susanna ... the goods...'

'You know that stealing is wrong,' I said, 'don't you?'

This time, he didn't even attempt to answer. His earlobes had started to turn red.

'I don't think she'll like it,' I continued. 'Especially now that you're buying a house together.'

Santeri's ears were now glowing, and I was beginning to worry that the sun might set them alight. Then he nodded the way little boys do when they've done something naughty.

'It is wrong,' he said. 'Stealing.'

'So you'll stop doing it?'

His cap rose then lowered again, rose then lowered.

'Promise?'

The cap rose and lowered again. Santeri's eyes were a little moist; now his whole face was ruddy. This wasn't his morning; things hadn't gone the way he had planned. If I hadn't been in such a hurry, I might have stayed and comforted him a little longer. But right now that was out of the question.

The confusion returned to his face.

'You can file the divorce papers,' I said, again trying to speak as clearly as possible. 'Eat the turkey, stop stealing. Three things. Will you remember them?'

'I...' he began, as though he was trying to sound as chipper as possible, 'I don't need a list.'

I looked at him a moment longer, then turned and got into my car.

35

I remembered Jarkko Mutikallio once telling me how he had turned the summer cottage he'd bought on the outskirts of Puhtijärvi into a home he could live in all year round.

It was hard to say whether this had really happened or not.

To me, the cottage still looked like a cottage. And near the small, wood-panelled, tiled-roof building stood two smaller constructions, dark brown, just like the cottage. The first, an oblong construction, looked like a barn; and the other was more like a shed or outside toilet. A little further off, nearer the shoreline, was a fourth dark-brown building. This was clearly the sauna – a wood-heated one, no less.

The dwelling was modest but impeccably tidy. Both the cottage and the two buildings next to it were in excellent condition. Even the sauna looked like it might have been freshly painted this summer. As well as looking after the company diary and eliminating his colleagues, Jarkko's organisational skills seemed to include property maintenance.

I stood on the spruce-covered hillside and looked down towards the cottage and its surroundings. I couldn't see any movement. This was to be expected. Jarkko was never late for work, and he was never ill. He was on site at Steam Devil from nine till five at the very least, and he guarded Erkki and his office door like a hawk.

I listened to the birdsong a moment longer, then set off down the rolling hillside, watching my step, as it was dotted with earth and sand and pine roots. When I reached the edge of his garden I stopped.

From here, I could see all four buildings and concluded that there was nobody here except me, a great crested grebe and its fledglings. The grebe must have noticed my arrival – it was leading its fledglings from the shore and into the water. The convoy of mini grebes set off almost in protest towards the protection of the birches by the shore a short distance away.

The air smelt of the late summer and the spruce forest.

I took out my phone, looked at it. Nobody had replied to my text message. I hoped I wasn't mistaken that there was still someone – and one person in particular – in Puhtijärvi who was interested in what I had to say for myself. I returned the phone to my pocket and walked towards the cottage.

I stepped onto the deck at the front, still watching my footsteps, and tried the door. It was locked. I moved towards the window, put my face against the glass and shaded my eyes with my palms so I could see inside.

I didn't know when I'd ever seen so many miniature models in one place.

Tanks, ships and cars were stacked on shelves, aeroplanes dangled from the ceiling. Dozens, at least, maybe hundreds of miniatures. The room was like a meeting of heaven and hell: heaven for someone who loved making small copies of old vehicles, and hell for those who wanted somewhere to rest their weary eyes and didn't find the sight of a Messerschmidt remotely relaxing.

Of course, I knew that being a miniature-model enthusiast didn't automatically make someone a serial killer – the existence of miniature-model retailers would surely have been brought into question long ago, if this had been the case – but on this occasion, I believed it pointed me in the right direction. I just had to find where I was going. And when I got there, I would be able to prove my innocence.

I returned to the door and tried it again. I pressed the handle down hard and pulled the door towards me with considerably more force than before. This time there was a small but significant movement. The tiny gap between the door and the doorframe widened very slightly – microscopically, but still. I looked around for some kind of tool, anything would do. There was nothing. The porch was tidy. Of course, Jarkko wouldn't leave his tools lying around; he would store them properly, for instance in...

The woodshed.

I turned. The woodshed looked unlocked. I headed towards it, feeling more hopeful with every step. The door wasn't locked; there was just a small wooden latch to stop it swinging open. Before touching the latch, I looked around and listened. I could have been in a quintessentially Finnish landscape painting: *An August Day in Puhtijärvi*. I needed two tools: something thin, sharp and firm to wedge between the cottage door and its frame, then something sturdier to hit it and twist it.

I opened the woodshed door, and peered inside, and thought that perhaps I wouldn't need those tools after all.

The collection of glues on the shelves lining the walls was breath-taking, both in breadth and quality. Some of the glues were, of course, perfect for building miniature models, but some of them were intended for more heavy-duty jobs. I knew most of these glues at least by name, and I knew that by combining different glues you could create the kind of adhesive that would work quickly and imperceptibly, was resistant to heat, and that would grip softer materials with such force that it would be virtually impossible to separate them again.

But the glue wasn't the only thing that confirmed what I had concluded some time ago.

There was something else in the woodshed too.

Just inside the doorway, propped against the left-hand wall, was a mountain bike with thick tyres, a very different bike from the one Jarkko usually rode. This one had thicker tyres with a larger, deeper tread. This was a bike that could withstand much rougher terrain. I didn't think I was jumping to conclusions when I assumed that this was the bike that had visited the lay-by, only walking distance from my own sauna. Behind the bike, hanging on a nail on the wall was a hoodie (large even by Jarkko's standards) in a deep shade of dark brown. Wearing this enormous garment with the hood pulled up, he could easily be mistaken for an elk, at least, that is, seen from a distance in the fading evening light and by someone whose attention was elsewhere, in this case on an ancient race at the Hockenheimring. To the right, on some form of worktop, was my knife in a resealable plastic bag. I hadn't noticed it missing, but I recognised it all the same. And just like the sauna ladle, this was engraved with my initials – and it would most certainly carry my DNA. It too was from my sauna; I'd last used it to make a birch whisk about a month ago. Presumably Jarkko had a plan for this knife, and because he was clearly intent on framing me for the murders, the knife must be intended for Kaarlo or Mirka.

I took out my phone. No missed calls. No new text messages.

I looked inside the woodshed again, at its contents, and made up my mind.

The message I'd sent on my way here had gone to Kiimalainen. It was short: *I WANT TO CONFESS*. And with it I'd included Jarkko's address. This was a bit reckless, it was going all-in on one card, but I knew I had a strong hand.

But now I was even more certain, so certain that I could just as well call the senior constable.

And I was about to press call when my hand stopped and my whole body froze. I felt someone behind me. I turned my head just enough to see part of the new arrival. I didn't need to see his face.

'You should have booked an appointment, Anni,' said Jarkko, wagging his long forefinger at me, the way he did whenever he wanted to chide or rebuke someone.

I moved instinctively. I didn't try to see what Jarkko had in his hand – more glue, a sharper sauna ladle or some other lethal weapon – but simply started to run. Behind me, I could hear him trying to catch me, then perhaps he tripped over – he let out a frustrated yell. I ran in the only direction possible: towards the shore and the sauna. I heard Jarkko get to his feet, he was on the move again now, hurtling after me. I kept my eyes on the sauna and hoped its door would be open too.

I reached the sauna, wrenched the door, it opened, and with that I was in the dressing room.

I hadn't thought any further ahead. I pulled the door closed, and only then realised that it couldn't be locked from the inside. I heard Jarkko's voice.

'You're a murderer, Anni,' he shouted. 'You think you can replace Erkki, but I won't let you. You wanted his...'

I couldn't make out the next words. I acted quickly. I opened the door to the steam room but didn't go inside. Instead, I lay down on the floor of the changing room and rolled myself under the long wooden bench, managing this at the last possible fraction of the last possible second.

Because Jarkko came barging in and continued barging right the way into the steam room. At that moment, I sprung up from under the bench, grabbed the bench itself and turned it so that one end hit the door to the steam room, pressing it shut, then I propped the other end against the opposite wall. It was the perfect fit. The steam-room door would not budge.

The beating of my heart left me short of breath. It felt like I hadn't breathed once since noticing there was someone standing behind me at the woodshed. My body was so full of adrenaline that I couldn't feel my limbs. I didn't know where my phone was; all I knew was that it wasn't in my hands, which felt both light and heavy and extremely shaky. I fumbled across the floor, groping for my phone, eventually found it, clenched it in my fingers.

I couldn't help it; I just had to lie down. On the very same bench that was keeping the door of the steam room shut and Jarkko in the sauna. Jarkko, whose voice I could hear now but whose words I still didn't have the energy to make out. I had the vague sense that everything that had happened in the last few days and weeks was still pent up in my body, all at once, and that it had all become so absurd that my current situation seemed almost natural: a murderer locked in the sauna, shouting and banging, and me lying on the bench to keep him there, in my hand the phone that I would soon use to make a call...

'Are you alright?'

The question betrayed a note of genuine concern. I squinted, looked at the dark figure that had appeared in the doorway, a figure I recognised instantly. I said I was alright. I heard Janne on his phone, saying he needed back-up and an ambulance. I said there was no need for an ambulance, the killer was in the sauna and the murder weapons in the woodshed, I was a little tired and was just resting here for a while. Janne didn't answer right away, he took a step closer, crouched down next to me and said I'd done something he had never seen before, that he was sorry, and that I was the bravest person he knew.

And that, if it was alright, he'd take the log from my hands now.

36

I dived into the cool, black water. I glided under the surface with long, calm strokes, and only when my lungs insisted did I come up for air and turn around. A soft light glimmered from the sauna windows. The lantern at the end of the jetty looked like a miniature lighthouse. On a calm, windless late-September evening like this, it was as though the turning of the seasons had momentarily stopped, as if providence and mercy themselves had shaped this evening and stopped the world, just for a moment.

I still wasn't quite used to the silence.

Many times, I'd found myself expecting to hear the high-pitched wail of engines, and each time I had to tell myself to relax, reminding myself that the days of car racing in this house were over. They were gone, as was Santeri, whom I only thought about in those brief moments when I heard news about his latest antics.

Santeri really did seem to have given up his short-lived criminal career, but this had come with its fair share of problems. Naturally, his earnings had plummeted, which in turn had affected the kind of house that he and the now acrimoniously separated Susanna could afford to buy. The last I heard, they were going to buy Jarkko Mutikallio's recently vacated cottage; its low price tag was partly because it had once belonged to a serial killer but also – as I'd suspected – the cottage really was just a cottage: there was no drainage, no running water, and it had to be heated with a wood burner. I knew Santeri, and I knew that rather than roll his sleeves up, he would keep warm by pulling on a vintage jumpsuit and would protect himself from mosquitoes in the outdoor toilet with Nigel Mansell's old helmet. I could see him sitting in the outdoor loo with the helmet on, Susanna begging him to install some plumbing, and decided that although I'd been through a lot, I'd still got off lightly.

I was free.

Even Kiimalainen had given up trying to put me in jail. He had even offered me an apology, albeit a subdued and reluctant one, but he'd still asked about the Great Elk's antlers. I hadn't told him that, at my father's express wishes, the antlers had been buried with him. The last time we went through the events at Jarkko's cottage, Kiimalainen was no longer constantly agitated or red in the face. Instead he seemed like a man who was more than ready for retirement.

As, of course, was Erkki. Erkki had made me Steam Devil's new CEO, and nowadays he seemed relieved that he no longer had to spend his time thinking about sauna stoves. He still spent a lot of time at the company though, and in his more lucid moments he prepared everyone – new and old employees alike – delicious lunches, usually from the fish he'd caught himself: zander, whitefish, perch, pike. When he was less lucid, he tried to organise afternoon dancing sessions and seemed genuinely upset at how little success these events had with the staff.

Kahavuori eventually bought the stoves – all sixty-four luxury, hand-made units – but he'd stayed in touch with me even after the sale had completed. He had his doubts about Jarkko's guilt and was still looking for the 'real' murderer, as he put it. And he'd been continuing his criminal profiling too. His latest theory was that the real killer must be someone who had recently separated from a partner who probably had a criminal background, someone who had recently come into some kind of money, someone who had just been promoted at work, for instance. Apparently, this explained the current lull in the murder rate.

And as for me ... What had finally saved me?

The shock I'd had? The sauna?

In normal circumstances, such a combination is not recommended. But when you have to confront a bulky killer in a sparsely populated area, both can come in handy.

Something moved in the water.

I swam closer to the shore, then stopped, allowing my legs to sink and trying to touch the bottom with my toes. I breathed as calmly as I could, listened to the ripples of the water, and felt it again. A gentle touch. The sauna's lights and the lantern's flame cast long, golden corridors across the surface of the lake, and I began to feel the cool of the September evening in my hands and feet. I waited a moment longer, sensed the dark water around me...

Janne pressed against my back, and after the chill of the autumnal lake the warmth of his body felt like sitting down by an open fire. He held me, brushed his lips against my neck and earlobe, and I was about to say something but realised that there was no need. Everything was already agreed. There were sprats for dinner, and we would fall asleep in each other's arms. It felt like a good plan, this evening and on all the evenings to come.

We pushed off, glided through the water, swam back towards the shore.

In the golden lake, side by side.

ACKNOWLEDGEMENTS

I want to thank the one and only Karen Sullivan at Orenda Books for publishing this book in the English-speaking world and for her support and kindness over the years. A warmest thank you and greatest admiration for the English translation to David Hackston, who makes translating Finnish seem like an easy, natural thing to do. (Which it is not, I assure you.) Thank you to West Camel for the brilliant editing on this novel and continuous support over the years. Thank you, the talented Mark Swan, for yet another fabulous cover. Thank you to Cole Sullivan for working tirelessly on behalf of my books in the UK and elsewhere. And a huge thank you to my agent, Federico Ambrosini, and everybody else at Salomonsson Agency. I'm so grateful for the work you do.

Thank you to the booksellers, bloggers, festival organisers and literary helpers of every kind – you are miracle makers.

And finally, thank you, Anu, I love you so much.